THE GHOST

Rumors From the Central Highlands of Vietnam

A Vietnam War Story

RICK DESTEFANIS

D1600631

THE GHOST

Rumors from the Central Highlands of Vietnam
A Vietnam War Story

Copyright © 2022 Rick DeStefanis

Excerpt from *The Birdhouse Man*
Copyright © 2020 Rick DeStefanis

All rights reserved.

ISBN: 978-1-7367120-3-0

Acknowledgements

As always, I received the help of friends while writing this story and wish to recognize them for their suggestions, edits, and ideas.

Carol Carlson is a friend from childhood who is currently working on a book for police mothers. A daughter, mother, and mother-in-law of police officers, Carol is well qualified for that endeavor. Her review of all aspects of this story as well as its plot and characters was indispensable. Thank you, Carol, for your hard work on this book.

Robert (Doc Enz) Enzenauer is a friend and beta-reader of the first rough draft of this work. As always, his input was valuable. Doc's qualifications: Brigadier General, Retired, United States Army, United States Military Academy, Class of 1975, 19th Special Forces, OEF2, FOB 195, July 2002-June 2003, Kabul, Afghanistan, 5/19th SFG (A), Colorado Army National Guard, 004. MD, MPH, MSS, MBA, Professor of Ophthalmology and Pediatrics, Chief of Ophthalmology, Children's Hospital of Colorado, Aurora,Colorado. Thanks, Doc, and *AIRBORNE ALL THE WAY, SIR!*

Elisabeth Hallett is the final editor who reviews my work. She can be contacted via email at soultrek@montana.com. Thank you, Elisabeth. I appreciate your work.

Todd Hebertson has designed all my book covers. His work stands out as unique when studying the bookstore shelves. You can see more of his covers and contact him through his website at www. bookcoverart.webs.com. Thanks for another great cover, Todd.

Also by Rick DeStefanis

THE VIETNAM WAR SERIES
Melody Hill
The Gomorrah Principle
Valley of the Purple Hearts
Raeford's MVP
The Birdhouse Man
Miss Molly's Final Mission

THE RAWLINS TRILOGY
Rawlins, No Longer Young
Rawlins, Into Montana
Rawlins, Last Ride to Montana

SOUTHERN FICTION SERIES
Tallahatchie

PROLOGUE

After Tet 1968, the war in Vietnam became a slugfest with American troops moving westward into the traditional strongholds of the North Vietnamese Army, the Central Highlands. Years before, this rugged, mountainous region of triple-canopied jungles and mist-shrouded landscapes had become the subject of rampant and varied rumors—entire patrols lost without a trace, enemy units led by mysterious white men, American soldiers held in bamboo cages, and myriad other unexplained sightings and events. It was a place of mystery where no man wanted to be separated from his unit.

This story is about one of those rumors. Few men who remain alive have first-hand knowledge of it, because all those involved were sworn to secrecy, lest a top-secret mission be revealed. And as with most tales, this one stretches the fabric of believability to the point where those who were there only cast sad eyes upon their buddies, shrug, and say, "Yeah, it sounds like some crazy shit, but you never know. It was a crazy war."

CHAPTER ONE

From the moment he arrived, Second Lieutenant Martin Shadows sensed his tour of duty in Vietnam might be different from anything he had ever been told. His orders, stamped CONFIDENTIAL, were to report to the commanding officer of intelligence at MAC-V—the Military Assistance Command—Vietnam, the very top of the food chain. Yes, most officers referred to it as the "chain of command," but since enlisting he had experienced so many ass-chewings, Martin figured "food chain" was more appropriate. He gazed out at the Vietnamese countryside, not yet decided which was worse, the putrid stench emanating from the ditches and canals or the ungodly equatorial heat that had him soaked with sweat.

Having just arrived in-country at Tan Son Nhut Airbase, the young lieutenant was on a green army bus bound for the MAC-V compound in Saigon. Stopping and starting, the spec-four bus driver negotiated the mass of humanity and almost every type of vehicle imaginable on a clogged Cach Mang Boulevard—the main drag between the airbase and MAC-V. Martin gazed out through the barred bus windows at the surrounding chaos.

Army vehicles competed with aged Citroën taxis, pedicabs, three-wheeled cyclos, and motor scooters, jockeying for position to get to only God knew where. A dingy pall of diesel fumes hung above the seething mass. Not to his surprise, Shadows saw occasional shell holes and multiple splintered pockmarks created by bullets along a stucco wall—evidence of the war. It wasn't so much unexpected as it was sobering.

Martin promised his mother back in Kentucky that his MOS, military intelligence, would keep him away from the worst of it, but this war was different. It had no lines of demarcation and the enemy looked no different from the hundreds of people he now stared at through the barred windows of the bus. Hell, from what he'd been told, many of them probably *were* the enemy. His mother cried that day, saying he was throwing away his college degree, even after he explained he was no longer protected by a college deferment. Martin enlisted for Army Intelligence School and later Officer Candidate School in hopes of avoiding his father's path, an infantryman's slog across France during World War II.

So far, the military intelligence path seemed to be working. After all, there were few places more heavily guarded than MAC-V headquarters, and when he arrived, two MPs escorted him into the main building and up to the office where he now sat. He waited patiently while a full bird colonel, clenching a cigar in his teeth, read his orders. The colonel folded the orders, set them aside, and gazed steadily across the desk at him.

"Welcome to the Republic of Vietnam, Lieutenant Shadows. What kind of name is that?"

"It's Lakota Sioux, sir."

The colonel bobbed his bushy eyebrows.

"That's interesting. Maybe we'll have time for a better introduction later, but my intention now is to expedite your movement to your first assignment. You will be issued new orders after you are properly briefed."

Reporting to MAC-V was a big deal but reporting directly to a full bird colonel and receiving a briefing from him was unheard-of for a cherry lieutenant. The adrenaline pulsed in his veins and his mind raced as he forced himself to focus on the colonel's words.

"As you may be aware, the military recently experienced some embarrassing incidents here in Vietnam—incidents that do not speak well of our men, our leaders, or our country. One involves the massacre of an entire village by US troops, and the other the murder of a Vietnamese civilian by Army Special Forces soldiers. My job is to get ahead of that curve and pre-empt any further such incidents.

"With this mission in mind, we are working with Army CID and embedding a number of intelligence officers in potential problem units. You are one of those men, and you will be operating incognito, so to speak. In other words, you are being assigned undercover as an enlisted man in order that you have closer contact with those you are watching. You will report to one of my officers, Captain Palmer, who will see that you are fully briefed and prepared before sending you into the field. Questions?"

"Where am I going, and exactly what am I looking for, sir?"

"Your first assignment will be at a small fire support base on the coast southeast of Chu Lai. That's Quảng Nam Province up in Second Corps. You will be looking for anything that violates the military code of conduct. Troops at this firebase have been found with all manner of expensive contraband—nothing new, but there are other troubling signs that point to something worse. We think someone there is sharing sensitive information and it's falling into enemy hands."

"So, my mission is to determine if we have soldiers selling information to the enemy, correct?"

A slight tick came and went on the colonel's jaw, but his crystalline blue eyes remained fixed hard and fast with a blazing glare that had no doubt wilted many a junior officer. Martin had no long-term plans with the military and for him, the colonel's ire was little more than an unintended aggravation. He had spoken too quickly. Best to remain silent and let him do the talking.

"Lieutenant, quick assumptions will get you in trouble where you're going, so I suggest you do more listening and less talking. This is a classified mission, and you are to share information with no one besides myself and your CO, Captain Palmer. When I say 'no one' I mean no one, to include higher ranking officers or civilians such as correspondents and people from the State Department, especially those connected with the Office of the Special Assistant. Whatever you learn will remain in house. Understood?"

"Yes, sir."

"As I said, MAC-V is currently dealing with at least two incidents with the potential for damaging the reputation of our troops and the United States Government. Should someone begin telling you about these or any other such incidents, you are to claim ignorance but listen closely and gather any information you can. That is all you need to know at this point.

"You are not to act on any information you may receive, other than to report it to us. Nor are you to interfere with any such actions by the men with whom you are embedded except where those actions may become a life and death matter. No one in that chain of command will know you are anything other than an enlisted replacement assigned to that unit. As I said, your CO here at MAC-V, Captain Palmer, will meet with you when he returns from a morning briefing. Leave your gear out there with my adjutant and go get some chow at the mess hall. Be back here at 1300 hours."

Martin wanted to ask a hundred more questions, but patience was the better part of good judgement for now. After saluting the colonel, he made his way to the officer's mess only to find his appetite lacking. This mission was nothing like he expected.

Army intelligence operations against a foreign enemy was one thing—but spying on his fellow soldiers was something entirely different. This sounded like a job better suited for the CID. The Criminal Investigation Department looked into this sort of thing, but for an army intelligence officer to do so seemed strange. And now, after all the hard work and sacrifice spent completing OCS, he was going to his first post as an enlisted man—even if not in fact.

Everyone back in the States who had been to Vietnam said it was a crazy place. Never had he understood the true meaning of those words until now. They were right. An American military officer spying on his own men sounded more like a political commissar in the Soviet Army. Martin was now a participant in something that violated the leadership trust he learned at OCS. Yet, like so many primrose paths, it seemed equally logical and necessary.

Three days later, army intelligence officer Second Lieutenant Martin Shadows had become infantryman Private First-Class Martin Shadows on his way to a detached infantry company guarding an artillery unit at Fire Support Base Suzy. The firebase was on a coastal peninsula, a few kilometers east of Highway One, near the South China Sea. All Martin's insignia, papers, and anything that might indicate he was a commissioned officer had been taken from him. He now wore PFC stripes on new green fatigues as he and two other replacements bounced along in a deuce-and-a-half on their way to FSB Suzy.

The army was becoming much like his life—one of conflicting cultures and confused loyalties. This mission had him feeling he was back to square one, a "half-breed" as a high school classmate once called him. With the light hair of his mother, but the dark brown eyes of his Lakota Sioux father, Martin had never considered himself any different from his classmates—until that day.

George Shadows, his father, met his mother when she went out to the Fort Peck reservation in Montana on a mission trip after World War II. Although she failed to capture his soul, she did steal his heart. Martin's father too had captured Lizzie Belle Riley's heart, and they traveled back to Kentucky where they were married. At her insistence they raised their son in the public schools of western Kentucky.

It wasn't a bad life, except Martin occasionally felt pulled between the two cultures, the most recent experience being a trip to Montana to visit his grandfather, Two Shadows. He was unsure what to think of it, except it was at the least *interesting*. It happened three weeks before he departed for Vietnam when his father, George Shadows, suggested the visit with this man Martin had seen only once as a boy.

That previous visit was when he was nine years old and expected his Lakota grandfather would be carrying a lance and have a full headdress of eagle feathers, but the old man wore a single braid in his hair and an old gray flannel shirt. He remembered little else about the visit except when Grandfather Two Shadows waved an eagle feather over his head and blessed him. At least that was how his mother described it—a blessing.

Martin figured the most recent visit only a few weeks ago had been an opportunity to take his mind off his coming tour of duty in Vietnam, and given the old man's age, it might have been his last chance to see him alive. They had smoked a pipe, while old Two Shadows told him of his many visions, but as a newly commissioned officer of the United States Army, Martin was left nonplussed by his grandfather's revelations—strange visions of leaping panthers and fire-breathing birds. Despite all this, he was glad he'd done it.

A cloud of dust filled the back of the deuce-and-a-half as it jolted to a stop. They'd arrived, and Fire Support Base Suzy was hotter than hell. Martin gazed out the back of the truck, faced with the sudden realization that he was again a half-breed, half officer, half enlisted man—not leading but spying on his fellow soldiers.

W ord was FSB Suzy was home to several 105-millimeter and two 155-millimeter Howitzers, thirty-four artillerymen, a few REMFs who filled various support roles, and a detached infantry company that provided base security. Arriving midafternoon with the other replacements, Martin jumped from the back of the deuce-and-a-half and looked around. Not a soul was in sight. The firebase seemed abandoned. A hot salty breeze blew in from the ocean, and a blazing sun hung high in the sky. The silence was almost spooky.

"Where *is* everybody?" he asked.

"Hell, they're probably staying out of this gawd-awful heat," the driver said. "I just haul supplies down here from Chu Lai, but I think the HQ building is up that way."

He pointed up a sandy road that ran between a row of sandbagged buildings.

"G'luck," he said.

Martin had learned his two counterparts' names during the ride. Paul Maziensky and Tim Gates gazed about like a pair of bastard buffalo calves looking for their daddy—a description he'd once heard his father use. Even if he was supposed to be an enlisted man, it was time to show some common sense. Throwing his duffle bag on his shoulder, Martin started up the road. The other two followed.

The firebase was small, about the size of a football stadium, and the only sign of life was a soldier's helmet visible in the guard tower at the main gate. Tilted forward, the helmet hadn't moved since their arrival—an almost certain indication its owner was sleeping.

"Where *is* everybody?" Paul asked.

"This is strange," Tim said.

Tim was right, but Martin was no longer surprised by much of what he saw in the army. And as if conjured by their worries, a soldier wearing sergeant stripes walked from between two buildings and strutted down the road toward them. He wasn't tall, but he was grim-faced to the point of looking angry. Martin figured he was just another NCO about to share some typical army love with the new replacements.

"Damned! That sonofabitch looks pissed," Tim said.

"I believe we're about to find out," Martin said.

Stopping, the sergeant stood with his hands on his hips, staring them up and down. "I reckon y'all must be the new cherries."

With his duffle bag on his shoulder, decked out in new green fatigues, and wearing un-scuffed jungle boots, Martin wanted to tell the little NCO he must be a first cousin to Einstein. He resisted the urge. Paul and Tim nodded dutifully.

"Okay, cherries, I'm Sergeant Kurbo, your platoon sergeant. Let's go. Follow me over here behind the mess hall. I'll take you to a hootch later. Right now, I gotta get you dumbasses squared away."

The grim-faced platoon sergeant spun about and strutted around the buildings as they hurried to catch up. He led them to a row of makeshift wooden tables.

"Let's go, cherries, hurry up. Come on. I ain't got all day! Get behind those tables. Line up and empty your pockets and duffle bags. Lay everything you got on the table in front of you."

Never was anything explained. It was the army way, and Martin didn't expect much more. Kurbo's greeting was typical—just more harassment for the new guys. He had always hoped for more, but each new duty assignment was the same bullshit. He set his wallet and newly issued military scrip on the table along with a zippo, his cigarettes, and a pocketknife. After opening his duffle bag, he dumped those contents out as well.

"Open your wallet, shithead!" Kurbo shouted.

The little sergeant was glaring at him. Martin took a deep breath. He had to play the role, but he would be damned if he was going to take crap from the likes of Kurbo.

"My name's not shithead, Sergeant."

He was bigger than the little sergeant—maybe five or six inches taller. Kurbo threw a confused glance his way. The little prick likely had never been challenged by a newbie.

"Open your wallet, private, or I'll make you wish you did."

Martin did as he was ordered. Kurbo eyed him for a moment before glancing inside the wallet. After shuffling through the men's personal belongings, he stepped back and stood with his hands again on his hips. It seemed to be his favored expression of the absolute authority granted him by his rank as an NCO.

"Okay, put that stuff back in your duffle bags. This is fair warning. Anyone caught with greenbacks, hard drugs, or any other contraband will go before the CO for an Article-15. Now, get your asses down to supply and draw your gear."

"How will we know what gear to draw, Sergeant?" Paul asked.

"They know what to issue you. Just don't load your weapon or fuck with any of the ordnance till you get back here. I'll go over it with you. Then we'll take a little patrol outside the wire. Now git!"

"Sergeant," Martin said.

Kurbo rolled his eyes. "What?"

"Do you mind telling us where supply is?"

Kurbo read the sarcasm in Martin's voice as he stared hard at him and pointed down the road. "Back that way, third building on the left."

Martin knew his attitude was going to lead to trouble, but he had already had enough of Kurbo. Regardless, he had a role to play and a job to do. Turning, he walked away. An hour later they were back, each with a rucksack, an M-16, twelve magazines, a cleaning kit, bayonet, entrenching tool, two canteens, two frags, two smoke grenades, trip flares, boxes of 5.56mm ammo, ammo pouches, poncho, poncho liner, insect repellent, flashlight, compass, and more crap than he could imagine ever fitting in the new rucksack. Sergeant Kurbo stepped from the sandbagged door of a hootch, yawned, and stretched. He eyed them as if it was the first time he had ever seen them.

"What now, Sarge?" Tim asked.

Kurbo again morphed into his bad-ass platoon sergeant mode.

"Yeah, well, just stay here and don't do anything stupid till I get back. Lieutenant Fitzer wants me to take you cherries on a little walk around the perimeter—get you some OJT. Dumbass is too lazy to do it himself. Get your shit together, but don't load your weapons. I'll get a squad together."

Martin looked around at the others and shrugged. Kurbo was a minimalist when it came to disseminating information, but it was clear he didn't respect his platoon leader. The men stuffed their ponchos and liners into their rucksacks along with the gun cleaning kits, entrenching tools, and most of the other gear.

"Where are you guys carrying your hand grenades?" Tim asked.

Martin shrugged and dropped his frags in the side cargo pocket of his fatigue shirt. "Put them in your pocket for now. Maybe somebody will tell us later. If we're going on a patrol, we better start loading our magazines."

"The sergeant told us not to load our weapons," Paul said.

"He didn't say not to load the magazines," Martin said. "I'm loading mine. You guys do what you want."

Tim shrugged and began thumbing 5.56mm rounds into a magazine. A few minutes later Kurbo came back down the road with five men. They gathered in a circle around the newbies while buttoning their fatigue shirts and lacing their boots. By the looks of their eyes, they'd been awakened from an afternoon nap.

"Okay, cherries. This is the rest of your squad. They can tell you their names later. Right now, the lieutenant wants me to give you a briefing. We're gonna get going so we can get back in time for chow call, so listen up. Our company has one job here on FSB Suzy. We protect those big guns back there. Those are one-oh-five and one-five-five Howitzers. That's it. Nothin' complicated. Any questions?"

"How do we protect them?" Paul asked.

Kurbo rolled his eyes as the old heads snickered.

"We don't. They don't need protectin'. There ain't been no VC around here in months. Oh, we find a booby trap once in a while, but that's just a gift from some local yokel who gets bored. Look, cherries, we got a pretty good gig here. Charlie don't fuck with us, and we don't fuck with him. We stay out of their villages, and they stay out of ours—know what I mean?"

"So, what do we do?" Martin asked.

"We hump out to the highway once or twice a month and trade with the locals for a little hootch and some pretty cool black-market stuff. The patrol is just something we do to show them we ain't toleratin' no shit. Right now, we're gonna do something a little easier. It's a perimeter walk—something the CO has one of our squads do three or four times a week. We just walk around the entire perimeter and look for shit like footprints or whatever. You know?"

"Footprints?" Martin said.

"Yeah," Kurbo said. "That's about all we ever find. Look, we've been doin' this shit for months, and there ain't nothin' hard about it. You got lucky when you landed here, so just be cool and you'll catch on. Now, saddle up and follow me down to the main gate."

"Should we load our rifles?" Tim asked.

"Wait till we get outside the wire. You can put a magazine in your weapon, but there ain't no need to lock and load. All we're gonna do is walk around the perimeter—get you used to walkin' a patrol."

"I haven't loaded my magazines yet," Paul said.

"You goddamn cherries got a lot to learn. Don't worry about it, shithead. Just put an empty one in your weapon. Believe me, their ain't been a gook with a gun around here in a while."

Martin wanted to say something, as the words of the drill instructors at Polk became a broken record skipping in his mind, *The Viet Cong are everywhere. Never let down your guard.*

"Taco, you take point. Douchie, you walk slack for him. Ernie, you stay behind me with the radio. Chief, you can walk drag and help me keep an eye on the cherries. You three dumbasses pay attention. Keep your weapons on safe and aimed away from the rest of us. What'd you do with your frags?"

Martin patted his side-pocket.

"Okay, just leave 'em there for now and don't fuck with them. I don't need anybody blowin' his ass away. The LT will be real disappointed in me if you do that."

The others laughed. The one named Douchie had the grating cackle of a chicken on steroids.

The nine-man squad turned onto a well-worn trail seventy-five meters from the gate and began circling the firebase. Much of the undergrowth was browned by Agent Orange, but a new growth of grass was already chest-high in places. This so-called patrol was nothing like the training Martin received back at Fort Polk. These men seemed to know what was expected, but they were acting like a bunch of boy scouts on a hike. With their M-16s slung over their shoulders, they stumbled along smoking cigarettes and talking.

The radio broke squelch as the RTO did a commo-check with someone he called Centurion One Romeo.

"Centurion One Romeo, that's the lieutenant," Kurbo said. "He's playing poker today with some of the artillery guys. He wants to know if you cherries took your malaria pills and salt tablets before we left."

Martin and the newbies shrugged in unison. Their fatigues were soaked with sweat as they slapped at the mosquitoes.

"Yeah, I know. I forgot to send y'all to see Doc Cowan. He's the company medic. Go see him when we get back. He'll hook you up."

He turned to the RTO, "Just tell Fitzer we got it covered."

The patrol had made it a third of the way around the perimeter when a sparkling rain began falling through the sunshine. It was as if thousands of diamonds were shimmering as they tumbled from the sky. Kurbo pulled off his helmet and let the rain hit him in the face.

"Ahhh," he said. "Wonderful rain. Get used to it, cherries. It rains every afternoon, and during the monsoon it rains all day and all night—never stops."

A thundering boom shook the ground. Martin's heart lunged into his throat as he dove for cover in the high grass. Lying on his back, he watched as a huge quavering smoke ring floated skyward over the firebase. From the trail came the snickering laughs of the old heads. He stood and pushed his way back through the grass.

Kurbo was gagging with laughter. "You, uh, you cherries, oh my god, y'all looked fantastic. I mean, y'all were like a bunch of cats with your asses on fire."

"That was one of our one-five-fives," Ernie said. "You dumbasses, better get ready. That was just a marker round."

As if cued by him, the Howitzers opened up with ground-shaking booms. The concussion alone was fearsome as they fired twelve rounds before going silent.

"What were they shooting at?" Tim asked.

"Who the hell knows?" Kurbo said.

"We mostly support the ROK Marines and ARVN troops patrolling out near Highway One," Ernie said. "If it's the ARVNs, they probably spotted a water buffalo in a rice paddy somewhere and wanted it for supper. If it was the ROKs, they probably took some stray sniper fire from a village, which is now a pile of burning straw."

"You're kidding, right?" Paul said.

"No. The South Vietnamese will call in an artillery strike on anything, even one of their own villages if they don't like the looks of it. And the ROKs, hell, they're just plain badass. Most of the time, the VC just let 'em pass and don't do nothin' 'cause they know they'll get their asses kicked if they do."

Kurbo nodded in agreement, before motioning toward the point man. "We need to di di if we're gonna get back in time for chow. Taco, let's just double back the way we came. It's shorter."

"The CO said we needed to circle the whole firebase this time," Taco said.

He wore buck sergeant stripes and seemed a little sharper than the others.

"You're a high-strung bastard, ain't cha?" Douchie said.

Taco shrugged. "We need to check out the whole perimeter."

"Be cool, Douchie," Kurbo said. "Look'a here, Taco, the

lieutenant don't give a shit, and the old man won't know shit if nobody tells him. Besides, there'll be another patrol tomorrow or the next day. We're gonna turn back. Let's move out."

Martin was beginning to think he had landed in hell. After all that the DIs on Tiger Ridge had said about the VC being slick bastards, this was crazy. Constantly, those drill instructors had taken them through realistic mockups of villages, led them through thick swamps, and harassed them with mock ambushes and sniper fire. And for what?

This so-called perimeter patrol was a stroll through the park compared to the training, but Martin kept his M-16 at the ready. Every one of the DIs at Polk wore a Combat Infantryman's badge on his fatigues, and every one of them talked of the VC with respect. They had been here, and they knew something these boys apparently hadn't yet learned.

A week turned into two while Martin, Paul, and Tim spent most of their days sitting in a perimeter bunker, playing poker, or lying around in the hootch. Two hot meals a day had them all gaining weight, and the only duty came when they had to pull the metal drums from beneath the latrines and burn the waste with diesel fuel. Martin had lost much of his military scrip in what were undoubtably rigged poker games with Douchie and the other old heads. The boredom was already grinding away at his psyche.

The screened door slapped shut that afternoon as someone came inside the hootch. Martin cracked open an eye from his afternoon nap. It was Sergeant Kurbo walking down the center aisle between the bunks. The little sergeant stopped halfway and stomped the floor. It was a makeshift floor of old pallets, and his stomp barely made a thump. Martin kept his eyes closed and tried not to smile.

"Okay, wake your sorry asses up," Kurbo shouted. "Fall out in zero-five minutes for a briefing. The platoon is patrolling out to the highway tomorrow, and you need to get your shit together. You cherries, bring your rucksacks and other gear so we can show you how to pack it."

A few minutes later Martin stumbled outside with his gear and walked to where the platoon was gathered beneath the palms. Kurbo stood with his hands on his hips and a cigarette dangling from his lips—kind of like he thought he was John Wayne. How he became a platoon sergeant defied explanation. He gazed down at Paul and Tim who were on their knees loading their rucksacks.

"What are you gonna do with all that shit?" Kurbo asked.

Paul looked up at him—red-faced and sweating. "I figured a couple changes of socks and some extra boxers would be smart to carry."

"Two days—that's all we're gonna be out. We hump out to the highway, do our shopping and bivouac one stinking night. Then we hump back here the next day. We'll be back in time for evening chow. Look, all you need is one change of socks, your poncho, and the liner. You can put the towel around your neck and leave the rest of that crap under your bunk. Besides, you want to leave room in your ruck for the cool shit you'll buy at the black market."

Taco, Ernie, and another soldier named Peebles showed up with several large cardboard boxes. After setting them on the ground and ripping them open, Taco pulled a deck of cards from his pocket and gave it a quick shuffle.

"Hey," Douchie said, "Let me shuffle the cards."

"No way, asshole," Taco said. "I got it."

He went around to each man, letting him draw a card. By now, there were seventeen men gathered under the palms.

"I didn't get a card," Tim said.

Paul stood and turned to Kurbo. "Me neither."

Martin already knew what was coming. The cardboard cases contained boxes of C-rations. Each box was marked "MEAL, COMBAT, INDIVIDUAL," with the contents listed below that. Most said things like "TURKEY, BONED, B-3A UNIT or "HAM & EGGS, CHOPPED B-1A Unit." Kurbo ignored Tim and Paul as he reached into one of the cases and pulled out three boxes of C-rations.

"Okay, who got high card?' he asked.

Douchie held up the Ace of clubs.

"Sonofabitch," someone muttered. "How'd he do that?"

Douchie handed the card to Taco and picked out three boxes of C-rations. When the men had chosen their meals, only a few boxes remained. Most were ham and eggs, boned turkey, or ham and lima beans in juices.

"Okay, cherries, y'all get the good stuff," Kurbo said. "Take three meals each and grab you one of those P-38s. Most of it ain't too bad if you load it up with Tabasco, but there ain't much you can do with those ham and muthas. That shit is just plain nasty."

Douchie let out one of his cackling laughs.

"Listen up," Kurbo said. "First Squad will lead, and Chief, I want you on point. We'll move out after chow in the morning and take the high trail south of the villages. Coming back, the LT wants us to come down the road along the paddies, closer to the villages and check them out. Y'all make sure you're squared away and standing tall in the morning. Lieutenant Fitzer's gonna inspect your weapons before we head out. Any questions?"

"I thought this was going to be a platoon patrol?" Tim said.

"And?" Kurbo said.

Tim glanced around at the others. "There are only seventeen of us here."

The usual snickers came from the old heads.

"The firebase takes priority," Kurbo said. "We're leaving some men behind to help with guard duty. Besides we have three dudes on R&R and one over at LBJ for assaulting an NCO. Any more questions?"

The old heads were busy swapping their C-ration peaches, fruit cocktail, and cigarettes. They ignored him.

"We'll go by supply in the morning and pick up Claymores, flares, wire, and anything else we need. When you cherries get through here, take all that trash down to the firepit."

Martin figured they would remain cherries until a new group of replacements arrived. This was to be his first patrol out to the highway since arriving, and despite all his apprehensions, he actually looked forward to it. He hoped Kurbo was right about the absence of enemy activity in the AO. Regardless, lying around smoking cigarettes, playing poker, and listening to the AFVN had grown monotonous. Anything would be better than that, or so he hoped.

The next morning Martin was beginning to think the patrol had been cancelled when Kurbo stomped into the hootch and shouted, "Fall out! Let's go. Bring your gear."

This wasn't the normal army first call. That usually came well before daylight, but here at FSB Suzy things were different. It was already bright outside, with the sun shining through the trees and the ocean waters glittering in the distance.

Lieutenant Fitzer stood with Kurbo while the men fell into a loose formation. Peebles and Douchie were the last to arrive, their bootlaces trailing in the dust and their fatigue shirts half-buttoned. Neither had shaved, and both had hugely dilated pupils—probably from smoking their morning weed. Martin cast a quick glance at

Kurbo, but the little platoon sergeant turned toward Fitzer.

"The platoon is ready for inspection, LT."

The lieutenant raised his chin and gazed past Kurbo.

"Good morning, men."

Fitzer, too, seemed oblivious to the two sad sacks as they knelt and laced their boots.

"This is the first time out for you newbies, so pay attention to the old heads, and you'll be okay. The platoon looks good to me, Sergeant Kurbo. Let's get ready to move out. You said first squad is taking the lead. Ernie and I, along with Doc, will follow you. Second squad can bring up the rear."

Martin, Tim, and Paul cast questioning glances at one another. They had spent half the night cleaning their weapons and preparing for this non-inspection. The patrol filed past the guard tower and out through the main gate. The one they called Chief seemed to take his point man position seriously. He and the man walking slack, Taco, carried their weapons at the ready, but the others lasted only a few hundred meters before going into boy scout mode.

Martin followed Douchie. Behind him were Tim and Paul, followed by Kurbo, the lieutenant, his RTO, and the medic, Doc Cowan. Peebles was at the rear of the squad. He and Douchie were now smoking cigarettes and walking with their M-16s across their shoulders, as were most of the guys in second squad. Martin could only bite his tongue and hope for the best.

The platoon walked atop a dike past a couple of hamlets before picking up a trail that swung further south. The column bunched up and spread out again as they passed through a grove of banyans and out into an open expanse of grasses. Martin studied his counterparts. None of them seemed particularly watchful, except for Chief and Taco. The patrol covered nearly four clicks before Kurbo called the column to a halt.

"Take five."

Martin gazed about as the men dropped their rucksacks, pulled out canteens, and fired up cigarettes. There was no regard for security. They were sitting in the open on the trail where it crossed a low grassy rise. Tree lines to the north and south loomed dark and shadowy. The point man, Chief, had walked thirty or forty meters farther down the hill before stopping. His slack man, Sergeant Taco, had joined him. They at least seemed to be scanning the wood lines before relaxing.

"We're just sitting up here like ducks in a shooting gallery," Martin said to no one in particular.

"Shut the fuck up, cherry," Douchie said. "At least up here we got us a little breeze."

Martin walked down the hill and sat closer to Chief and Taco. Fifteen minutes later Kurbo shouted for the platoon to saddle up and move out.

CHAPTER THREE

When the platoon arrived that afternoon, Highway One was plugged with people and military vehicles. A column of ARVN trucks had stopped, partially blocking the road while its men milled about in a roadside market. Thatched hootches sat along the highway where black-toothed mama-sans chewed betel nuts and squatted behind makeshift tables and ground cloths filled with almost every black-market product imaginable—everything from Pentax cameras and Seiko wristwatches to American C-rations, bottles of Coca Cola, and K-bar knives.

The platoon broke ranks and wandered amongst the vendors along with the South Vietnamese troops. The ARVN soldiers were buying bowls of fermented fish heads with rice. They scooped the rice with their fingers and gnawed the fish heads like candied apples. Tim and Paul watched them as if they were seeing Siamese twins at a roadside carnival. For Martin, the sight of the soldiers eating the fish heads would have been bearable had it not been for their stench. He had to look away.

Lieutenant Fitzer and Sergeant Kurbo had walked down the highway toward a jeep where two ARVN officers were standing. Gazing about at the thick palms and vegetation on the hills to the west, Martin took pause. The sun-glared paddies and scores of thatched huts were ideal locations for the Viet Cong to spring an ambush, yet no one seemed particularly concerned. No security had been posted. He eased to within earshot of the officers gathered behind the jeep.

One of the Vietnamese offices was a major with mottled burn scars on both forearms. The other was a colonel who was speaking fluent English. Sitting in the shade against the tire of a deuce-and-a-half, Martin took a swig of lukewarm water from one of his canteens. He listened to their conversation. The ARVN colonel was asking questions about the firebase, which Fitzer and Kurbo were answering, seemingly without reservation.

"Yeah," Fitzer said, "the artillery boys finally got that part the other day, so they have both one-five-fives operational now. Only problem now is their FD&C officer rotated out, and the new guy is still learning the ropes."

"Ah, let me see," the colonel said. "Ah, yes, the Fire Direction and Control officer."

"Ha! Yeah," Kurbo said. "You better tell your boys to keep their heads down when they call in fire-missions."

The colonel cast a disgusted glare toward the little sergeant.

"I suppose your mortars will be more accurate, Sergeant."

"Yeah, we wish, but they ain't gonna do us much good right now. We got a requisition in for more rounds, 'cause the salt started corroding the old ones. A couple of our clowns let the wind blow the tarps off the crates during the monsoon and they got soaked for a week before we noticed. We're not sure they're safe. Besides, if you're outside of three clicks we're not supposed to fire 'em anyway."

It would have been useful to see the Colonel's eyes, and Martin wanted to look their way, but he didn't want to be obvious. He wasn't sure who the Vietnamese officers were, or why Fitzer and

Kurbo were so needlessly sharing information—too much of which could be used against them if it fell into enemy hands. And why was this ARVN colonel so interested, anyway?

"Where will you make your position tonight?" the colonel asked.

"We're heading up the highway to the river and set up there with your boys guarding the bridges."

"Yes. That would be wise, but I believe the only open positions are those on the hill to the west of the railroad bridge," the colonel said.

"Good enough," Kurbo said, "as long as we're inside the wire."

A few minutes later, Tim and Paul came walking up the side of the highway. Like kids at a county fair, they were grinning and drinking bottles of black-market Coca Cola while comparing new sheath knives they'd bought.

"Hey Martin, check out these badass K-Bars," Paul said. "Lady said she got them from a Marine up at Chu Lai."

"I'm strapping mine on my leg like a boot knife," Tim said.

The two sat beside Martin.

Tim motioned with his head toward the officers. "What are they talking about?"

Martin glanced up to see the Vietnamese colonel and Lieutenant Fitzer looking his way. The colonel had him fixed with a hard stare. It was time for damage control.

"Aw, hell. I don't know. Officer stuff I suppose."

After a moment the officers seemed satisfied and returned to their conversation.

"You brought only two squads with you today," the colonel said.

Kurbo glanced around at the men wandering about the roadside market. "That's my whole platoon. They promised us some more replacements, but the company is short right now."

"Did you see those gooks eating the rotten fish heads?" Paul asked.

The colonel again cast a quick glance their way.

"Shut up, dude!" Tim hissed. "That gook officer heard you."

"Hey," Kurbo said. "You clowns take your asses back up there with the rest of the men."

Martin climbed to his feet, while Kurbo and the South Vietnamese colonel stood watching in stone-faced silence. He retrieved his M-16 and walked back up the shoulder of the road. Paul and Tim hurried to catch up.

"What's his problem?" Paul asked.

Paul was somewhat of a dolt, but not wanting to alienate him, Martin remained silent.

"You just called that ARVN officer a *gook*, you idiot," Tim said.

"I didn't call *him* a gook. I was just saying—"

"Yes, you did. You—"

"Why don't you guys give it a rest," Martin said. "Were any of these people selling liquor?"

"Yeah, there's one old gook over there with two or three cases," Tim said, "but they were going like snow cones in July."

A string of green Huey gunships suddenly appeared as they came thundering down the highway from the north, passing low overhead, before rising, tilting on their sides, and turning west out over the hills. Their main rotors cracked as the turbine engines screamed. Paul raised his fist and gave a loud, "Yahoooo!"

Martin found the old man selling the liquor, but there were only four bottles remaining—one bottle of Cutty Sark Scotch, one of Jose Cuervo Tequila, and two bottles of Wild Turkey 101. Likely stolen from some army installation, the bottles still had the original military seals on the caps. Martin could hardly believe his eyes—Kentucky Bourbon nine thousand miles from home. Things were looking up.

Douchie walked up behind them. "When that old gook had three full cases, he was selling that shit for five bucks a bottle. He's wanting ten now. I'm stickin' with weed."

Martin picked up the Cutty Sark. "How much?"

"Ten dolla," the old man said.

Martin frowned and waved him off. Setting down the Cutty Sark, he picked up one of the Wild Turkey fifths. The crowd of soldiers had thinned, and most had wandered over to the shade beside the big trucks.

"What about this one?" he asked.

The leathery-faced old man squinted but said nothing. Martin set the bottle down and started to turn away.

Clearly flustered, the old man ran his knotty fingers through the remains of his thinning gray hair. "Five dolla," he said.

"Okay," Martin said. He paid the man and pushed the bottle into his ruck sack.

The ARVN troops began climbing aboard the trucks as their engines roared to life and belched clouds of black exhaust. Kurbo came up the shoulder of the highway shouting, "Fall in."

"Looks like we're moving out," Paul said.

Tim turned slowly and gazed at him. "You are a damned genius, Maziensky. You know that?"

"Shut up," Kurbo shouted. "Fall in. Chief, take point. We're moving up to the bridges, where we'll set up our NDP inside the wire with the ARVNs. They've been told to expect us, but make sure you signal them before we get too close—don't want the crazy fucks opening up on us."

Martin studied his fellow soldiers as the platoon formed up. The men were almost schizophrenic with their actions—one moment as if they were in the deepest boonies and the next like they were on an outing at the park. The sun was low in the sky when the patrol arrived at the bridge outside the ARVN wire. After a brief discussion with a Vietnamese sentry, he directed them westward to a knoll above the railroad bridge where the remnants of several old bunkers remained. Lieutenant Fitzer walked down to visit with the CO of the ARVN company guarding the highway bridge.

Kurbo stood with his hands on his hips gazing around the hillside. "Douchie, you take two men and go over there to that old bunker on the river. Chief, you take two back that way by the railroad. Lopez, you and two more head to that bunker back the other way."

Martin began noticing shell craters everywhere, mostly overgrown with grass and vegetation, but some were fresh. Several of the bunkers had been blown apart from within—probably by sappers with satchel charges. There had been a hell of a fight here. A high wooded ridge rose steeply to the west—a perfect place for an assaulting force to fire rocket-propelled grenades and recoilless rifles directly down onto the little hilltop.

"Shadows," Kurbo shouted. "You and the other cherries get to be king on the hill. Y'all take that bunker up there on the west side. Rotate watches. One man stays awake at all times."

"Brilliant, just fucking brilliant," Martin mumbled.

"You say something, Shadows?"

"I said vigilant, Sarge. We'll be staying vigilant."

"That's good. Now, get your ass moving."

CHAPTER FOUR

Paul and Tim followed Martin to the top of the hill where they stood over the open remains of a bunker. It was now a hole in the ground. The remaining sandbags were shredded and there was the faint stench of something dead. Martin realized it was likely the overlooked remains of soldiers who had been manning the bunker when a Viet Cong sapper tossed a satchel charge inside.

The sun was setting, streaking the western sky with purple and orange. Someone on the hillside below had tuned a transistor radio to the AFVN, and the golden-voiced Tony Williams and The Platters singing "Twilight Time" echoed across the green hillside. The radio's tinny echoes quickly evaporated into the surrounding vastness of the hills as Martin sighed deeply and gazed out at the horizon. The "deepening shadows" of this night weren't gathering any "splendor."

The drill instructors at Polk knew exactly what they were talking about. He heard their words again, especially the part where they said Nam was a crazy place. The truth in those words was growing more apparent each day. Men like Paul and Tim depended on their leaders to help them see the next sunrise, yet they were being sadly neglected. Three new men, their first night in the boonies, and the only thing they were told was this destroyed bunker was their position for the night. Martin realized he had to take charge.

"I'm going to ease out there to the wire at the base of the ridge and set out a trip flare and a Claymore. Why don't you guys use your entrenching tools and dig the dirt out of that shell hole over there?"

"Why can't we just sleep in this hole where the bunker was?" Tim asked.

"It smells bad," Martin said.

Paul jumped down into the hole.

"Pheww! It does sort of stink down here. Smells like a dead rat or something."

"Do you guys know how this bunker was destroyed?"

They glanced at one another and shook their heads in unison.

"Most likely a VC sapper threw a satchel charge inside."

"So?" Paul said.

"So, what do you think happened to the men who were in there?"

"I'm pretty sure they were killed," Paul said.

"More like blown to smithereens," Tim said.

"That's right, and that odor is from the pieces of them they couldn't dig out of the dirt," Martin said.

Paul scrambled from the hole and stood gazing back down inside while wiping his hands on his fatigues.

"Now, go dig us a position in that shell hole over there while I put out this trip flare and a Claymore. Will you?"

"Sure, Martin," Tim said.

"Yeah, sure," Paul added.

When Martin returned with the wire to the Claymore, the last light of day was fading into nightfall. Paul and Tim were still digging madly, and the hole was now chest deep.

"That's probably deep enough. Let's take a break and eat our C-rations. Which one of you wants first watch?"

Neither answered. Martin shrugged. "Hell, let's eat. We'll decide when we're done."

It was Martin's first night outside the wire of the firebase, and despite his two companions, he was feeling terribly alone. He broke open a carton of C-rations. If there was one thing he missed besides his family, it was his mother's cooking. Originally from the outskirts of a rural Mississippi town, she never forgot what she had learned in her mother's kitchen. Whether it was the most perfectly fried chicken served on a Sunday afternoon, or homemade biscuits smothered in sausage gravy for breakfast, his mother did food right.

Army chow-hall food wasn't too bad, but the first time he had C-rations was during training at Fort Polk. When Martin punctured a can with a P-38, he could only describe it as the odor of a rank fart. For two days he refused to eat C-rations, giving in only when he realized surviving on cigarettes alone wasn't possible.

But that was then. He doused the can's contents with Tabasco and devoured them as if they were Mama's own country ham and butter beans. And it wasn't because he had lowered the bar for the C-rations. Hell, he'd thrown the damned bar away—no expectations, no disappointments. Tim and Paul demonstrated the same practicality as they wolfed down beans and wienies and turkey loaf. After licking the congealed grease from his plastic spoon, Martin stuck it back in his pocket.

The nighttime silence was shattered by a sudden but distant series of explosions followed by the crackle and pop of dozens of weapons. It was coming from across the river to the north. The chug of an M-60 machinegun sounded continuously above the chatter of the other weapons. Martin stood beside the hole with Tim and Paul, gazing at the flashes of grenades and RPGs reflecting against the night sky. It was a sobering sight—the first firefight they had witnessed.

Martin caught sight of someone walking up the hill toward them. "You guys get in the hole," he whispered.

Kurbo and Fitzer hadn't bothered giving them challenge and passwords, but one of the men was wearing an American helmet. "Get in the hole, *now*," he whispered. "Hurry. Someone is coming up the hill."

Despite the distant sounds of the firefight, Martin heard a distinct click as Tim thumbed the safety on his M-16.

"Wait!" he whispered. "I think it's Kurbo. Put your weapon back on safe."

The three men remained motionless, Paul and Tim in the hole and Martin kneeling beside it. Kurbo came up the hill but had walked to the edge of the old bunker where he stood with his head jerking about.

"Hey, where are you cherries at?" he said in a loud voice.

"Over here, Sarge," Martin answered in a subdued voice.

"What the fuck are you doing over there?"

"We made our NPD over here because the old bunker is silhouetted at the top of the hill and it stinks," Martin said.

"I told you dumbasses to use this bunker."

He walked their way while the firefight on the distant hilltop continued sputtering and roaring. By now several parachute flares were drifting eerily across the night sky.

"You see that shit? Well, do you?"

"We see it," Martin answered.

"Charlie is kicking somebody's ass. You fuckers better start listening to what I say. You need to stay awake tonight."

"Don't worry, Sarge," Paul said. "I'm not about to sleep—not with that shit going on."

"Good. Now, get your sorry asses back over there to that bunker."

"Sarge," Martin said, "I've already set out a Claymore just down the hill there, and if—"

"Who the fuck told you to put out a Claymore?"

"It's the way we were trained at Fort Polk. I thought it was standard procedure."

"You don't do shit, cherry, unless you ask me first. You understand?"

"Yes, Sergeant. Do you want me to go out there and get it?"

"Just stay here where you're at and stay awake. I'll deal with you idiots when we get back to the firebase."

Kurbo stomped away down the hillside from where he had come.

"Man, that sonofabitch is really pissed," Tim said.

"Don't worry about it," Martin said. "I'll tell him it was all my idea. Now, who wants first watch?"

"I'm not sleeping tonight," Paul said.

"Me neither," Tim added. "You seem to know a lot about this shit, Shadows. How come you know so much?"

"I suppose I paid attention to the drill sergeants back at Polk."

"Where are you from?" Tim asked.

"Western Kentucky, just north of Bowling Green. How about you guys?"

"I'm from Cincinnati," Tim said. "How about you, Paul, where are you from?"

"Pennsylvania," Paul said, "near Harrisburg."

The men wrapped themselves in their poncho liners to ward off the mosquitoes that were now feeding voraciously on their exposed skin.

"What kind of name is Shadows?" Tim asked.

"Indian," Martin said. "My father is full-blooded Lakota Sioux."

"No shit?" Paul said.

Martin had decided that despite Paul's simple-mindedness, he was really a nice guy.

"No shit, Paul. He's from Montana originally, but my mother lived near a little town east of Bowling Green and didn't want to leave Kentucky, so my father settled there, and they got married."

"Man, that's cool," Paul said.

"So, what did you do back in Kentucky before you ended up in the army?" Tim asked.

Knowing instinctively that neither Paul nor Tim had been to college, Martin didn't want to tell them he had graduated from Western Kentucky.

"I did a little construction work after high school, some fishing, and some hunting. My father started me hunting when I was a kid. He was a natural, and we hunted in the hills around home. He never was a man to say much, but he taught me a lot. How about you guys?"

"I got drafted right out of high school," Paul said. "I flunked fourth grade, so I was a little bit older than the others, and the army got me first."

"I tried to get a job in Cincinnati after high school," Tim said, "but I got drafted, too. They said this damned war was about over, so I figured on outlasting the draft board, but they got me anyway. Me and my girlfriend are going to get married when I get home. She's the best girl ever—sorta like that Temptations song, "My Girl," you know? I'm going to make it through this shit because Annie's waiting for me."

Tim blanched, suddenly self-conscious. Pulling off his helmet, he scratched his head.

"Sorry. Didn't mean to sound all mushy or whatever. So, what kind of hunting did you do back in Kentucky?"

"Hey, don't be sorry. I'm jealous," Martin said. "I wish I had a steady, but yeah, we hunted most anything my mother would cook—rabbits, squirrels, even deer during the fall. Me and my father butchered the deer and put the meat in the deep freeze. We put up at least two every year."

"You really killed a deer?" Paul asked.

"I started hunting when I was twelve. My father took me. I've killed five or six since then."

"Wow. That's awesome," Paul said. "I've always wanted to go deer hunting. I killed a pheasant one time on the railroad track near my house, but I've never shot a deer."

"There wasn't much hunting where I lived," Tim said. "Besides I was pretty busy with my girlfriend."

He pulled a neck chain with a silver medal from inside his fatigue shirt.

"This is a Saint Xavier medal Annie gave me. She's such an optimist, always finding the silver linings. She went to college there at night. Xavier is a men's school, but they're supposed to let the girls start going during the day, next year. That's so 'Annie.' She's really dedicated, and, oh sorry—didn't mean to get off the subject. I wouldn't mind trying to deer hunt someday. Maybe we can all meet at your place after this war is over and go hunting."

The last thing Martin wanted to do was stifle their dreams.

"Sure. Maybe so, but deer hunting isn't easy. You have to be really quiet, keep your eyes open, and move slow. It takes a lot of patience. Deer hunting teaches you how to move in the woods and how to read sign. My father taught me a lot, too. One of the most difficult things is learning how to see a deer. A big buck can be standing right in front of you sometimes and you won't see him till he takes off like a rocket. Not much chance of getting a decent shot then."

The firefight to the north slackened as a red stream of tracers appeared from the sky above the hilltop. A few seconds later the distant buzzing sound of a minigun arrived. It was a Spooky gunship circling above the battle.

"Damn!" Tim said. "Did you see that?"

It was said Spooky could put a round in every square foot of ground for a thousand meters. Some called them "game changers," while others called them saviors from heaven. C-47 and C-130 gunships, they flew patterns around besieged firebases and perimeters, showering the encircling enemy troops with a devastating rain of lead.

"We better keep our voices down," Martin said. "There's no telling who might be out there listening."

"Yeah, you're right."

Martin picked up the clacker for the Claymore and handed it to Tim.

"Take this. You know how to use it, right?"

"Yeah. Where are you going?"

"I'm going to get down in this hole and sleep a few hours. Do not under any circumstances go to sleep. If you hear something out of the ordinary, wake me up. You two stay awake till midnight, then I'll take the rest of the night. Is that okay with you?"

"Sure," Tim said.

"I'm still not sleeping tonight," Paul said.

"Okay, I just need you to stay awake till midnight."

Paul shrugged. "Sure."

"All right then. If I wake up and you guys have fallen asleep, I'll scalp you both."

Paul eyed him for a moment before his teeth showed with a white grin in the darkness. "Aww shit, Shadows, you're just jokin' around, but don't worry. We won't fall asleep."

"He just said he's half Injun, Maziensky. I don't think he's kidding."

Martin wrapped his poncho liner over his head and closed his eyes. Paul was going to have a long year in Vietnam—if he made it out alive. His only hope for survival was for someone to take him under a wing and watch after him. For a moment Martin almost wished he could be that person, but the thought lasted only a moment. He had his own problems to deal with.

It seemed no more than twenty minutes passed before Martin jerked awake. Someone was lying against him, breathing heavily. Pulling the poncho liner from around his face, he shoved the comatose Paul away. Tim was still standing and gazing out toward the perimeter wire.

"What time is it?" he whispered.

"It's almost midnight," Tim answered. "Did you get a good nap?"

"Yeah. How long has numb-nuts been sleeping?"

"Hell. He passed out twenty minutes after you went to sleep."

The two men continued whispering.

"Have you seen or heard anything?"

"Nothing. It's been quiet."

Martin climbed to his feet and peered out over the edge of the foxhole. A milky fog had risen from the river, blotting out everything beyond twenty meters.

"Get some rest. I'll take it till daylight."

Tim sat down and covered his head. Within minutes he was breathing heavily along with Paul. It was as Tim said—real quiet. Martin couldn't help but wonder if Kurbo was checking on the other men. As lax as the platoon sergeant was with discipline, the entire platoon was probably asleep by now. With everything shrouded in fog, a sliver of new moon created little more than a slight contrast in the night shadows.

After a while Martin tried to look at his wristwatch. The phosphorescent dial said it was after 0100 hours. It was a long time till daylight. There came a pop from down near the wire. The fog below began glowing. Something had tripped the flare. Martin's heart pounded with an infusion of adrenaline as he reached for his M-16 and thumbed the safety to fire, but he remembered the words of one of the drill instructors. *Never fire your weapon at night unless you must because you will give away your position.* He laid the M-16 at the edge of the hole and pulled a fragmentation grenade from his pocket.

CHAPTER FIVE

Martin was frozen with indecision. What if it was one of their men out there wandering around? He slid his middle finger into the grenade's ring. There came another sound. It wasn't much—perhaps someone running softly in the grass. Off to his left he spotted movement in the fog. Someone was coming up the hill at a full sprint toward the empty bunker. Snatching the ring on the frag, he held the spoon in place and waited. The runner threw something toward the bunker and dove to the ground.

It dawned on him—a grenade. He ducked as the explosion flashed bright in the night sky. The man was on his feet again, running back the way he had come. Martin threw his grenade as hard as he could down the hill and again ducked below the edge of the foxhole. It seemed forever but was probably less than four seconds before it detonated with a flash and a boom. Slowly he raised his head and stared into the fog and shadows. Paul and Tim were now fully awake, standing beside him with their weapons at the ready. The trip flare was still burning down the hill, casting an eerie white light into the fog. Holding his M-16 steady, Martin waited.

"What was it?" Paul asked. "Did you see somebody?"

"Sshhh," Tim whispered. "Not so loud."

"Here," Martin said. "Take the clacker and stay down. When I give you the word, blow the Claymore."

"Did you throw those grenades?" Tim hissed.

Martin raised a hand to silence him. After a couple minutes he whispered in Tim's ear. "I think it was a sapper. He threw a grenade into that old bunker. That's all I saw, and he ran back down the hill toward the wire."

"The sonofabitch thought we were in that bunker," Tim said.

"Yeah. I know."

"What are we going to do now?"

"We wait to see if there're more of them."

"I don't know about you," Tim said, "but I'm staying awake till daylight."

"Me too," Paul said, "but I sure wish I had a rifle."

He was the squad grenadier and toted the M-79.

"Do you have any flechette rounds for that thump gun?" Martin asked.

"Yeah."

"Put one in the chamber."

The hours crept by, and it seemed an eternity before the stars faded, the moon set, and behind them, the eastern sky glowed with a pre-dawn orange. Martin figured Kurbo or the lieutenant would have checked on them, but no one had shown up and his frustration had now morphed to anger. There wasn't a thimble-full of leadership between them, but he had to remain silent and play his role as a Private First-Class.

The fog still clung to the hillside as the light of dawn slowly lit the perimeter. Behind him came the sound of footsteps and Martin glanced over his shoulder. It was Kurbo and Taco coming up the hill. The little platoon sergeant was shaking his head in disgust as he walked up and stood with his hands on his hips.

"Well, you cherries totally freaked out your first night in the bush, didn't you?"

Taco laughed.

"It sounded like one of your grenades went off pretty close. Anybody hurt?"

Paul wagged his head.

"It was a sapper," Martin said. "He—"

"Bullshit!" Kurbo shouted. "You dumb fucks let your imagination run away with you, and you kept us all awake."

"It was a sapper, Sarge," Tim said. "He—"

"Did you actually see him?" Kurbo asked.

Tim shrugged. "Well, no, but—"

"No! No, you didn't. I didn't think you did. You pussies just got scared of the dark and started chunking frags, didn't you?"

"I threw one grenade," Martin said.

"Don't add to your problems by lying, cherry. I heard at least two explosions."

"That's right. The sapper threw a grenade first."

Kurbo pressed his lips into a flat smile of skepticism.

"Yeah. So, you saw this guy?"

"Yeah, he tripped the flare down there, and I saw him running toward that old bunker over there on the left. He threw a grenade into the hole and ran back toward the wire. That's when I threw my frag."

"How come you didn't just hose him down with your sixteen?"

"I didn't know if he was alone, and I didn't want to give away our position."

"Taco," Kurbo said, "what do you think? Is Shadows blowing smoke up my ass?"

Taco was buck sergeant Ray Lopez, a fourth-generation Mexican immigrant, from San Antonio, Texas. He glanced around and shrugged. "Maybe we should walk down to the wire and see if we can find something."

Kurbo gazed down the hill. "We'll wait till this fog burns off. You cherries better eat some C's. We're moving out as soon as we can see. I'm going back to tell the LT y'all ain't dead. I'll be back in a little while."

Martin dumped packets of coffee, sugar, cocoa, and creamer into his canteen cup, added water and heated the concoction with a heat tab. While it warmed, he opened a can of beans and weenies for breakfast. Tim and Paul were eating their C-rations as well.

"Man, this is some awful shit," Tim said, spooning a solidified concoction of ham and eggs from the green can.

Paul nodded, but both were eating like wolves on a deer carcass. A few minutes later Kurbo and Taco came walking up the hill with Lieutenant Fitzer. The sun had risen, and the fog was thinning. Sitting at the edge of the hole, Martin gazed up as the three men approached.

"Good morning, sir," Martin said.

Fitzer's eyes were bloodshot.

"Is it?" the lieutenant asked. "Sergeant Kurbo tells me you boys came up with some cock and bull story about a VC sapper sneaking inside the wire."

Fitzer was probably about the same age as Martin, but taller and more muscular—probably played football for some small college. He carried himself with the casual swagger of a jock whose ego elevated him above the peons.

"So, tell me, how did you manage to see this sapper at night in the fog?"

Since enlisting, Martin had met a number of men who had questionable IQs. Someone like Paul, a kid from rural Pennsylvania with a high school diploma, was understandably not the brightest person, but from men like Kurbo, an E-6 platoon sergeant, and Fitzer, a first lieutenant platoon leader, he expected more—not a lot more, but at least some level of inquisitive analysis before drawing conclusions. He eyed them in silence.

"Thinkin' 'bout changin' your story, are you?" Kurbo said.

"I'm not changing anything, Sergeant. It happened the way I said." Martin stood and turned toward Fitzer. "Lieutenant...*sir*..." He made a point of pausing to display his growing anger, but he could not step over the line. "The sapper hit the trip flare down by the wire and there was a little bit of a moon out last night. I heard him running and saw his silhouette over there on the left when he threw the grenade into the old bunker position."

Kurbo rolled his eyes and turned his head to one side in a childish show of doubt.

"Who authorized you to put out a trip-flare, private?" the lieutenant asked.

"I didn't realize using my infantry training for the proper method of securing our night defensive position required special permission...*sir*."

It was clear that Martin's intentional delay before emphasizing "sir" left Fitzer feeling his authority was being challenged. The lieutenant squinched his lips into a tight circle but seemed at a loss for words.

"LT, since this cherry seems to think he knows so much, why don't we let him walk point back to the firebase?"

Fitzer slowly nodded.

"Good idea, Sergeant Kurbo, but let's walk down the hill

anyway and take a look around. Sergeant Lopez, you take the lead."

Martin turned to follow them, but the men stopped and looked back at him.

"Shadows, you and your buddies stay here," the lieutenant said. "We'll be back in a minute."

Fitzer, Kurbo, and Taco walked down the hill and milled about for several minutes while Martin and Tim watched. Paul had opened a can of apricots and was oblivious to what was happening. They were probably a couple hundred meters away, when Taco pointed at something. Kurbo and the lieutenant came over and looked down at the ground. The men were now standing just inside the pile of concertina at the base of the hill, but a mist of light fog partially obscured them.

"I think they found something," Tim said.

Martin nodded. "We'll see."

A few minutes later they came back up the hill.

"Shadows," Kurbo said, "you and your buddies gather your shit and get your asses down to the CP. You'll be on point today. Gates, you'll walk slack for him."

"Slack?" Tim said.

"Your know-it-all buddy, PFC Shadows, can explain it to you. Now, get your asses in gear."

"What did you find down there?" Martin asked.

"We didn't find shit," Kurbo said.

Taco stared at the cocky little platoon sergeant. Martin saw it in his eyes. They had found something, but why did they refuse to admit it? It was strange. Even stranger was the memory of something his grandfather had said during their recent visit. The old man had foreseen a conflict somewhat like this in one of his visions, but Martin almost laughed at the thought. Two Shadows had made a predictable guess and there was so much more that was so farfetched he refused to worry about it.

CHAPTER SIX

Tim and Paul finished their C-ration breakfasts and began gathering their gear for the trek back to the firebase. Martin though was lost in thought as he recalled his visit with Grandfather Two Shadows in Montana. The old man's prognostications may have been farfetched, but it was uncanny how he had predicted this conflict with his leaders. Even Martin's mother, a devout Christian, had agreed with his father and encouraged him to learn more about Lakota beliefs.

He later described the visit to his mother as an "eye-opener." A highly respected elder amongst his people, Grandfather Two Shadows lived on the Fort Peck reservation, where they called him a wicasa wakan. The best Martin could figure, the old man was somewhere between a shaman and a preacher of sorts.

Martin's mother said Two Shadows was the only reason Martin's father had survived World War II, and she encouraged her son to listen to the things he said. It was clear she was willing to try anything to help him survive the war in Vietnam. Martin put little stock in ancient superstitions, but because it pleased her, he went along with it.

It wasn't that he was ashamed of his heritage. As a kid he reveled in being the Sioux brave—counting coup on his enemies and hunting buffalo on the Great Plains. But like most childhood games, they gave way to the reality of adulthood, college, and the military. Fresh out of OCS, he was now a commissioned Army officer, and he had to act like one. The military was an exacting business, and there was no room for superstition or anything outside the military code of conduct.

The trip to Montana was inevitable, and it was the least he could do for his mother and father, especially after all they had done for him. Making up his mind to tolerate old Two Shadows's feather-waving and chanting for a few days, he tossed his duffle bag into the pickup truck, bid his mother goodbye, and headed west. Purchasing a plane ticket and flying would have been easier but traveling by road gave him time to think. It also had the more immediate pleasure of closer intercourse with the cornfields, forests, rivers, and mountains—the things he loved most about the country.

The sun was low in the Montana sky that afternoon when he arrived—its glare dulled by a dusty amber haze. A front was moving in and like Martin, the weather was growing restless. He hoped to make a good impression on his grandfather, but he wasn't quite sure why it was so important to him. It had been over twelve years since he had last seen him. Martin wished now he had worn his dress uniform. He wanted to show him he was no longer a kid. Besides, the old man would be impressed with all the braids and brass buttons—or so he thought.

An old woman stood on the stoop of a clapboard house—one that Martin didn't remember as being so small. Parking the pickup in the front yard, he got out and walked to the porch. His memory was hazy, but he recognized his grandmother. She looked up at him with the grayed eyes of age and opened her arms only slightly. He pulled her close and she laid her head against his chest.

"It's good to see you, grandmother."

But after a quick hug, she stepped back as if she had taken undue liberties.

"Your grandfather is waiting inside."

He bussed her lightly on the forehead and the old woman's eyes lit up as if the sun had risen in them. She held his hand for a moment longer before letting go. The door creaked as his grandmother passed silently into another room, closing the door behind her. Two Shadows's face was lit by a small lamp, where he sat beside a woodburning stove. The room was hot and smelled of woodsmoke and tobacco. The old man, wearing a brown flannel shirt and leather work boots, sat close to the stove. Martin realized his grandfather was even older than he imagined and needed this warmth even in the summertime.

He stood at a respectful distance. The old man motioned with his hand for him to come closer.

"I am happy you saw fit to come visit me, Martin."

"Grandfather, it isn't that I simply saw fit, but that I needed and wanted to come. I wanted to see you and Grandmother."

The old man had been crouched close to the stove until that moment, but it seemed his frail body became suddenly energized as he sat upright and inhaled deeply. For the first time their eyes met, as Two Shadows took his full measure.

"You are indeed my grandson, Martin Shadows. Come, sit here beside me, and feel the warmth of my fire. I have much to say to you about my many visions, but that must wait until after we go to the sweat lodge tomorrow to pray for health and well-being. When we are done, we will share Chanunupa Wakan. It is a good one."

The old man motioned to a decorative leather sheath hanging on the far wall. Inside there appeared to be a pipe, and Martin was now glad he had begun smoking cigarettes since joining the army. Perhaps smoking the old man's pipe wouldn't make him sick.

"My lodge on the prairie is also good. I cut the birch poles on the river and the skins I have collected for this occasion. It is a small tepee, but it will make a good shelter for us while we smoke the pipe and talk of your coming journey."

Sweat streamed down Martin's face. It was going to be a long week staying in this small house with these two ancient people, going to his grandfather's sweat lodge, and smoking a pipe in a tepee. His military training had been a bitch, but it hardened him—hopefully enough to tolerate the coming days. He remembered his first day of Basic and the words of his drill instructor, *"If you keep your sense of humor, you can make it through this."* He would keep that in mind while allowing the old man his rituals. After all, it might be an experience he could someday share with his children.

CHAPTER SEVEN

Martin found it difficult to believe that Lieutenant Fitzer had agreed with Kurbo's suggestion that he take point. And it wasn't so much his fear of being on point as it was knowing several idiots were behind him with loaded weapons. To make matters worse, Tim was walking slack—the number two man in the column who was supposed to help spot ambushes and such, while Martin searched the trail for booby traps.

Two newbies with almost no in-country experience were leading the platoon that day, and it all seemed like fun and games for Kurbo and the Lieutenant. Martin's only reprieve was Kurbo left Taco up front behind Tim to make sure they went in the right direction.

At the ARVN colonel's suggestion, they were taking a different trail back to the firebase, one that ran along the river and skirted the backside of the villages. The vegetation here was thick, although much of it had died and regrown after being sprayed with Agent Orange. Three hours into the patrol, Kurbo called for a halt. Not a breeze stirred, and the heat was merciless. The villages at the top of the ridge were quiet.

After easing back to where Tim knelt with Taco, Martin toweled the sweat from his face and lit a cigarette. The rest of the platoon was strung out for forty or fifty meters back down the trail.

Kurbo and Fitzer were talking and making no effort to modulate their voices. Taco and Tim remained silent. Martin shook another cigarette from the pack and offered it to Taco.

"Thanks."

Martin lit it.

"What did you see when you walked down the hill this morning?" he asked.

Taco inhaled deeply from his cigarette and glanced back toward Fitzer and Kurbo. They were too far away to overhear the conversation.

"The wire down there was cut, and that frag you threw must've got that fucker good, 'cause there was a helluva blood trail."

"Really?" Tim said.

"Yeah. I think they're a little spooked. It's the first time we've had anything like that happen in months."

"Why did they say they didn't see anything?"

"You guys are cherries. They didn't want to look stupid for not believing you when you said you saw a sapper."

"They don't seem very worried about it now."

"Yeah, I know. The LT is brand new—been here maybe a month—and he does whatever Kurbo tells him. Kurbo, I don't know how he got to be a platoon sergeant. He has no sense."

"What about the CO? Doesn't he see it?"

"He got here a couple months ago. He's a good man, but he's a juicer—bad on the bottle. They said his infantry company got ambushed by NVA regulars up near Pleiku in '67. He got hit bad, lost his RTO and First Sergeant, but managed to get most of the company out alive. They say he's a hero, but he doesn't care about much of anything—lets the platoon leaders run things."

"I suppose that explains a lot," Martin said. "When was the last time you guys were in contact?"

"We haven't fired a shot in three months, but we did come out to the bridge back there a week or so ago after VC sappers killed a bunch of the ARVNs. I guess you saw the bunkers all blown to hell."

"Saddle up!" Kurbo shouted. "Let's move out."

"Thanks, Taco."

"Call me Ray. That Taco shit is something Kurbo came up with."

"Yeah. No problem."

Martin again took point and started down the trail. The trail was crossed by numerous paths coming down to the river from the villages along the ridge. He was no expert, but this route back to the firebase looked a lot riskier than the one they had taken coming out. The villages were on the high ground on one side and the river was on the other. Even a dumbass second lieutenant could see coming this way was a bad decision. He focused on the surrounding undergrowth, but his grandfather's words came back to him as he thought of that day in Montana.

The next morning, they had driven his pickup for miles up a gravel road deep into the reservation. Martin was wondering if they were going all the way to Canada when Two Shadows finally motioned for him to stop. He pulled the pickup off the road. They were in the middle of nowhere. The old man got out and stared into the distant hills. Martin shut off the engine and also stepped out. He retrieved a large brown paper bag from behind the truck seat. It contained something his father said the old man treasured— Kentucky tobacco.

A hawk soared high above, its screeching calls echoing across the hills. The air was clean and fresh, and the bird's amber breast glowed in the sunlight as it rode the summer thermals, climbing until it was high in the clouds. Martin gave his grandfather the bag. The old man glanced inside and smiled.

"It is a fine gift, grandson. It will bring me great pleasure. I thank you."

Two Shadows placed it on the truck seat.

"We will leave it here for now. This morning we are going to the sweat lodge."

The old man motioned toward a coulee, and Martin saw another pickup truck parked below, near a small, dome-shaped structure—the sweat lodge, he figured. It was covered with hides and tarps. Two men were there tending a fire. Martin followed his grandfather down the hill toward them. Standing back while they greeted one another, Martin waited until his grandfather turned and motioned him forward.

"Dogs Running and Thomas Bear, this is my grandson, Martin Shadows." They were old men, but not as old as his grandfather. Both nodded. "They will help us with our sweat lodge, today. Now take off your clothes and step inside."

Martin hadn't thought of this, and hesitated.

"All of them?"

"If you have undershorts, you may wear them, but the less you wear the better you will tolerate the sweat lodge."

Suddenly glad he wasn't wearing his tighty-whities, Martin stripped down to his army issue O.D. green boxers. Dogs Running and Thomas Bear collected his clothes and tossed them in the back of the pickup. If his fellow Army Officer Candidate School grads saw him now, they'd laugh their asses off. He felt like a fool—miles out in the middle of a Montana Indian reservation wearing nothing but his boxers.

He followed his grandfather as they stepped through the tiny opening into the steaming hot shadows of the little sweat lodge. A tarp, apparently placed by one of the men outside, closed over the opening. Martin sat on hides opposite his grandfather as a salty sweat trickled into his eyes. Two Shadows began chanting in a sing-song voice and combed the air with a large eagle feather. Martin wiped more sweat from his forehead.

The old medicine man chanted tirelessly, and Martin was beginning to feel like the steamed lobster he'd had a few weeks ago at a restaurant in Maryland. He watched as his grandfather took something from a small pouch and tossed it onto the glowing coals. It had been at least an hour, but the men outside continued pushing heated stones through a small hole at the base of the lodge, and dousing them with water. The air was thick and moist, and Martin became lightheaded as the old man's chants continued. He was beginning to understand the source of Two Shadows's visions.

After a while the chanting ceased, and silence reigned. It lasted until time and consciousness melded as one and there was no longer a before or after. Despite his loss of time, Martin was certain they had been in the lodge three or four hours. Beginning to fear he might lose consciousness, a wave of relief washed over him when the tarp was drawn from the opening. He squinted against the bright light.

His grandfather stood and motioned for him to follow. Wobbling on unsteady legs, he stepped out into the glorious Montana fresh air. Martin's world was aglow with a sense of relief as he sucked in the cool clean air. At least now he wouldn't have to explain to the army how he suffered heat stroke while on leave.

Grandfather and grandson rested and ate a small lunch of dried elk meat and Saltine crackers. When they were done, Two Shadows went to the pickup truck and returned with his pipe. He cradled it in his arm as if it were some sacred religious object.

"Come. Follow me."

Martin followed his grandfather over a small rise, where far out on a grassy flat there stood a tepee. Numerous animal hides covered the lodge and were painted with glyphs resembling men, animals, the sun, and the moon—symbols that no doubt carried meanings for those who understood such things. He followed the old man on a rocky path out to the shelter.

"We will make a fire," the old man said, throwing back the hide that covered the opening.

"A fire, Grandfather?"

It was summertime and they'd spent the entire morning in the sweat lodge. His body only now was beginning to cool.

"Yes. It is necessary for us to speak with the spirits."

Martin glanced around and drew a final breath of fresh air before stooping through the opening. After a few minutes the pungent odor of burning cedar and juniper filled the lodge. Two Shadows unsheathed his pipe and began stuffing the bowl from the contents of a deerskin pouch. A hazy smoke filled the interior of the tepee. Outside a prairie wind arose, buffeting the lodge while the men passed the pipe. Martin felt his head again becoming light as he realized the pipe might contain something besides tobacco.

The flames of the small fire licked around the logs, providing a dim light. Two Shadows's ruddy face and dark brown eyes glowed as a godlike visage in the shadows. They passed the pipe and they smoked. After a while Martin felt as if he had downed several glasses of his father's favorite bourbon—Four Roses. After the agony of the sweat lodge, it was a nice mellow feeling.

Nearly a half hour passed, and the old man had yet to speak, but it was not Martin's place to break the silence. He waited while considering his situation. He never imagined he would actually sit in a tepee and smoke a pipe. It reminded him of a Hollywood western, except this was not some movie director's imagination. It was the real thing. He had sweated that morning until he sweated no more. And he was here with a real descendant of the Lakota

Sioux nation—a man whose father had seen his people die while fighting for their lands.

Each time the old man restuffed the bowl and relit the pipe he inhaled from it before passing it to Martin. Martin hoped to survive without burning his vocal cords beyond recognition. It seemed another hour passed before Two Shadows set the pipe aside and tossed him a bottle of water. The cool water had the effect of a snow-melt stream on his parched throat, and his head was now swimming in a world of euphoric peace.

"My visions of you, my grandson, have been many since your father told me you joined the army. It is important that a man know himself better than his enemies. You have much to learn about yourself if you are to survive. So, listen, and I will tell you of the things I have seen.

"My first vision is one of a quest you must face—one far more difficult than that of your fellow soldiers. Some of them you will have no choice but to betray. Yet, it is your leaders whom you will face first. It is them you will confront, but they will lead you into a trap. You will feel great anguish, for some of those who follow these leaders will die with them. I have seen these visions, but I do not believe you will die because I have seen you carrying their bodies. Yet you too will face great suffering."

Well, this was good news. He was going to survive Vietnam, or so it seemed, but betraying his men was out of the question. He would never do that.

"I don't understand, Grandfather. I'll never betray any of my men. How do you see these things?"

It was immediately apparent that he'd offended the old man as Two Shadows fixed him with eyes that must have been akin to those of Jesus facing his Doubting Thomas. The old man took a deep breath but showed the same patience as Jesus when he invited the Twin to touch his wounds.

"The Great Spirit, Wakȟáŋ Tȟáŋka, takes many shapes and is within all things that inhabit the earth—the mountains, the streams, the antelope, and the buffalo. He has shown me these things and many more, but some I will not share because I know not what they mean."

"What others are there, Grandfather?"

"As I said, there are many. One such vision came to me only recently in a dream. I saw it clearly but could not understand it. You will find safety in a dark world filled with water from which you will bring war on your enemies. This is a strange place that I did not understand, because the rocks there cry, and those who hear their wails believe they come from the spirit world.

"I could make my own assumptions about this, but they may be incorrect. And another, my last vision—or maybe it was dream—I don't quite remember, but it too was equally as strange because I saw you with your warriors riding the fiery breath of a great thundering bird high into the mountains. I know these things must sound strange. As I said, I do not understand them, but be patient, my grandson. You will someday find their meaning."

More than anything else, Martin wanted to maintain respect for his grandfather. The old man was from another generation, another culture, and perhaps from another world, but he would not allow his doubts to show. Wailing rocks and riding the breath of fire-breathing birds were both visions well beyond the pale, yet he genuinely hoped for the day when he would understand his grandfather's culture and its strange symbolisms.

CHAPTER EIGHT

Martin tensed and froze mid-stride as he gazed up the trail. Something had left him spooked, and he was still having a tough time with the things his grandfather had said. Much of what Two Shadows predicted was easily explainable. His grandfather's visions were of things expected of men at war. Martin's very purpose for being here was a betrayal and a confrontation of sorts—and not necessarily unexpected given the current circumstances. After all, this *was* Vietnam, a world with a rationale not unlike Lewis Carroll's story about Alice and her trip down the rabbit hole.

Still, his grandfather's revelations predicted something even more ominous. Facing Kurbo and Lieutenant Fitzer seemed to have fulfilled one prediction, but it was the next words Two Shadows had spoken that now haunted him, *You will feel great anguish, for some of those who follow these leaders will die with them.* His rational mind, that of an army officer, again took over. He was being a fool. He had a job to do, yet he was standing on the trail, frozen in place, unable to move. His every sense was saying something wasn't right.

Martin was uncertain what had made him stop—a sound perhaps, or a subliminal flash of movement in the shadows, or perhaps some sixth sense that said something in his surroundings was out of place. There were no birds flitting about—no insects buzzing—only the shuffles and grunts of the careless men coming up the trail behind him. He had to trust his instincts. Turning, he motioned for them to kneel. Ray, Tim, and a few of the others dropped to a knee. But several, including Kurbo and Fitzer, remained standing while gazing impatiently up his way.

A slight breeze finally arose and stirred the thick vegetation around him. He could barely feel it on his face, but the wind brought with it an odor—that of rotted fish. He almost explained it away because of the river down below, but there was another— that of human body odor—and it wasn't his, but it was close.

Martin's neck tingled as he thumbed the safety on his M-16 to auto. Moving only his eyes he searched the undergrowth for something, anything that was out of place, and he saw it. The metallic taste of fear shellacked his mouth. A Chinese Claymore mine was less than ten feet away—just off the trail, and he was directly in front of it, but there was no trip wire—only the electrical lead wire to a remote detonator. His reaction was instantaneous.

Army training for men caught in an ambush always seemed counterintuitive. Charging directly into it with suppressing fire was best described as the least lethal option, yet the best one for escaping the kill-zone and surviving. The only thing he wanted to do now was to leap past the mine before it was detonated.

Glancing back at Tim and Ray he found his throat constricted to a point where he was barely able to croak "Ambush!"

Martin lunged up the slope past the Claymore as he sprayed the ridge above with his M-16. Pushing blindly through head-high palms, he sprinted thirty meters beyond the Claymore before realizing it hadn't detonated. Little more than three or four seconds had elapsed since he first spotted the mine. Fractions of seconds became eternities while the adrenaline overload had him dizzy, panting, and second-guessing himself. The Claymore was a directional mine, normally command-detonated, but had he really seen it, or was—?

"What the fuck?" Kurbo's voice came from the trail below. Martin knew now that he had overreacted. Perhaps the mine was an old one.

"Goddamit! You dumb cherry fuck, what the hell are—"

The mine detonated with a crashing boom that sent leaves, limbs, and hundreds of ball-bearing pellets toward the trail, shredding everything in their path, including the men below. Another, then a third mine detonated, but they were farther up the trail beyond the first one—harming no one. The clack of AK-47s came from higher up the ridge as the air became a hornet's nest of cracking green tracers zipping past.

Seeing flashes of movement above, Martin raised his M-16 and mashed the trigger. Nothing. He had already emptied the magazine. Fumbling, he pulled another from an ammo pouch and dropped the empty magazine from his weapon. The enemy stopped firing as the sound of men running came from above. By the time he slapped the new magazine into the rifle and released the bolt, there was only a shrill and unceasing scream coming from the trail below. It was the worst thing he had ever heard—the sounds of another human dying in agony.

"Shoot!" came Fitzer's voice—timid and hesitant. "Shoot, I said." This time his voice cracked but came with less uncertainty.

There was one, then two shots, followed by an inundating roar of M-16s firing in all directions. Leaves fluttered down around him as Martin curled into a ball. At any moment he expected a round to pass through him, shredding his guts and ending his life.

"Cease fire," he croaked. His throat still refused to open. The rounds thudded into the dirt, kicking clods into his eyes. Certain he was about to be silenced forever, his feeble voice suddenly found strength, and he yelled again, "Cease fire, dammit! Cease fire!"

"Cease fire!" someone below shouted. It again sounded like Fitzer's voice.

"They're gone," Martin shouted. "There's no one up here but me."

Metallic clacks of fresh magazines slapping into place came from below.

"You okay?" It was a barely audible voice coming from the brush a few feet below. So as not to raise his head, Martin peered beneath his arm. His eyes met those of Ray Lopez—wide and glassy with fear.

"Go on up the ridge where you can see better and stand watch. I'm going back down to see who was hit. I'll send a couple more men up here in a minute."

With that, Ray slid back down the hill. A few minutes after reaching the top of the ridge, Martin heard a slight rustle in the brush below. It was the soldier Kurbo called Chief. The silent one, he spoke to almost no one. Martin had heard someone call him Thunders and figured he was Indian, but he was otherwise a mystery. Although Chief seemed like an old head, he was still a buck private.

"You seen anything?" he asked.

Martin wagged his head. Chief's eyes searched the cover. A thick growth of ferns, palms, and saplings covered the ridge.

"Kurbo's dead," Chief said. "Damned Claymore caught him in the guts. It got that other cherry who was with you on point, and our RTO, Ernie. Him and Kurbo were walking up to you guys and walked right into that Claymore."

"Tim? Tim Gates is dead?"

"Yeah. I think that's his name. He was right in front of the Claymore. So were Ernie and Kurbo—pretty much made a mess out of all of them. He should have followed you and Taco up the hill. What's your name?"

"Shadows. Martin Shadows."

"Better get your shit together, Martin Shadows. Taco's in charge now. He put Douchie on point, and they're coming up through here with the rest of the platoon. We're turning south and humping over to the other trail other side of the villages where it's more open."

"Anybody wounded?"

"Only that other cherry, but it's not bad. He caught a piece of shrapnel across his arm, but he's okay. Doc wrapped it. He'll probably get a bunch of stitches when we get back."

"We aren't calling for a medevac?"

"Can't," Chief said. "Ernie's radio got fucked up when he was hit. It's dead. We have to hump the bodies back to the firebase."

Martin drew a quavering breath. He was certain now. This group was SNAFU personified—System Normal All Fucked Up. A contact from MAC-V was supposed to be at the firebase in a few days. They hadn't said how he was supposed to recognize him— only that the contact would find him. His first request was going to be for reassignment somewhere far away from this madness. He noticed Chief gazing steadily at him. Their eyes met.

"You have some Indian blood in you, don't you?"

Martin nodded. "Yeah. My father is Lakota Sioux from Montana."

Chief raised his brows.

"I am Lakota. I'm from the Rosebud Reservation in South Dakota. What's your father's name?"

"George Two Shadows."

Chief fished an unfiltered Lucky Strike from the red and white pack. He shook out another and offered it to Martin. Martin opened his Zippo carefully to avoid the loud ping and lit both cigarettes.

"Ray told me Kurbo insisted on calling him Taco. Is that how you got your name?"

"I prefer Thunders or my Jesuit name, Joe, but Kurbo didn't give me the choice."

Martin exhaled the smoke into the ground at his feet.

"I'll call you Thunders."

From down the hill came the rustle and grunts of the platoon approaching. Groups of four, including the lieutenant and Paul, were struggling with three sagging ponchos carrying the bodies of the dead. Paul's bloodied right arm was wrapped with a field dressing. Ray Lopez and Fitzer were at the front corners of the first poncho.

"Shadows," Ray called out, "come get hold of this one with the LT. Chief and I will walk point."

Lieutenant Fitzer looked dazed and seemed satisfied with Ray's decision. He didn't argue. Martin could only speculate how this man had completed officer training school and what influence had bought such a dumbass a commission as an Army officer.

CHAPTER NINE

It was late afternoon when the platoon walked through the gate at Firebase Suzy. A medevac chopper was called for Paul and to transport the dead. Dazed and exhausted, Martin was ready to go to his hootch and crash, but he saw Doc Cowan behind the mess area, alone and wrestling with the mangled bodies.

He was trying to slide them from the ponchos into body bags, but the medic was becoming frustrated as he picked up an arm that had become separated from Ernie's body and tossed it into the bag. No one was helping. Martin stood stunned while watching as Doc pulled a bloody coil of black wire from the remains and tossed it aside. It was the handset cord from Ernie's radio.

"Come on," Ray Lopez said, motioning to Douchie. "Let's go help Doc."

"Hell no! You're crazy, Taco," Douchie said. "No way I'm going over there. You go. He doesn't need two of us."

Ray gazed Martin's way and perhaps it was his officer training kicking in, but Martin had seen enough. It was time to take charge. "He's right, Ray. Y'all were pretty tight with those guys. Just stay here. I'll go over there and give him a hand."

A small crowd of the artillery men had gathered against one of the buildings forty meters away.

"Hey," Ray called to them. "Can some of you guys come over here and give us a hand?"

Their eyes widened in unison as the gawkers were caught off guard by the request. Some looked away, while others slowly shook their heads and slunk away back between the buildings.

"Well, just fuck you, assholes!" Ray shouted.

"It's okay," Martin said. "Go get us a truck to take them over to the chopper pad."

Ray gazed at him with tortured eyes. "But—"

"Just go, Sarge. I got this."

With bloody hands and arms, Doc Cowan was on his knees closing one of the bags. He glanced up with watery, bloodshot eyes as Martin approached, but he was focused on something far beyond where Martin stood. It seemed as if he was somewhere light years beyond the moment in which they now existed, fighting to find an explanation or a remnant of sanity.

"What can I do to help?" Martin asked.

His words seemed to bring the medic back to the moment. Their eyes met as if Doc only now realized he was standing there. The medic looked down at the body bags and up at Martin. He cocked his head to one side and gestured toward two of the bags.

"I already put Ernie and Kurbo in those, but you can help me with that fella there."

He motioned to a bloody heap of fatigues, boots, and body parts. Martin knew then he had made a mistake. He didn't need to be here. He didn't need to see what kneeling directly in front of a Claymore mine did to a man. After gazing at Tim's remains for a terribly long while, he looked back at Doc Cowan. If there was something he needed to do, he had no idea where to begin.

"It's okay," Doc said. "Just wait. We'll have to work together and pour him from the poncho into the bag."

A salty onshore breeze blew across the compound, stirring

the sand and dust. Despite his nausea and the horrific pulse of adrenaline that had his head spinning, Martin never felt so alive as he did now—alive in body but dead in soul. The sun was still shining brightly. Beautiful white cumulus clouds towered high out over the ocean, and the swaying palms never seemed so green. He was breathing, and his heart was beating, but why? He had been but four seconds and several quick steps from eternity, from being where Tim was now. It was all so arbitrary and so eternally final.

Doc motioned for him to grasp the poncho that held Tim's remains, but Martin spotted something shiny. He looked closer. It was the Saint Xavier medal Tim's girlfriend had given him.

"Wait. Wait a minute."

He reached into Tim's remains and pulled out the bloody medal and chain.

"I didn't see that," Doc said. "Put it in that bag there with his other personal effects."

The ringing in Martin's ears was nearly unbearable as Doc closed the body bag and they finished. It would be a closed casket funeral, and Tim's girlfriend, Annie, would probably stand there with his family and say goodbye. He wondered if she would get the Saint Xavier medal. The flag would be folded and given to his mother. Taps would be played, and seven white-gloved soldiers would aim their rifles skyward and fire three times in a 21-gun salute. That would be it. Tim would be a memory.

By the time he reached the hootch that afternoon, the choppers had come and gone. Kurbo, Ernie, and Tim were on their way to a GRU, Paul to a field hospital, and Martin was pretty certain he was on his way to hell. No one was around when he pulled the bottle of Wild Turkey from his rucksack, cut the seal with his knife, and pulled the cork. Hundred proof bourbon never went down so smoothly as it did now. When he lowered the bottle, a quarter of the contents were gone—but the pain remained.

He set the bottle on the floor beside his bunk and unlaced his boots. A late afternoon thunderstorm had blown in off the South China Sea and the rain thundered on the tin roof while sheets of water ran off in sandy pools outside. After throwing his boots against the wall, he lay back and stared at the ceiling. It had been eighteen hours now without sleep. If he lived through eleven more months of this shit, his next assignment would be in an army hospital with a padded room and massive doses of Thorazine.

———————————

Martin didn't remember closing his eyes, but he was suddenly aware of someone softly poking his shoulder. He jerked awake and rolled over. It was Taco, or as he regained his senses, he remembered it was Ray—Ray Lopez. The sergeant was shaved, wearing clean fatigues, and looking rested.

"You okay?"

Martin blinked and looked around.

"Yeah. You already showered and changed? What time is it?"

"It's oh-seven-hundred, and the CO said he wants to meet with us this morning at oh-eight-hundred."

"This morning?"

"Yeah." Ray held up the bottle of Wild Turkey. "I'm assuming this is yours?"

"Yeah."

"Where's the cork?"

"The cork?"

Martin looked around only to realize it was still clutched

tightly in his left hand. He gave it to Ray and sat up.

"You must have slept pretty good."

The previous day's memories flooded in, and Martin found himself staring at the sandbagged walls of the hootch, but all he saw were the bodies. An officer was never supposed to cry, and he swallowed hard, forcing the lump in his throat to sink back into his gut.

"Come on. Don't think about that shit right now. You need to get moving."

Fifty-five minutes later he had showered, shaved, and donned clean fatigues. He was lacing his boots when the hootch's screen door slammed shut. It was Ray returning.

"Let's go, Shadows. The CO is waiting on us."

As the two men walked up the sandy road toward the company HQ, Ray gave him the skinny on their meeting.

"Captain Bowman saw some pretty bad shit over around Kontum and Pleiku, so he's a little zoned out, but he knows his shit. He's going to ask me first for my verbal report. He'll ask questions, and he may ask you to tell your side of what went down. Just stick with the facts—no speculation unless he asks for it. Lieutenant Fitzer is already up there with him doing his debriefing, so a lot of what we tell him he'll already know."

There was much he could say—wanted to say, but Martin was again in a position where he had to keep his mouth shut and play his role as an enlisted man. The CO was still meeting with Fitzer when they stepped inside the HQ hootch.

"Come on in, men, and take a seat," the captain said. "Grab that chair out there and bring it in here."

The CO turned his attention back to the lieutenant.

"So, you and Sergeant Kurbo met with Colonel Nguyen, and he suggested you take the trail along the river?"

"Yes, sir."

The CO was a lean and wiry man, probably less than thirty

years old, but he had the weary eyes of an old man—a very old man. He cast them on the young lieutenant.

"Seems that was a bad suggestion."

Fitzer's face reddened.

"When we got there, the colonel saw us coming down a paddy dike to the highway and said we were becoming predictable and needed to take a different trail going back. Sergeant Kurbo and I discussed it and thought it was a pretty good suggestion, so that's what we did."

Martin noticed the slight tick that came and went in the captain's eye, but the old man must have been a pretty good card player because he revealed little else. He was certain the captain thought Fitzer was a fool for taking the ARVN colonel's suggestion, but he said nothing. He turned to Ray and gazed at him for several seconds. Ray shifted in his chair and sat up straighter. The captain's eyes moved to Martin.

"You were walking point, is that right?"

"Yes, sir."

"Why did you stop where you did?"

"I'm not sure, sir. Something didn't seem quite right, so I signaled for everyone to get down. That's when I saw the Chinese Claymore there beside the trail."

"And so, you yelled 'ambush' and charged past it up the hill. Why?"

"Because, sir, that's the way I was trained. They said the best way to counter an ambush is to—"

"Had the enemy begun shooting at that point?"

"Uh, no, sir. I saw the Claymore, figured it was an ambush, and knew I was on the wrong side of it."

"There were two more Claymores that went off further up the trail," Ray said, "but they didn't hurt anybody. The men in front of the first mine were Shadows and Gates, and me—at least until Sergeant Kurbo and Ernie ran forward. If it hadn't been for Shadows the whole platoon would have been wiped out."

The captain glanced over at Fitzer.

"Why did Kurbo run to the point when Shadows had just shouted there was an ambush?"

Fitzer squirmed and cast an accusatory glance at the others. Martin wanted to answer for him. He wanted to tell the CO it happened because Fitzer was an idiot and not fit to be a platoon leader. Instead, he gritted his teeth and remained tight-lipped.

Sergeant Lopez responded. "I'm not sure, sir. I believe the LT thought since PFC Shadows was such a new man, he was simply over-reacting to something he saw."

"Why did you have a new man with no field experience on point?"

Bowman was staring hard at Fitzer.

"We, that is Sergeant Kurbo and I, thought it would calm him down, because of the previous night when—"

The captain held up his hand. "That's enough. Put it in your AAR, lieutenant."

He fixed his eyes on Martin.

"You did well, Shadows. I believe Sergeant Lopez is right. Your quick reaction saved the rest of the platoon from annihilation. I'm recommending you both for Bronze Stars with V devices. When Lieutenant Fitzer has the recommendation completed, I will forward it with my approval to the battalion commander."

He turned his attention to Fitzer.

"I'll expect your AAR and the medal recommendations for PFC Shadows and Sergeant Lopez here on my desk by 1600 hours. Write the others up for Purple Hearts, including that new kid, Maziensky."

Bowman stood and turned to Sergeant Lopez. "I need four men to help unload the inbound supply truck. Send Shadows. It seems the driver is a friend of his and was asking about him. You are dismissed, gentlemen."

Martin knew immediately the request was from his MAC-V contact. The men stepped out of the HQ hootch, shading their eyes from the morning sun. Lieutenant Fitzer said nothing as he hurried away. Ray grinned at Martin and pointed down the road toward the supply hootch.

"No breaks for heroes, Shadows. Get moving."

Martin turned and started down the road, but Ray called out to him. "That's the army way: medal winner today, shit burner tomorrow. Don't let it get you down. I'll send some more guys down there when I get back to the hootch."

"No problem, Sarge. Thanks for the plug with the captain. Hell, who knows? They might make me a general, someday."

Lopez laughed aloud and shook his head.

"You know something, Shadows? I like you."

CHAPTER TEN

Martin walked down to the supply hootch that morning where a deuce-and-a-half was backed in to unload. Two soldiers, a Spec-4 and a buck sergeant, were standing at the back of the truck talking. The sergeant had his cap pulled low across his face. He stepped forward and extended his hand as Martin approached.

"Hey Martin, how ya' doing, ol' buddy. I got word you were over here and dropped by for a visit."

The soldier raised his head enough for Martin to recognize him. It was Captain Palmer, his CO from MAC-V.

"Is there someplace around here we can get a beer?"

"I'm afraid not. Besides, I'm on duty."

"Too bad, but it must be nice with the beach so close. Can we walk out that way?"

Martin caught his drift.

"Come on. We'll go over to the other side of the firebase where you can get a better view."

"Hey," the driver shouted, "what happened to the men who were supposed to help me unload this shit?"

"They should be here in a few minutes," Martin said.

"We won't be gone long," Palmer added.

The two men walked past the gun pits where the one-five-fives sat idle. A couple of the artillerymen sat on the sandbags with M-16s across their laps. They watched as Martin and Palmer sauntered down to a bunker near the wire and stood gazing out at the ocean.

"So, how's it going?" Palmer asked.

"Not good."

"How's that?"

"No discipline around here, and we lost three men in an ambush yesterday."

"Yeah. I heard you were there."

"I was on point."

Palmer turned and stared at him, his eyes shadowed with incredulity.

"You were walking point?"

"Yeah. It was my slack man that got killed, along with the platoon sergeant and his RTO. They walked point blank into a Chi-Com Claymore. It pretty much made a mess of them."

"Umm. Sounds like you were lucky."

Palmer shook a couple of Marlboros from a pack and gave one to Martin.

"Have you seen or heard anything?"

"We humped out to the highway the other day where we met an ARVN infantry convoy. The platoon sergeant that was killed, Kurbo, and my platoon leader, Lieutenant Fitzer, seemed to know the ARVN colonel who was there. There was a major with him, but it was the colonel who was asking questions—lots of them."

"What sort of questions?"

"How many men were in our platoon, where we planned to set up for the night, if one of our one-five-fives back at the firebase had been repaired yet. Sergeant Kurbo and Lieutenant Fitzer pretty much spilled their guts, even volunteering that we have a shortage of 82-millimeter mortar rounds on the firebase."

"Jesus! I'm assuming this colonel spoke pretty good English. Did you get his name?"

"Not till my debriefing with Fitzer and the CO this morning. The lieutenant said his name was Nguyen. He also said it was Nguyen who suggested we take the river trail back to the firebase because we were becoming too predictable."

"The trail where you were ambushed?"

Martin nodded.

"What did the CO think about him taking Nguyen's advice?"

"He didn't seem happy about it, but he didn't say much in front of me and Sergeant Lopez."

"Well, it sounds like we may have found a possible leak."

Martin tried to hide his elation.

"Does this mean my work is done here?"

Palmer drew hard on his cigarette and exhaled as he gazed out at the emerald swells crashing ashore a couple hundred meters away.

"Not yet."

Martin masked his disappointment.

"We'll do some follow-up on this Colonel Nguyen, but we have to be careful. If he's working for the VC, we don't want to tip him off. You say your platoon RTO was one of the KIA, right?"

"That's right."

"I want you to try to volunteer for the job. I also want you to get closer to the enlisted men who have been here a while, the old heads—strike up some conversations and try to get their opinions about the officers."

"Anything in particular I'm trying to learn?"

"Yeah. Try to find out what they think about the current platoon leader as well as the previous one."

"My understanding is Fitzer hasn't been here that long, and the men haven't made up their minds about him."

"Do they ever talk about the previous platoon leader?"

"No, sir, not that I've overheard. Why?"

"He was killed by a fragmentation grenade we think was tossed by one of his own men. That lieutenant had been with the platoon less than six weeks."

Martin found himself suddenly fighting back a flash of anger. Why? Why would they have not told him about something like this in advance? He drew a calming breath before speaking.

"That would have been something useful to know in advance, sir."

Palmer squinted and again gazed out through the trees toward the South China Sea. A sampan with dirty white sails was far out on the horizon, rising and sinking on the swells.

"We thought it better not to tell you about it, because we wanted you to keep an open mind."

"With all due respect, sir, I believe that was a mistake. The more I know the better I can perform this mission. Is there anything else I haven't been told?"

Martin studied his CO, realizing they were much alike, just cogs in the gears that ran the system.

"The initial thought was to limit the information we gave you so you would look under every rock—so to speak. I agree it was a mistake, and yes, there's more I can tell you. Bear with me on this. It may sound a bit strange.

"The platoon you're in here on Suzy was used as a leper colony of sorts. Troublemakers from throughout the regiment were sent here, supposedly for rejuvenation. This came out when we began investigating Lieutenant Branch's death. If you've seen the old movie *Twelve O'clock High*, you'll know what I'm talking about. That practice was stopped, but CID has hit every manner of stonewall with their investigation. If anyone in the platoon knows anything about Branch getting killed, they're not talking."

"So, when and where was Lieutenant Branch killed, and why is army intelligence involved?"

"At the time of Branch's death, he was performing pacification patrols in the surrounding villages, but the locals were close-mouthed, and he kept coming up empty-handed. We believe he was being compromised by someone in the ARVN or Vietnamese Special Police units he was working with. Frankly, we still don't know if he was killed by the enemy or some of his own men.

"The only thing confirmed about his death was that an American fragmentation grenade killed him. Sergeant Kurbo said he thought the grenade might have been set as a booby trap the lieutenant tripped when he went into the bushes to relieve himself. Does that sound strange to you?"

"Why would a booby trap be located off the trail?"

Palmer nodded. "Exactly."

"Could it be someone got spooked that day when he left the trail and thought he was the enemy?"

"Possibly, but the stonewalling by his men led CID to think otherwise, and your information on this Colonel Nguyen resurrects the other possibilities. Nguyen is the battalion commander in charge of the ARVN units that were working with Branch and his men."

There was no need to ask more questions. Most of what Captain Palmer said was speculation, but the implications were clear. Martin was inside a trick bag of possibilities that included both murder and espionage.

Later that afternoon Martin saw Ray Lopez again. He was sitting on a picnic table under the palm trees making out the duty roster.

"You mind if I join you?"

Ray looked up. "No. Have a seat."

"Have they decided who will replace Ernie as RTO?"

"Nah. That'll be the LT's call. Why? You interested?"

Martin shrugged. "Yeah, maybe."

Lopez stopped writing and looked up at him. His eyes spoke volumes of doubt.

"You sure? That's kind of a risky position."

"Why do you say that?"

"Well, several reasons. The RTO is the first man the gook snipers take out, and that Prick-25 is a heavy bastard to hump."

"Anything else?"

"Yeah. You have to stay real close to the LT."

"Why is that a problem?"

Lopez mopped the sweat from his face with a green towel.

"I take it you haven't heard about our last platoon leader getting fragged."

"Fragged? No shit?"

"No shit."

"Did they catch whoever did it?"

"Nope. Nobody seems to know. Kurbo said it was a booby trap. I'm not so sure."

"Do you think they'll frag Fitzer, too?"

"Don't know. If he keeps fucking up like he did taking us on that river trail, they might."

Martin opened a pack of Camels.

"Want one?"

"Sure."

He lit two and gave one to Lopez.

"Still want me to put your name in to the LT?"

Martin didn't want to sound over-zealous.

"Not sure, but if I'm RTO and you're the platoon sergeant, maybe we can keep him from doing something else stupid."

Ray seemed to think about it a moment before nodding. "Hell, if you're willing to take the chance, that's not such a bad idea. I'll see what Fitzer says."

The names and faces of the platoon members ran through Martin's mind. Any of them could have been involved in the killing of Lieutenant Branch, but one name kept coming back to him again and again—one he had overlooked until now—Douchie. Suspicion was a long way from proof, but why was he so focused on this one? Although Douchie was an immature dipshit, he seemed too smart to do something that might land his ass in Leavenworth for the rest of his life. Yet, the more Martin thought about it, the more Douchie seemed to fit the role.

According to Ray, Douchie got his name because he was a douche bag of a human being. No one liked him—not even the other dregs. Douchie was relentlessly loyal to one person, and that was himself. His only talent was riffling a deck of cards and cheating his buddies at poker—likely one of the many reasons they didn't like him. But that was small potatoes if Martin's gut instincts were correct. Douchie was capable of far worse.

The platoon was on firebase support for the next month. This meant bunker duty, guard tower watch, KP, and shit-burning detail—essentially whatever needed to be done. The plus side was other than an occasional perimeter patrol, there would be no humping to the villages or out to Highway One. That was left to the other platoons. This would give Martin the time he needed to get closer and spend time with the men in his own unit.

CHAPTER ELEVEN

Martin crawled beneath his mosquito net that night as a muggy wind blew in through the screens of the hootch. He thought back again to that week in Montana when his grandfather was telling him tales of Sioux warriors from years ago, counting coup and hanging eagle feathers from their lances. He enjoyed listening as Two Shadows talked of buffalo hunts and of ancestral battles with other tribes and the American cavalry, but it was the visions that left Martin now wondering what he might have missed. He wished he'd listened more closely and hadn't been so doubtful.

Lying awake for a while, he heard the faraway rumble of artillery somewhere in the highlands. Despite his doubts, it now seemed as if Two Shadows's visions were actually coming true. The old man had foreseen the conflict Martin had with his new leaders and how they would lead him and the other men into an ambush. Two Shadows had even seen him carrying their bodies in the ponchos. But how? And yet, many other things from his visions were so outlandish they were beyond the realm of logic. There was no way they could fit into this world that was Vietnam.

Martin tried to remember more as he drifted deeper into

a netherworld of memories and dreams. That day when they smoked the pipe, there came a moment when the wind outside the lodge had died, and it seemed the prairie silence was endless. His grandfather stopped talking and seemed lost in thought, until he suddenly began again, telling so much of what then had seemed fanciful and almost nonsensical.

"A warrior must find his spirit—the one that is without fear. He must allow his spirit to find its true center. Martin Shadows, you will have many spirits—the bear, the rabbit, the wolf, and the cougar. I see this. You will adapt well and call upon the one that is best for you to defeat your enemies."

Martin's head swam with the effects of his grandfather's tobacco as his doubts gave way to curiosity.

"Which of these spirits is best, Grandfather?"

"There is a time for each of them—the bear stands to fight, the rabbit runs to outwit the fox, the wolf depends upon his pack, and the cougar travels alone and uses his stealth. The best one is the one your enemies least expect. It will strike fear in their hearts. You will have many battles in which you will take many forms, but I see the cougar—the great cat whose strength is stealth—as your warrior spirit who stalks his enemies in the shadows. The cougar will take you to your greatest accomplishment."

Again, Martin tried to mask his feelings. The army by its very nature voided the maverick, the individual who couldn't work with a team. The army was the consummate wolfpack. His grandfather was more than a soothsayer from an ancient culture, but his beliefs had little in common with modern warfare and military structure. Despite his efforts to better understand these things, Martin's skepticism remained.

He reminded himself again that he was a United States Army officer, and this was the 20th Century. He was not Crazy Horse defiantly riding his pony along the cavalry lines, seemingly impervious to the enemy bullets. In Vietnam the North Vietnamese soldiers were shooting AK-47s with thirty-round magazines. Heroes died quickly in modern wars, and Vietnam was no different. And when he thought the old man's visions could not get more bizarre, they did.

"My grandson, what I have to tell you now causes my heart deep pain because I know not what it means or how it ends. My dreams are many, but I had another where you found a friend in a dark place. This seemed good, but something happened, and you left with your friend on a boat that took you to another place where you sprang like the cougar from a tree to kill your enemies with your knife."

Martin closed his eyes lest they give him away.

"Čaŋgléska Wakȟaŋ represents that which tells us all that is our universe is connected. I tell you this because I saw something that was not from our Lakota beliefs but a spirit of the ancient tribes from the north called Bekaakwaabewizidn. I saw you as this spirit with little flesh on your bones, and you fought your enemy with a knife and their own weapons. It is noble for a Lakota warrior to fight so well. My only hope comes with the vision that you will follow Wakan Tanka and do good things with your life."

Martin was certain now the old man had stuffed the pipe with a hallucinogen of some sort. Peyote, hemp, or whatever, it was causing his stories to become more outlandish by the moment.

"I don't understand what this Bekaakwaabewizidn is you are talking about?"

Two Shadows handed him the pipe. Martin was well beyond the realm of normal consciousness and fighting to find something meaningful in his grandfather's words. He drew hard on the pipe and exhaled the smoke into the haze floating around them.

"As I said, my grandson, it is a mystery to me also."

Martin closed his eyes. He had to think of a way to respond without hurting his grandfather's feelings. He had been raised a Christian by his mother. He had graduated from college and the Army Officer Candidate School, but he was now under this deep and influential spell cast by his grandfather—one he would need to shed before going to Vietnam.

The third day of his visit they drove far out on the reservation, where they sat atop a hill and watched a small herd of pronghorns feeding in the distance. A meadowlark's flute-like melody floated over the wind-stirred grasses while crows called from the cottonwoods down by the river. Two Shadows was explaining more about one of the visions, when he somehow detected Martin's skepticism. The old man merely smiled.

"It is okay, Martin. Perhaps you will better understand with the story of the blind man. You see, a blind man walks the same path every day. He does this despite knowing the world around him is constantly changing, and that one of those changes could rise up at any time and strike him in his face. In this life we are all this blind man. We go about every day as if every tomorrow will always come, yet we never know when something will change or possibly end our lives here forever.

"We do this because to do otherwise is to always live in fear. Like the blind man, we cannot allow our lives to be paralyzed by fear of things we cannot see. For a soldier, such events can occur more often, but you must find a way to do your duty. I believe this is the reason the Great Spirit has shared these visions with me—so that I might help you walk this path without fear. I hope you will listen."

In a few days he would return to Kentucky and spend the last week of his leave with his mother and father. There would likely be interesting discussions forthcoming, because he had a war to fight, and jumping from trees like a cougar wasn't how it was done. For now, he didn't respond to his grandfather's story. He remained silent.

When Martin returned home from Montana there were seven days remaining before his departure to Vietnam. He stood gazing out his upstairs bedroom window at the Kentucky hills, while absentmindedly picking up one of the model airplanes from the shelf above his desk. He watched as his mother pulled into the front driveway.

No doubt, she had gone to the grocery to get the fixings for his favorite meal: fried chicken with mashed potatoes and gravy. He heard her coming up the steps and turned as she stepped into the open doorway. On the way home from Montana, he had debated telling her about his grandfather's visions. Smiling brightly, he walked over and wrapped his arms around her.

"I was at the grocery store," she said.

"Let me guess. You got a chicken and potatoes for supper."

She pinched his cheek.

"Of course. How was your visit with your grandfather?"

It was the inevitable question, yet one for which he had yet to find a suitable answer.

"It was good. Grandfather helped me see some things I never considered."

She gave him the knowing smile of a mother who saw through his vague response.

"Come on down to the kitchen. I have a pitcher of fresh tea fixed for you, and your father will be home soon. He'll want to hear about your trip to Montana."

Martin sat at the kitchen table sipping his tea, while his mother began preparing supper. She no doubt wanted to know more, but he wasn't sure how to tell her. It was all so far-fetched, yet there was something haunting his subconscious—something that made him believe there was more to his grandfather's visions than the ramblings of an old Indian medicine man.

"Your grandfather is a good man who has seen some bad things in his life, but I worry about his influence on you."

"Mama, I know you have doubts about Grandfather and his ways, but you don't have to worry."

"Son, I just don't want you thinking you have to be some great warrior."

"I know what I'm getting into, and I don't plan on being a hero. Vietnam is a mess, but I probably won't even be in a combat zone. An intelligence officer gathers information to share with those who are. Now stop your worrying."

She gave him a sad-eyed smile.

"Worrying is what mothers do. We worry about our men."

"Well, it doesn't accomplish anything, and it doesn't help me."

"What would you have me do?"

"Take care of Dad, write often, and send me lots of your cookies and fruitcake. Everything is going to be fine."

Martin awakened and lay there in the hootch staring into the darkness. He had to write his mother and tell her things had changed. Everything he had told her about being safe was no longer true, and had he listened more closely to his grandfather, he might have better realized it then. He had to tell her he was now on a firebase where there were risks. That was the best he could do, because telling her the entire truth was out of the question. He would write just enough to let her know it wasn't the cakewalk he promised without telling her he was now stuck in a quagmire of danger.

CHAPTER TWELVE

P aul Maziensky had begun wearing a silver crucifix with his dog tags since the ambush. It was something given to him by a chaplain at the field hospital where they stitched up his arm. He and Ray Lopez discovered they had both been altar boys at their Catholic churches, and Ray took to watching after him. The one-on-one attention not only boosted Paul's confidence but helped him discover a newfound skill that took him beyond "cherry" status.

A few days earlier Ray had taken him outside the wire with a few dozen rounds for his M-79, to train him. By the time they finished, for all that Paul lacked in IQ, he made up for with his ability to shoot the thump-gun. As Ray put it, *the boy has talent.* Paul could hang four grenades in the air before the first one hit the ground and drop them all in an area no larger than a barroom dance floor.

Lieutenant Fitzer had the platoon standing at ease in formation that morning while he explained the next mission. With eight new replacements, the ranks had swollen to twenty-three men, and Martin was officially no longer a cherry. He had been working with Fitzer and Lopez learning his new RTO duties, but more importantly, he was learning a lot about his fellow platoon members, including Robert "Douchie" Greyman.

"We are not going out to the highway tomorrow," Fitzer announced, "but into those villages along the river—the one near where we got ambushed a few weeks back."

A rippling murmur of curses rolled through the formation.

"At ease," Ray Lopez said. Though firm, his voice was low and restrained. He had been given a staff sergeant's stripe and was now the official platoon sergeant.

"It shouldn't be a big deal," the lieutenant said. "We'll have an ARVN interpreter with us while we poke around, do some interrogations, look for weapons and contraband, and just show the local yokels we're not putting up with any more of their shit. The reason I had you fall out with your gear is so Sergeant Lopez can do an inspection. He'll also give you my new SOP while we're out on patrol—which means there'll be no more grab-ass. You're going to start acting like real soldiers.

"A-ten-hut!" Fitzer shouted. He turned to Ray. "They're all yours, Sergeant Lopez."

When the lieutenant was gone, Ray lit a cigarette.

"Stand at ease, men. Smoke 'em if you got 'em and open the actions on your weapons."

A brief rain shower that morning had left the air thick and humid, and one of the cherries stood with his eyeglasses fogged as he fumbled with his M-16. Ray stopped in front of him, but the soldier seemed oblivious as he struggled to open his weapon. After a moment Lopez waved a hand in front of the man's face and the soldier looked up. His eyeglasses were opaque with condensation. Red-faced and sweating, he stood with his mouth agape and his upper teeth bared.

"Having troubles?" Ray asked.

"Uh, no sir. I mean no, Sergeant. I got it now."

Ray took the man's weapon and examined the action.

Peebles and Douchie laughed.

"Dumb fuck," Peebles mumbled.

Ray shoved the weapon back into the man's hands.

"Looks good," he said. "What's your name?"

"Hale," the soldier said. "Fred Hale."

"His name is cherry," Douchie mumbled.

"Well, Private Hale, I suggest you wipe the fog off your glasses if you intend to aim that rifle at anything."

Douchie stopped laughing when Lopez stepped in front of him. Peebles elbowed him. "You done gone and done it now, Douchie. You done made Sergeant Taco mad."

Peebles, one of the old leper colony members in the platoon, wore a smart-alec grin while picking at his overgrown afro with a long-toothed comb. He and Douchie traded fist bumps and high fives. Martin studied them. It was a mutual masturbation of insecurity. Neither could stand alone.

"You're right," Lopez said. "He's a cherry, and he doesn't know much, but if we get in another firefight, you idiots might wish he did. So why don't you help these newbies learn what the fuck they're doing?"

Douchie's face reddened as he and Ray stood nose to nose. "Ooouuuwwweeee," he said. "The great Sergeant Taco has spoken."

Ray's face turned to stone, while Douchie cast a quick glance at Peebles.

"I'll give him a hand," Martin said.

"Yeah, that'll work," Douchie said, "the blind leading the blind. What'cha gonna teach him, how to get your slack man and the platoon sergeant blown away?"

Martin's mind short-circuited with rage, and he lunged at Douchie, but Ray tackled him, pinning him to the ground. With Ray's knee in his back and a hand gripping his neck, Martin came to his senses. Sand and dirt coated his face, and he had nearly blown everything. Closing his eyes, he drew a deep breath. After a moment, Ray carefully released his grip and pulled Martin to his feet.

Douchie's cackling laughter continued, until a voice came from the rear of the formation. "Why don't you shut your mouth, Greyman?"

It was Joe Thunders. The entire platoon including Douchie went suddenly silent. For the first time that morning, Robert "Douchie" Greyman's eyes revealed a nervous doubt as he tried to make eye contact with anyone who would look his way. They were all fixated on Joe Thunders. He seldom spoke, but when he did, his quiet voice demanded everyone's attention. It seemed they feared him.

"If you don't do better, you're going to wake up one morning strapped to one of those ant hills outside the wire," Thunders said.

No one spoke, and the silence was broken only by the distant pounding of the surf out on the beach. Martin knocked the dust off his fatigues, and a tone of cooperation ensued for the rest of the morning as the platoon prepared for the next day's patrol. Only later, when several vehicles came through the main gate, did Martin realize matters were taking a turn for the worse. It was the ARVN Colonel Nguyen and his XO Major Thanh. They were probably coming to meet with Captain Bowman.

Martin wanted to hear what was discussed and to see if the captain would mention tomorrow's patrol to Nguyen and his protégé. The HQ building also housed the Command-and-Control center—a room across the hall from the captain's office. As soon as the two Vietnamese officers entered, Martin followed. The officers glanced back at him but seemed unperturbed as he went into the C&C room where a sergeant sat monitoring the radios.

The sergeant looked up from his copy of *Stars and Stripes*.

"What's up?"

Martin used his new RTO position as an excuse. "Nothing much. Just thought I'd sit and listen to the radio procedure some more."

Someone had hung a poncho over the wall maps.

"What's that about?" he asked.

"The captain ordered it a few minutes ago. I don't think he trusts the gooks."

Through the partially opened door Martin could see across the hall where the CO was facing Nguyen and Thanh.

"Where will you use my interpreter?" Nguyen asked.

Captain Bowman cast a wary glance at the ARVN colonel.

"We want to make an interpreter a permanent part of our SOP," Bowman said.

Nguyen eyed him as if it were a high-stakes poker game, except here the chips were the lives of men.

"I am not certain I can allow you to have him permanently. He often works for other American units. When do you next need him? I will send him then."

It was a cat and mouse game—one with potentially lethal consequences.

"I'm not sure," the CO said. "Can you leave him with us this week or until we get one permanently assigned?"

Nguyen grimaced. Doing little to mask his frustration, he crammed his half-smoked cigarette into a butt can.

"He will stay a week. That is all I can do for you."

"I suppose that'll have to work. Thank you, Colonel."

Not another word was spoken as Nguyen spun about and strutted out. Martin turned away from the open door. His eyes met those of the sergeant sitting in front of the radios. When they were gone, the sergeant leaned toward Martin.

"Sounds like the little bastard was pissed," he whispered.

"About what?" Martin said.

"Like I said, the captain doesn't trust him."

The patrol departed the firebase the next morning shortly after daybreak. Ray's influence was immediately apparent as the men maintained good noise discipline and separation. The interpreter walked behind the lieutenant and Martin, who was packing the radio. Joe Thunders was on point. Ray posted men on each flank as the main column followed the road out to the village on the river.

Arriving midmorning, the platoon deployed in a line between the road and the village. Fitzer studied the hootches through his binoculars. It was strangely quiet—no chickens squawking or pigs squealing, and no children playing—nothing but an eerie silence. With the livestock secured and the children inside the hootches, it was obvious someone had warned them of their arrival.

"Do you think Nguyen told them we were coming?" Martin asked.

Ray shrugged. "I hope not."

"He probably didn't expect us this soon," Fitzer said. "Let's move out."

"I think we should watch the village a while before we go in," Ray said.

"It's hot as hell, and I don't want to stay out here all day. Let's move out, Sergeant, now. Get the men moving."

Martin glanced at Ray. The platoon sergeant probably felt the same as he did. Fitzer had gone from being an insecure screw-up to a George Patton wannabe.

"Tell your men watch for booby traps," the interpreter said.

"These people seemed to know we were coming," Ray said.

"Do you know why?"

"Yes," the interpreter said. "I here yesterday with Colonel Nguyen. He tell the village chief you come maybe soon."

"Damn!" Ray cursed.

"Doesn't matter," the lieutenant said. "Our orders are to search the village. Now, do as I said and get the men moving."

Ray walked out to the lead element where the men had taken a knee. They had stopped short of a slime-filled canal that ran along the front side of the village. Martin followed Lieutenant Fitzer as he walked toward a small wooden bridge crossing the canal. Joe Thunders was there kneeling beside Paul. A wooden gate was across one end of the bridge.

"Okay, let's move out," Fitzer said. He motioned Thunders toward the bridge. "You lead. We'll follow."

"I wouldn't cross that bridge, sir," Martin said.

Thunders hadn't moved. It was Tiger Land jungle warfare training one-oh-one. The drill instructors said you never entered a village through a gate or over a bridge, because they were almost always booby-trapped.

"Why?" the lieutenant asked.

"It's probably booby-trapped."

Several men up and down the line had already waded into the slimy canal up to their waists, and several were already struggling to climb out on the other side.

"Chief," Fitzer yelled. "Check out that bridge for booby traps."

Thunders didn't move.

"Okay," the lieutenant said. "I'll deal with you later. I need someone with balls. Maziensky, get up there and check out that bridge."

Paul stood and started toward the bridge.

"Hold up, Paul," Sergeant Lopez shouted.

Paul stopped and glanced at Lopez.

"What the hell do you think you're doing, Sergeant?" the lieutenant said.

"I think we're making a mistake, sir."

"Oh, for the love of Christ!" He started toward the gate. "You chickenshits can wait here while I go check it out. Come on, Maziensky."

Paul came to his feet and followed the lieutenant. Stopping at the gate, Fitzer studied the little bridge carefully. Thunders eased down on his belly and hugged the ground. Martin followed suit but raised his head and watched. After a few moments the lieutenant reached out and gingerly pushed the gate open. The blast blew him and Paul backward into the air. Tumbling like rag dolls, they landed in bloody heaps several feet away. The bridge was vaporized, and the concussion sent Martin's helmet flying as shrapnel stung his face.

Lumber clattered to the ground around him, and despite the instant flood of adrenaline and the roaring inside his head, Martin keyed the mic on the handset of the radio.

"Centurion One, this is Centurion Romeo Alpha. O'er."

Barely able to speak, he waited. It was probably no more than three or four seconds, but it seemed forever, and Martin was about to call again when the CO answered from the Command-and-Control center back at Suzy.

"Centurion Romeo Alpha, this is Centurion One. Go ahead. Over."

"Centurion, we've got two men down f'om a booby trap. We need dust-off ASAP. O'er."

"Okay, I need you to put Centurion Romeo Actual on the horn."

"Can't do it, sir. He's down."

"All right, son. I need your exact location. Can you find the platoon sergeant?"

"We a'e at point Alpha oh-one, sir. I can send the coo'dinates in the open if you need them."

"That won't be necessary, Centurion Romeo. Good job. Are you under fire?"

"Negative, Centurion One. So far it's just the booby trap. O'er."

"Roger, Centurion Romeo Alpha. A medevac will be on the way shortly, and we'll try to get you a couple of Cobras overhead as well. Be ready to pop smoke when they contact you. Standby. Over."

"Roger, Centurion One. Standing by. O'er."

Someone slapped his back. Martin turned. It was Joe Thunders.

"I got a dus'-off coming," Martin said. His head was pounding, and he couldn't speak clearly.

"Maziensky and the lieutenant won't need it," Thunders said, "but you might."

"Just a li'le dazed is all."

"I'm not so sure. You're bleeding pretty bad from that hole in your jaw."

Martin touched his cheek, and for the first time he felt a sting of pain.

"S-it!"

Thunders snatched the field dressing from Martin's web-gear and tore it open.

"Medic!" he shouted.

Martin spit a mouthful of blood off to one side as Doc Cowan and Ray Lopez ran up.

"Aw shit," Lopez said. "How bad is it, Chief?"

"Not sure."

"Let's get the radio off his back. We'll call for a dust-off."

"Al-weady did," Martin said.

Ray stared at him as if he were a ghost.

"I can't find any more wounds," Doc said. "Open your mouth."

Chief held the field dressing against his jaw while Doc Cowan swabbed his mouth with gauze.

"His tongue and teeth are all good. I can't tell where the damned shrapnel went."

Despite stars darting before his eyes and the continuous roar in his head, Martin realized Ray had brought the men back from the village and deployed them along the canal.

"Ray." He stopped to spit. "If the basta'ds are going to ambush us, they're pro'ly waiting for the dust-off to come in first."

It was a classic Viet Cong tactic—something he learned at OCS. After a booby trap was triggered, they would lie in wait to ambush reinforcing troops or inbound medevacs.

"You need to stop talking, Shadows," Doc said.

"They're pro'ly o'r there 'cross the road," Martin said, again garbling his words.

Ray glanced out toward the low rolling terrain south of the road.

"He's right," Thunders said. "We need to get a couple squads over there ASAP."

"Okay. I'll take care of that," Lopez said. "You and Doc get him back to the road for the dust-off."

The radio broke squelch. "Centurion Romeo Alpha, this is Centurion one. Over."

Ray grabbed the handset. "This is Centurion Romeo Sierra. Go ahead."

"Roger, Sierra. Your dust-off is twenty mikes out, and your Cobras will be right behind him. Give me a Sit-Rep. Over."

"We have two Kilo India Alpha and one Whisky India Alpha. I'm securing a Lima Zulu for a dust-off. Over."

Realizing he must have passed out, Martin awakened to stinging sand and dust and the whining roar of a turbine engine as a Huey helicopter landed a few meters away. Green tracers cracked past, but the zippered roar of a Vulcan minigun answered as a Cobra gunship thundered by overhead. He closed his eyes against the spray of sand, but his ears couldn't shut out the sounds of the surrounding battle. The whoosh of a rocket-propelled grenade passing close was punctuated by its explosion in the field behind them. It was followed by the metallic clacks of shrapnel striking the thin-skinned chopper.

"Jesus!" the crew chief shouted. "That was close."

Martin felt the strong arms of his buddies lifting him on board. He opened his eyes as the poncho-wrapped bodies of the lieutenant and Paul were shoved onto the floor beside him. The whine of the turbine increased along with the rhythmic thunder of the rotors as an awful odor assaulted his senses. It brought with it the same revulsion he had experienced that day when he helped Doc with Tim's remains—a visceral reaction to the odor of a desecrated human body. It had remained in his sinuses for days before eventually fading. Now, it returned.

A moment later the helicopter's churning downdraft brought relief as it sucked the air from the cabin, but Martin couldn't take his eyes off the obliterated bodies beside him. There was no thinking, no wishing—nothing but this moment searing his psyche with what he already knew would be a deep and permanent scar. The chopper lifted skyward, and he tasted his own blood—seeping warm and slick inside his mouth.

CHAPTER THIRTEEN

Martin awoke to find gauze stuffed between his cheek and gum and a bandage taped to his jaw. The odors were mostly of iodine, chlorine bleach, and rubbing alcohol, and it was quiet. He raised his head to look around, only to realize he had a monumental headache and was surrounded by occupied hospital beds. Some of the men around him read magazines while others slept. There were no IVs or heart monitors, and none of them seemed in particularly bad shape. A woman in army fatigues sat at a small table on one end of the room—probably a nurse.

Rolling his legs off the side of the bed, he sat upright. The pain intensified and he rubbed his forehead. The woman was coming his way. He started to open his mouth to speak, but a shooting pain stopped him cold. It seemed as if it spilled out of his left eye and ran down his jaw. He reached up to touch it, only to realize his jaw and eye were massively swollen and wrapped in gauze.

"Where are you going, soldier?"

Her brows were raised, and she gave him a flat smile. She seemed pleasant enough. Martin squinted and looked down. A catheter tube ran from beneath his gown into a bag hanging beside the bed. He again tried to speak but managed little more than a garbled grunt. She flipped a paper on her clipboard and gave him a pen.

"Here. Just write on this, but I want you to lie back and take it easy. Now that you're awake, we're going to change out the gauze pack in your mouth. A doctor should be around any time now."

Martin studied her for a moment—a nurse, no doubt. He scribbled on the clipboard: "*I have a headache. Do you have aspirin? Did you find the shrapnel that did this?*"

He was convinced the shrapnel had penetrated his jaw and was embedded somewhere in his brain. The nurse took the clipboard and studied it.

"The doctor will be here shortly, and he will decide what kind of pain meds you can have. Other than the wound on your cheek, you received a pretty bad concussion. I'm not sure what you're asking about the shrapnel."

She grabbed his record hanging at the foot of the bed and studied it.

"Hmmm, says T&T shrapnel wound, 4.2-millimeter, exiting left jaw. That's pretty small. I'm not sure. I wasn't here yesterday when they brought you in, but it must not be too bad. This is a ward for men with minor wounds who are expected to return to their units within a week or two."

A short time later a doctor appeared at the end of his bed. After injecting novocaine into Martin's jaw, he began extracting a seemingly endless string of blood-soaked gauze through his mouth.

"Open wide as you can," the nurse said.

The doctor dropped the bloody gauze into a stainless pan and held a small penlight, shining it into his mouth.

"Looks pretty good. Have him rinse his mouth with the antibiotic solution and repack it—not as much this time. Let's put some more ice on it, too."

"Yes, sir. He was asking if we found the piece of shrapnel."

The doctor turned to Martin. "That wound is an exit wound to the outside of your jaw. Best we could figure is your mouth was open when a tiny piece of shrapnel came in at an angle from your right side. You were lucky it didn't take out any teeth or your tongue. Barring any infection, you'll probably be back with your unit in a week or so."

———————————

Martin awoke from an afternoon nap to find his MAC-V commander, Captain Palmer, standing beside the bed. He was feeling better and had spent the last two days walking around the medical compound. His mission at FSB Suzy now seemed useless, and he hoped Palmer would give him another duty assignment.

"Nasty bruise there," Palmer said, pointing to his face. "The doc said you'll be released in a day or two. Feel like taking a walk?"

"Sure."

They stepped out into the bright afternoon sunlight. It was quiet except for the laughter of several men and women nearby, drinking beer and cooking burgers on a charcoal grill.

"How are you?" Palmer asked.

"I'm okay, but those damned hamburgers smell like heaven. If it weren't for chicken broth, cream of wheat, and ice cream I'd be starving."

"I'm sorry to hear about your platoon leader and the other guy. It sounds like you were lucky."

"He used bad judgement. We tried to warn him. And that kid, Paul, he didn't have to die. I mean…."

Martin went silent, unable to continue. He was right. Paul didn't have to die, and had he said something, he might still be alive. He could have looked out for him. The colonel at MAC-V had said he could blow his undercover role when it was a life and death matter, but he'd hesitated, and Paul was dead.

"Bad judgement seems endemic to that bunch," Palmer said. "What have you learned?"

It preyed on his mind, gnawing at his psyche, and Martin couldn't shake it. Paul died because he hadn't been smart enough to step in when it was time. He should have stopped him from following Fitzer to the bridge.

"You still with me, Shadows?" Palmer asked.

"Huh?"

"Have you learned anything new?"

"Oh, sorry. I was a little zoned out. Factually, nothing, but I can offer some speculation."

"Go for it."

"This Colonel Nguyen has a lot of flies swarming around him."

"Yeah," Palmer said. "We still haven't found anything on him. Tell me what you're thinking."

"Our platoon has made two patrols, one to the highway and the other to that village, and both times we got into trouble. I'm not sure why, but Nguyen was asking a lot of questions both times before we were hit. This time it was about when and where we planned to use his interpreter. Captain Bowman played his cards close to the vest, but I think Nguyen figured it out. He knew we were going into that village, and it would likely be soon."

"So, you think Bowman doesn't trust him, and you're still thinking Nguyen's the leak—an ARVN colonel?"

Martin read Palmer's doubt.

"I was brought up to believe when the windows of a house are glowing orange and smoke is coming from the gable vents, there may be a fire."

"It sounds like you've got some pretty strong feelings about him. We'll keep investigating on our end but keep me updated if you learn anything else. What else do you have?"

"This guy Robert Greyman—they call him Douchie. I suppose

it's the same with him. I don't have anything other than a gut feeling, but if I had to pick one man who might frag an officer, he'd be the one."

"Hmmm. I wish you had something more than your gut feeling. Anything else?"

"No, sir."

"Well, we'll do some background checks on Greyman. Is that it?"

"Yes, sir."

"Okay. Keep your eyes and ears open. We'll work on it from our end as well, but our options are limited with the ARVN colonel. Since Tet, we've come to realize the South Vietnamese army and government are riddled with spies. We've eliminated a bunch of them, but we have to be discreet. If this Colonel Nguyen *is* a VC sympathizer and we start asking questions, he'll likely just disappear. I'll let you know if we come up with anything."

———

Martin never imagined his Army Intelligence MOS would leave him playing cat and mouse with a possible enemy spy. This was surely a job for someone with more experience and bigger kahunas than his. He wasn't qualified for this mission, and worse, he wasn't even in charge. The more he thought about it, the more it seemed he was struggling in a pit of quicksand. A few days later he returned to Fire Support Base Suzy.

The battalion commander flew in and pinned him with another Bronze Star and a Purple Heart, but it was his new platoon leader, Lieutenant Jake Randal, that gave him some small element of hope. The day Martin returned, the young lieutenant came to the hootch, sought him out, and shook his hand. Randal was a drastic change for the better, compared to Kurbo and Fitzer.

Randal chose his words carefully and seemed introspective as he asked questions—not the usual mindless crap about how the chow was, or if Martin was writing home regularly, but meaningful questions. Jake Randal genuinely wanted to hear his thoughts and ideas. They talked for nearly an hour, and Martin came away knowing the platoon now had a leader with at least some common sense.

Later, Ray Lopez said much the same thing when he explained how the lieutenant asked him a hundred questions about the men and the platoon's operations. Randal was especially interested when Ray told him about Colonel Nguyen. The new platoon leader was meeting that afternoon with Captain Bowman and the visiting battalion commander to discuss the matter. Martin wasn't sure what they could do about Nguyen, but at least they were now aware future missions might be compromised by him.

———————

Two weeks later, Martin was eating regular food and back to full duty status. Lieutenant Randal had taken the platoon out to the beach for a game of jungle rules volleyball—something that made rugby look like child's play. The morale improved, and no further patrols were sent out to the highway or into the villages along the river. The CO was focused on immediate firebase security, which meant only the daily perimeter patrols were being performed.

It was near sunrise that day when Martin and his squad from First Platoon passed quietly through the main gate to begin their perimeter patrol—the first since his return. Lieutenant Randal, who had worked closely with Ray Lopez to improve the platoon's performance, accompanied them. Only two problem children remained—Douchie and Peebles.

At Ray's suggestion, Randal put them in the column to his immediate front where he could watch them. Joe Thunders was on point with Martin walking slack. Most of the cherries had gotten past their newbie jitters and things were going well as they followed the trail westward.

Lieutenant Randal ran his platoon as it was taught in OCS at Benning and infantry training at Polk. There was no screwing around. Noise discipline was expected, and readiness was demanded. He made sure everyone knew their jobs and understood the mission. A light mist of fog hung high in the palms that morning, and the sky in the east was ablaze with another South China Sea sunrise.

The LT directed Thunders to lead the squad past the usual perimeter trail before they began circling the firebase. It was a smart move, because it reduced the possibility of booby traps by making their route less predictable, but it also added considerable distance to what was normally a quick and easy patrol. It also required cutting new trails in places—pushing through high grass and fighting tangles of "wait-a-minute" vines.

The sweltering midmorning heat had begun taking its toll when word was passed for the men to take five and rest in place. Lying around the field hospital and the firebase for several weeks had sapped Martin's stamina. He dropped to his knees and opened a canteen, gulping the warm water. Lieutenant Randal walked back to check on the newbies. A few moments later a red-faced Douchie and his sidekick Peebles walked up and sat beside Martin and Joe Thunders.

"I thought the LT said for us to maintain our intervals and rest in place," Martin said.

"I want to be as far away from that gung-ho bastard as I can be," Douchie said.

"You got that shit right," Peebles said. Sweat poured from

under his helmet leaving his black skin glistening in the blistering hot sun. "Mutha fucka thinks he's John Wayne or something—walkin' us all over hell's half acre this way."

Douchie lit a cigarette and exhaled. "He keeps this shit up, and his ass is gonna end up like that other John Wayne we fragged."

"You got that shit right," Peebles said.

"You guys fragged somebody?" Martin asked.

"You're fuckin' A, we did," Peebles said, "and we'll frag yo' sorry ass if you don't act right. Yeah, my man Douchie here rolled that sweet little green potato right under John Wayne's ass while he was takin' a shit. Boom! No more morning PT. No more extra duty."

Martin's mind raced. He had to draw him into saying more. "I suppose Randal better get his shit together if he doesn't want a free ride to the hospital like that guy."

Douchie squeezed his cigarette between his thumb and finger and squinted across a distant rice paddy. Four hundred meters away a lone farmer was knee-deep in the water, trudging along behind his water buffalo. Nam at times could be a beautiful place, or it could be an ugly one. Today, as Martin listened to Douchie, it was the latter.

"Sumbitch is going to get a free ride all right enough," he said, "but it won't be to no hospital. It'll be a ride to the GRU just like that bastard Branch got."

"You got that shit right," Peebles said.

He and Douchie slapped palms and bumped fists.

"Branch?" Martin said.

"Yeah," Peebles said. "That was John Wayne's name."

"Oh well," Martin said. "That's too bad. Maybe this new guy will settle in and calm down in a month or two."

"We'll see," Douchie said, "but he better hurry up. I'm already belly-full of his gung-ho bullshit."

Word came up from the rear to saddle up and move out. They stood and helped one another with their rucksacks. Martin's hunch had been right, and now he had Joe Thunders as a witness. And the idiots had simply come out and bragged about it. Perhaps his luck was changing, but he had to get word to Captain Palmer before they acted on their threats.

There was a plan for emergencies whereby Martin declared his actual identity and requested a special broadband frequency to contact MAC-V using the firebase C&C radios, but this was not yet an emergency. The remaining option was to wait for Palmer to contact him again. That would be next week. He would keep close tabs on Douchie until then.

After they returned to the firebase that afternoon, Martin walked with Joe Thunders out to a sandbagged gun pit near the perimeter. Pulling the bottle of Wild Turkey from his cargo pocket, he held the amber liquid up to the sun and examined it before pulling the cork. It was his first drink in nearly a month. The heat of the day had given way to a gentle onshore breeze. He offered Joe the bottle.

"You should know, we redskins don't do well with that stuff."

Martin laughed and replaced the cork, but Thunders pulled the bottle from his hands.

"I'll try to behave."

Removing the cork, he took two long swallows from the bottle and gave it back to Martin. Martin lit two cigarettes and gave one to Joe. Both men sat gazing out at the purple hills to the west.

"What'd you think about what Douchie and Peebles said today?"

Joe maintained his focus on the distant horizon.

"We pretty much assumed it was one of them, but nobody knew for sure. The CID investigators wore us out about it. They kept asking the same questions over and over, but none of us saw anything. You're not going to say something, are you?"

Martin shrugged but said nothing.

"I'm not sure I would," Thunders said.

"Why?"

"Douchie and Peebles are vicious bastards. If the CID doesn't think they have enough to prove a case, they might turn them loose after questioning, but they're going to know you said something. You might be next."

"I have a hard question for you."

"Yeah?"

"If I take this to the CO will you testify to what you heard?"

"Give me your bottle, Shadows."

He took another swig and handed it back. Martin did the same.

"I'll testify," Thunders said. "They'll have to kill both of us."

CHAPTER FOURTEEN

The following day Martin was up at first light. It was a non-duty day for him, but he went in search of Lieutenant Randal. The platoon leader was coming out of the showers wearing boxers and unlaced jungle boots. Rubbing his head with a towel, the lieutenant looked up in surprise when Martin walked up.

"You're not on the duty roster today, Shadows. Why are you up so early?"

"Good morning to you too, sir."

The lieutenant laughed.

"Sorry, I forgot my proper war-time etiquette. Yes, it is a damned good morning, PFC Shadows, even for Vietnam. So, what's up with you?"

"I'd like to meet with you and Captain Bowman."

The lieutenant stopped drying his head and gave Martin a sideways glance.

"Oh. So, how did you hear about it?"

Martin was going to tell him about the conversation with Doochie and Peebles, but the lieutenant was talking about something else. No one was around, and the firebase was quiet.

"Hear about what?" Martin asked.

"Why are you wanting to meet with us?"

"It's about something I overheard."

"About a patrol?"

His plan to tell him about Douchie and Peebles went out the window—at least for the moment. First, he wanted to know more about this patrol.

"Yes, sir."

"Well, it's true but we're trying to keep it quiet. We're calling you, Joe Thunders, and Sergeant Lopez in for a briefing in a couple hours, but you can't say anything about it to anyone. You'll learn more about it then. Remember, don't say a word to anyone."

Martin decided to wait and tell the lieutenant about Douchie and Peebles later. Shortly after breakfast, he got word to report to Command-and-Control. C&C had been cleared of everyone when Martin, Joe Thunders, and Ray Lopez arrived.

"Grab a chair, gentlemen," Captain Bowman said.

He and Lieutenant Randal were already seated and waited while the others pulled up their chairs.

"Shadows, you're getting an early promotion to Specialist 4th Class. Your orders will be issued soon. Thunders, I've already issued orders restoring your rank to E-4. You've earned it. Just stay off the liquor."

Joe glanced at Martin and gave a subtle bob of his brows. Thunder's ironic humor didn't escape him as Martin fought to keep a straight face. He also realized he was due for promotion to First Lieutenant and wanted to tell Joe of that irony as well. It would have to wait till another time.

"Men, we have a situation to deal with, and what we discuss here must not be mentioned outside this room. Is that clear?"

The men nodded in unison.

"It involves the ARVN colonel named Nguyen. I believe you all have seen him at one time or another. Right?"

Again, they nodded.

"The brigade commander wants us to undertake a recon mission. It's a stretch, but he hopes we can determine if Nguyen is an enemy sympathizer. Here's the plan: Lieutenant Randal is going to take you guys through the wire later tonight. You'll be going up the road to the village where Lieutenant Fitzer and PFC Maziensky were KIA. You will establish an OP where you can see anyone who comes and goes in the ville'. Sergeant Lopez, you will carry the radio, while Thunders and Shadows will provide security.

"First thing in the morning, I'm contacting Colonel Nguyen and asking him for the same interpreter we used the last time. I'm telling him we're going back into that village the day after tomorrow. If Nguyen enters the village before then, I hope to have you in place where you can see who he meets with. That's it. You won't take any action, except to observe and report. You will exfiltrate after dark, and report back here. Questions?"

"What if we see him talking with armed VC?" Martin asked.

"It's already been discussed at brigade level. The Vietnamese Special Police will be notified, and a contingent will be here to meet him when he arrives at the firebase."

Martin was light-headed with another adrenaline buzz. His orders were to avoid active participation and simply observe and report. Suddenly, he was a participant in something having possible lethal consequences. He was originally told his mission was to prevent further embarrassing incidents like the Green Beret Project Gamma affair that resulted in the execution of a suspected NVA spy. Yet, he was about to participate in a mission that, if it went sideways, could have similar results.

Keep me updated. Palmer's words kept running through his mind as Martin silently walked through the firebase gate that night, but perhaps he was already aware of this mission. He hoped so. Considering the possible ramifications, it seemed certain the higher-ups with the 4th Infantry would have cleared it with MAC-V.

Joe Thunders was on point, and Martin brought up the rear. The four men walked on the shoulder of the sandy road to muffle their footfalls. Insects, frogs, and lizards provided a muted chorus from the surrounding rice paddies. The few remaining tall palms stood starkly against the night sky—their wounded remains drooping with the effects of Agent Orange.

Martin hoped to contact Captain Palmer upon their return to the firebase, but his only hope for now was to prevent a major mistake by these men. If Colonel Nguyen didn't show up at all, it wouldn't hurt his feelings, but his gut said otherwise. Nguyen would likely come to the village in the next twenty-four hours to warn them of the Americans' return. Lieutenant Randal would follow orders, but Nguyen's reaction if they were discovered was the big question.

Despite moving cautiously, they reached the village after a couple hours. Wading across the canal, they climbed atop a berm at the village edge and hid in the brush. With a good view of the road behind them, the newly rebuilt bridge, and the center of the village, it was an ideal observation post—or so it seemed.

The night hours passed slowly as sweat soaked the parts of their fatigues the canal hadn't, and mosquitoes whined incessantly. At dawn a rooster crowed, and there came the sound of someone chopping wood only a few meters away. The four men lay motionless in the grass as the man's grunts sounded with each swing of his axe. The sound of splitting wood was followed by a clack as he tossed each piece into a pile. The morning light revealed they were perhaps too close, but it was too late. They had to remain in place.

After a while the odor of morning cook fires filled the stagnant air. There was little movement in the village until after sunup when a jeep approached on the road from the west. It slowed and turned down the trail toward the village. When it stopped, Lieutenant Randal studied the two men in the vehicle through his binoculars. One remained with the jeep, while the other walked toward the canal bridge. Randal gave Ray Lopez the binoculars.

"That's Nguyen coming this way," Lopez whispered.

"Do you recognize his driver?" Randal asked.

Ray continued gazing through the binoculars.

"Yeah. That's his XO, Major Thanh."

Joe Thunders elbowed Martin's ribs. "Look."

A guerrilla with a floppy hat and an AK-47 walked from behind a hootch and met the colonel as he crossed the bridge. Three more appeared in the doorway of a hootch barely fifty meters away.

"Jesus! There's a bunch of them here," Lopez whispered.

The Americans remained frozen, knowing their slightest movement would be detected. Nguyen's meeting was brief, but as he turned back toward the bridge, the sound of men running came from somewhere down the berm. Martin turned as several hand grenades sailed in arcs toward the recon team. A VC patrol had come up behind them.

"Grenade!" he shouted.

Diving off the side of the berm, he scrambled for cover. Several guerrillas fired their weapons, and ear-splitting cracks of AK-47 rounds filled the air as the grenades detonated. Martin was crawling toward the nearest hootch, when he spotted Nguyen running back into the village. If Nguyen escaped now, he would likely disappear forever. The colonel ducked into a nearby doorway, as another Chi-Com grenade thudded into the dirt a few feet from Martin. He rolled into a depression and buried his head in his arms.

Totally disoriented, Martin's head was roaring as muted voices surrounded him. They were speaking Vietnamese, and only then did he realize he had been unconscious. The dim light revealed he was inside a hut—probably dragged there by the ones standing over him. Through the dust and sweat in his eyes, he saw the dimly lit face of Nguyen. The colonel motioned for the guerrillas to grab him, and they shoved him into a hole. The musty odor of freshly dug dirt and unbathed men filled his nostrils, and he realized they were dragging him into a tunnel.

It seemed several minutes must have passed when he again felt himself jarred back to consciousness. This time he was in water, choking and gasping for air. He spat and opened his eyes. He was in the river below the village. A moment later someone grabbed his fatigue shirt and snatched him into a boat. Again, the lights faded.

CHAPTER FIFTEEN

The intense odors of rotted fish, mildew, and salty ocean air filled his head as Martin slowly became aware of the rise and fall of the boat on gentle swells. He was enveloped in darkness and an oven-like heat. Slowly raising his hand, he touched his face only to discover he was blindfolded. His arm brushed against something hot, and it dawned on him—he was under a canvas tarpaulin.

Pushing at the tarp, he tried to sit upright, but lightning bolts of pain shot through his body. His scream manifested itself as little more than a dull grunt as he fell back. It seemed a miracle that he might still be alive, but if he wasn't already in hell, he was damned close.

Nasally voices cracked somewhere above, and the deck beneath him vibrated as if men were jumping down to where he lay beneath the tarp. It was snatched away, and the ocean breeze brought heaven-sent relief from the oppressive heat. His blindfold prevented him from knowing anything other than that it was still daylight. A moment later it too was snatched away, and he held his arm across his face, shielding his eyes from the sunlight. Someone jerked his arm down and shoved a canteen to his mouth.

He needed no encouragement as he sucked down the warm

water. His crusty lips and tongue were suddenly rejuvenated by the joyous moisture. The canteen was pulled away too soon and he reached out, only to have his hand batted away. Still squinting in near blindness, he shielded his face again from the glaring sunlight and glanced about. The sun was high in the sky, and Martin realized he had been unconscious for a long while—perhaps as much as a day and a half, maybe more.

He'd been stripped of everything but his fatigue shirt and trousers. One of the men was wearing his boots, another his hat. Despite an awful headache and every muscle in his body aching, he found no shrapnel wounds. The shallow depression back at the village must have saved him from the worst of it, but he was pretty sure he had another concussion.

A sparkling, blue-green ocean stretched away in every direction beneath piles of towering white cumulus. Off the port side, the dark green outline of the coast stretched along the horizon. The wooden boat was old and reeked of dead fish, as well as the body odors of its sweaty crew. There were also odors of gasoline and motor oil, indicating a gasoline engine was likely somewhere below deck, but they were under a full battened sail for the moment. Creaking and groaning, the junk plowed through gentle swells.

The dark-tanned men around him wore mostly black clothing. Some were shirtless. All had weapons, mostly SKS rifles and AK-47s. They glared at him from dark brown eyes—accusatory eyes that said they had already seen battle with the American military. And there was Nguyen still wearing his ARVN camo fatigues. He was sitting in an aluminum lawn chair on the upper deck. His façade was grim, but his eyes glowered with satisfaction, as if he were the proud lord and commander of this miserable scow.

"Tell me, PFC Shadows, who are you?"

Martin didn't want to talk. After a few moments, Nguyen nodded and smiled.

"I knew you were a problem the first time I saw you. Now, you want to play coy, but don't worry. Where we are going there are men who will encourage you to talk. They will make you glad to tell us who you really are."

Martin couldn't imagine how Nguyen would know he was anything other than an army grunt. He was probably fishing for answers. That was the only explanation, but it didn't matter. As soon as nightfall came and everyone was asleep, he planned to slip overboard. If he failed to make it to shore, it no longer mattered. It was better to die in the ocean than be tortured to death in an NVA prison.

———————————

Martin awakened on his back, realizing he had again fallen asleep. Opening his eyes, he stared into a glittering purple blanket of stars that stretched back into eternity. He tried to sit up only to find his arms and ankles were tied. Trussed like a hog, he could do little more than roll on his side. Most of his pain had subsided but escaping overboard was now impossible.

The sail had been struck, and the quiet chug of the gasoline engine came from below deck. The sea was dead calm. Thirst again gripped him, but he was determined to ask for nothing. He would die first, and he recalled those long hours spent in the sweat lodge with his grandfather. In some small way it had prepared him for this. Martin closed his eyes, resigned to save his strength, if only to see what the next day might bring.

When he again awakened, the stars were fading. The deep purple night sky was now a slate gray—a precursor to dawn. Someone knelt beside him and jerked his head upright. The canteen was again shoved to his mouth, and he drank. The water had cooled somewhat during the night. The man let him drink as much as he wanted, and when he was done, the guerrilla cut the cords from around his wrists, but he left his feet tied. A small cardboard box was tossed into his lap.

"Eat some of your American C-rations," a voice said. It was Nguyen sitting in his chair on the rear deck.

Martin dumped the carton's contents in his lap and fished out the P-38 on his dog tag chain. The guerrilla with the canteen grabbed the cigarettes along with the cocoa and coffee packets. Martin began opening the tin of peanut butter and crackers, as he cut his eyes out at the ocean. A few dim lights twinkled far out across the water on the port side. The boat was still heading north along the coast. He guessed they had been underway for two days and two nights.

He intentionally dropped a cracker and turned to retrieve it. This enabled him to see over the bow. A strange formation, a distant island, jutted from the ocean, much as Devils Tower in Wyoming did from the western landscape. *Matȟó Thípila* his Lakota father had once called it, home of the bears. It rose over twelve hundred feet above the prairie, but this island looked little more than a hundred and fifty feet high, and the upper portions of its cliffs were laced with vines and vegetation.

"That is to be your new home, PFC Shadows," Nguyen said.

He had seen Martin looking.

"Yes, we are off the coast of what your people call North Vietnam. In a short while, you will understand why your air force and navy consider this an unoccupied island and ignore its existence."

Just before sunup the sound of crashing surf indicated they were nearing the island, and a short while later the boat glided into a narrow channel among the rocks. Upon reaching the cliff wall, the canal turned and paralleled the cliff until it turned again into the mouth of a cavern. Inside was a hidden estuary where several boats were moored. One was a small runabout with an Evinrude outboard motor. Another was a junk similar to the one he was on, but the third was a gray, forty-foot launch—a modern highspeed patrol boat with antennas and multiple armaments.

A uniformed soldier standing on a rock shelf held a flashlight—its beam slashing the shadowy light inside the cavern estuary. Beside him stood another man who threw a coil of rope to the boat crew. A guerrilla snatched Martin's arms behind his back and again tied them with parachute cord. Afterward the cords were cut from around his ankles, and he was nudged ahead with the barrel of an AK-47.

Martin remembered another of his grandfather's visions—one he thought ludicrous until now. Two Shadows had said, *"You will find safety in a dark world from which you will bring havoc to your enemies."* What doubts he still harbored about the old man's powers were again subject to another strange coincidence. This was most certainly a dark world, but he wasn't so sure about its safety nor his ability to bring havoc to his enemies.

From somewhere in the depths of the cave came the hum of a generator—probably the power source for the strings of dim lightbulbs hanging from a zig-zagging flight of metal stairs. The stairs climbed sixty feet up a vertical wall at the back of the estuary. Martin could little imagine a more surreal experience as the footfalls of the men echoed from the rock walls, and the cavern glowed with the eerie amber light of the bulbs.

They pushed him toward the stairway, but stiff and sore, Martin stumbled and fell to his knees. He quickly recovered only to have one of the guards club him with the butt of an SKS. Stars danced before his eyes, and Nguyen barked something at the guards. They took Martin by the arms and helped him climb the stairs. It was clear the colonel wanted him to remain alive—at least for now.

When they reached the top of the stairway, there was another opening leading into a long corridor where more strings of naked bulbs hung from the ceiling. Martin shook free of their grasps and walked on his own. One of the guards gave a grunting laugh, probably knowing this show of rebellion would soon be crushed, but Martin prayed that his grandfather's visions predicted otherwise. These bastards would pay. If he could, he would bring them the havoc Two Shadows predicted—one the likes of which none of them had experienced.

This new passageway was another cavern, with barred cells hollowed out in its walls. Most were empty except for two. One held several dark-skinned Asians—small men who seemed on the verge of starvation. Their brown eyes followed him with curiosity as he walked past. From another cell farther down the corridor a ragged wraith gazed out at him—a white man who was a near skeleton of a human being. He stared from sunken blue eyes, and his long beard indicated he had been imprisoned for a long time, possibly years. Martin's vow of revenge suddenly seemed premature.

Voices echoed in the cavern as two men approached from the opposite direction. One wore the uniform of an NVA officer, the other an olive drab one that Martin didn't recognize. They stopped at the next open cell door and Nguyen motioned to the guards, who cut Martin's restraints and shoved him inside. Maintaining his balance, he quickly spun about to face his captors. One cast a smirk his way, while another set a small porcelain cup of water inside and slammed the steel door shut. Unlike the others with bars, this door was solid, and except for cracks of dim light around the edges, it sealed the dank cell in near total darkness.

CHAPTER SIXTEEN

When the American prisoner, Shadows, was safely locked away that morning, Colonel Nguyen met with the prison commandant and a Chinese interrogator named Cháng. The Vietnamese commandant, Linh, appeared competent, but there was a strange paranoia about him that seemed related to Cháng. Tight-lipped and formal in the Chinaman's presence, Linh's trust seemed tenuous at best. When Cháng finally left the room, the commandant lit a cigarette and smiled. He had said little about the prisoner, and Nguyen realized it was more than distrust—a conflict, perhaps.

He sat with Linh in a small office, a spartan affair as the Greeks might describe it. The furnishing consisted of a desk with chairs and a framed photo of Chairman Ho. Nguyen's officer quarters in Saigon were a penthouse suite by comparison. Capitalism did have its benefits. He chose to remain silent and allow his fellow officer to speak first.

Colonel Linh offered him a cigarette—one of the aged ones left behind by the French—the previous madmen who thought they could colonize Vietnam. They were vanquished as would be the Americans—if not in battle, then by their own people who had been protesting in the streets since the people's massive Tet

Offensive. Nguyen smiled. After the few Marlboros left in his pack, all he had remaining were a couple packs of Chesterfields, but a filtered Marlboro was a way to establish an edge of superiority. He pulled the pack from his pocket and offered one to Linh.

"So, tell me what it is that makes you believe your prisoner is one we must thoroughly interrogate," Linh said.

Nguyen watched while Linh inhaled the luxurious flavor of the Marlboro and paused, before exhaling through both nostrils and his mouth. He seemed immersed in pleasure—almost as if the cigarette were laced with Thai opium. Nguyen stifled the urge to smile. His counterpart had been too long in the North.

"Colonel Linh, I have spent many months working with these Americans. Many are imbeciles, but some are not. This one is not. He is different. I saw it in his eyes and in the manner in which he carries himself. I cannot say with certainty that I am right, but he demands our closer scrutiny. It was with only the barest of luck I escaped capture, because I believe they discovered my true identity."

"Your instincts serve you well, Colonel Nguyen. I sent your prisoner's name to Hanoi, and they radioed me with extensive information. There are indeed some interesting facts and even more interesting inconsistencies discovered about him by your fellow agents in the South. Some of the report is still being decoded as we speak. We must wait until that is completed to determine what warrants our immediate attention. However, we have one small issue."

Nguyen studied his colleague with a curious but respectful eye.

"I am under orders to provide our esteemed Chinese advisor the first opportunity for interrogation."

"How is this an issue as long as we get the information we need?" Nguyen asked.

Linh gazed at his cigarette as he spoke. "We Vietnamese seek first to address the immediate problems that hinder our army in the South. The Chinese seek something different—something, let's say that addresses the geo-political issues of the entire region. Comrade Chang's intent is to change the hearts and minds of his prisoners, whereby he claims the information is more likely to be accurate and useful. My complaint to him has been that his methods are slow and produce information that is often dated beyond usefulness. Telling him so was a mistake."

"What you say sounds logical, so why was that a mistake?"

"We had two American Green Berets brought here for interrogation. They were captured along with four of their Bru mercenaries about a year ago. Hanoi knew these prisoners could provide valuable tactical information about their operations in Laos, but Mister Cháng insisted he be allowed to first use his methods.

"I suppose it was my fault for expressing a need for urgency, because he accidentally killed one of the Americans. My prison cadre thought the death of this man was a bad thing, and they claim to still hear his dying screams coming from the jungle. Cháng scoffs at their fear of the spirits, but I am not so sure."

"So, are you saying that we must continue to allow Cháng his methods?"

"I am afraid that is the case."

"I suspect many of our agents in the South are in danger of being discovered by others like my prisoner. What if he accidentally kills him? It could be costly."

"We have no choice. I must follow orders, but I have demanded Chang take greater care. I have also reported this to Hanoi and our leaders have informed me that he may be recalled. Our leaders fear his government is seeking to undermine ours and use their power to take control. It seems relations between our countries are weakening."

"That is not surprising. After all, we are old enemies with the Chinese."

"For now, we have no choice but to stand aside and allow him his way. Perhaps when you return south you can warn others. If we are able to obtain useful information, I will make certain it reaches you."

Nguyen gritted his teeth and mashed his half-finished Marlboro into an ivory ashtray. Linh gazed at the smashed cigarette as if it were a blasphemy—a symbol of terrible waste and decadent Americanism. Nguyen saw this immediately, but if those were his counterpart's thoughts, he no longer cared. After all, they were merely jingoisms for the masses. What mattered were the lives of the leaders—the ones who led the revolution—those like his fellow agents in the South.

"Our people die while the Chinese make buffoons of us," he said.

Linh slowly lifted his eyes from the ashtray. "I agree. The needless killing of the first American caused us all great concern. Two of my men have disappeared since then, one that very day, and we do not know the reason. Even our leaders in Hanoi expressed to Cháng their displeasure, but he only responds with ridicule. Regardless, I believe he will use greater care now, and we will get whatever information we need much sooner."

Mister Cháng made his presence known the next morning as Colonels Nguyen and Linh took a breakfast of dried fruit and coffee atop the escarpment. A mild breeze blew off the ocean, rustling the trees overhead as he strutted toward them with the rigid bearing of a military officer. Nguyen valued the image of a stalwart soldier, and Cháng, despite the absence of rank on his uniform, was the epitome of one. His red star and impeccably tailored uniform were mere garnish to his deportment.

Refusing to sit, Chang stood gazing out at the ocean while inserting a cigarette into an amber holder. He cupped his hands against the breeze and struck a flame with an American Zippo lighter.

"Good morning, Mister Cháng," Linh said.

Cháng exhaled through his nostrils and simply nodded. "So, tell me, Colonel Nguyen. Why do you believe your prisoner is of such value?"

Nguyen eyed the Chinaman carefully. He seemed deficient of even the most rudimentary elements of courtesy.

"Perhaps, you will join us for some fruit and coffee, Mister Cháng?" Linh asked.

"I took my breakfast at first light, an hour ago."

Nguyen was quickly discovering the source of Colonel Linh's animus. Cháng was an arrogant man.

"Ah, so you are ready to work immediately on our new prisoner, correct?" Nguyen said.

"I have already begun my work."

"And, my esteemed advisor," Linh said, "what work is that?"

Nguyen stifled a smile. Colonel Linh was sparring with an equal display of arrogance.

"He is in a dark cell and will remain there with no contact for a few weeks."

Nguyen was compelled to make Cháng understand how any delay could be costly. If the Americans were infiltrating their units with undercover agents, many more An Ninh agents like himself would be discovered.

"I believe this man is not simply a common soldier, as he wishes to represent himself," Nguyen said.

"And what is it that makes you believe this?"

"One of my contacts—that is one of this prisoner's comrades, a soldier in his own unit, told me he feels this is the case."

"And you believe this other American soldier is telling you the truth about what he feels?"

"I have no reason to doubt him."

"And what motivations has he for reporting his comrade?"

"This soldier is stupid and takes pride in talking about his fellow soldiers because he is not happy with the American army. It makes him feel important to speak freely with a Vietnamese colonel."

"What evidence did this soldier give you that your prisoner is more than another soldier?"

"He witnessed him talking with a soldier visiting his base, and they seemed secretive."

"And what was it these two soldiers discussed?"

Nguyen glanced at Linh, but his counterpart turned to gaze out beyond the cliffs toward the glittering waters. There was no help to be had there, and Cháng was pushing him into a checkmate.

"The soldier said he could not hear what they were discussing."

Sighing deeply, Cháng snatched the cigarette butt from the holder and tossed it into the ferns.

"Colonel Nguyen, I have a much more valuable prisoner needing my attention. He is an American Special Forces soldier your army captured in Laos. I have worked with him for months, and only now has he found the good reasoning to join the people's revolution. He is telling me much, and he is my first priority, but if you insist, you and Colonel Linh should question your prisoner, and perhaps I can assist."

This was what Nguyen had hoped for, but Colonel Linh now appeared sullen. It was clear he had taken offense to Nguyen's interference and felt his authority as prison commandant was being usurped.

"This decision is Colonel Linh's, Mister Cháng. My only concern is that we get information quickly so we might prevent further damage to our agents in the South."

Linh raised his chin. The gesture seemed to have worked.

"You begin your journey south, Colonel Nguyen, and I will join with Mister Cháng to work on your prisoner. Our contacts in Hanoi will update you with the information we obtain."

Nguyen was satisfied with the arrangement but had to impress upon them the need for urgency.

"Comrades, I do not wish to sound melodramatic, but my old battalion from the 66th Regiment has been ordered eastward into the highlands south of Chu Lai. I am joining them there to plan our strike on an American artillery base near the coast. I therefore hope you understand the urgency for obtaining whatever information we can from this prisoner."

"I wish you safe travels, Colonel," Cháng said. "I assure you we will work with diligence to get from him whatever information we can."

CHAPTER SEVENTEEN

Martin lay on the cold rock floor of his cell, staring into an opaque wall of darkness. The steel door had apparently been draped with something to prevent even a hint of light from entering. Thoughts of his mother came as brief but comforting respites from his dilemma, but it was his grandfather's words that occupied his mind most—words he now wished he had listened to with greater care. Several days, maybe even a week, had passed since his capture. He was uncertain how long it had been, and there were only two sounds that broke an otherwise interminable silence.

One was a constant but regular drip-drip of water, followed by a pause, then another drip-drip...drip. It echoed quietly, but in a constant and repetitive pattern from somewhere below, in the labyrinth of caves. The sound wasn't particularly offensive, but it was a clock ticking away the seconds of his life. His only relief came when the drips grew into the sound of rushing water—probably created by rainfall on the island above.

The other sound he heard was different, and the first time he heard it, he sat upright. It was sporadic and occurred only twice, but it wasn't something natural. Both times the slight taps of a rock striking the wall came in a brief staccato, ending in silence.

The second time it occurred he realized it was a quick and metered type of code—Morse Code perhaps, but try as he might, he could make no sense of it.

After a while, he began to recognize a benefit to the silence. The ringing in his ears had faded, and he was beginning to recognize the slightest nuances of sound—things he hadn't heard since the ambush outside the village. The damage caused by the explosions was beginning to heal as his headaches faded. The first things he heard from his cell were the gentle clank of a steel door somewhere far down the corridor followed by the quiet tread of a sentry's boots on the rock floors.

He searched for the porcelain water cup in the darkness, but his fingers told him it was dry. It had been that way for two days. The pangs of an empty belly and parched tongue were playing havoc with his mind. He closed his eyes in hopes of sleep disguising the pain and thirst. If he didn't get water soon, he would likely die. The drip-drip...drip was an agonizing tease, but it lulled him into a catatonic rest. His thirst remained as he drifted in and out of a fitful sleep.

That day back in Montana, Martin wanted to show his grandfather that he was no sissy. They had smoked the pipe for several hours, and his throat was parched, but he refused to let Two Shadows see his discomfort. He cleared his throat while the old man gazed steadily at him with eyes that were neither intimidating nor sympathetic but filled with deep wisdom. They seemed to stare into his very soul.

"Your Lakota blood serves you well, Martin Shadows. You will leave your warrior's mark on your enemies. Mask your pain as you have, and they will fear and respect you."

Martin nodded respectfully.

"And fear not the thirst caused by Chanunupa Wakan as it is symbolic of the relationships of the natural world where there is

balance in everything we know. Your thirst will be relieved in good time."

His grandfather gave him a teasing smile and reached for the water bottle at his side, but a blinding light filled Martin's eyes, and he thought he had stepped from the tepee, only to realize he had been awakened by men shining flashlights in his eyes. They said nothing as they snatched him to his feet and shoved him toward the door.

Jabbing rifles in his back, they pushed him up the long corridor. Eventually they reached a massive underground room lit by hundreds of light bulbs and lined with terraced wooden walkways, balconies, and doors. The guards motioned him toward a doorway where there stood one of the men who first met Colonel Nguyen at the cell door.

"Good day, Private Shadows. I am Colonel Linh. I am the commandant here and have many questions for you. Please, step inside and we will begin what I hope will be a fruitful discussion."

He motioned Martin into a room where a single naked bulb hung above a small table with two folding metal chairs. The gray walls were bare. Martin stood while Linh sat behind the table and lit a cigarette. For nearly a minute, he relished his cigarette with theatrical pleasure. After a while he glanced Martin's way.

"Oh, by all means, please be seated. Perhaps you would like a cigarette?"

Martin studied him carefully.

"Or you would like something else, water perhaps?"

Linh must have known he had been without water for days.

"A cigarette will do."

The Vietnamese colonel failed to hide his surprise as his brows rose slightly while he shook one from a pack of Chesterfields and gave it to Martin.

"Your captor, Colonel Nguyen, was kind enough to share with

me some of your American cigarettes. Hopefully, because I too share, you will grant me your cooperation in return."

Taking a Zippo from his pocket, the colonel lit the unfiltered Chesterfield. Martin noticed the engraving on the lighter. It was the Army Special Forces dagger with crossed arrows and the motto *De oppresso liber.* The lighter was no doubt taken from some unfortunate Green Beret. Martin gritted his teeth. He wanted to snatch the little bastard across the table and kill him.

Linh held the lighter in front of Martin's face, allowing its yellow flame to burn.

"What do you fear, Shadows? Fire, perhaps? All living creatures fear fire. Did you know that a man can be burned to death very slowly, little by little, for many weeks?"

Linh snapped the lighter shut and dropped it in his pocket. Martin sent his mind off to Montana and his grandfather's lodge in the hills. There was pain coming, and he had to find a way to deflect it.

"There are many ways to find a man's deepest fears. Do you know what *I* fear? I fear drowning in water because I have never learned to swim. That surprises you, no? We all have our fears. So how shall I find yours? Perhaps you will cooperate, and none of this will be necessary."

His greatest fear was something Martin had never considered, and the answer wasn't readily apparent—even to himself. He was being held in this prison cave on an island off the coast of North Vietnam, but Kentucky had abundant caves. He had spent his boyhood days exploring them and remembered the time when his flashlight failed, and he had lost his backup light. A maze of side tunnels with twists, turns, and obscure off-shoots left him thinking his skeleton might someday be found by another generation of spelunkers.

That perhaps was his closest encounter with fear bordering

on panic. By its very nature, this prison was probably what he feared most—being lost forever, his family having no clue where he had gone. And it wasn't as much for himself as it was for his mother and father. The only way he had survived that day was by stifling his panic and carefully thinking through his situation. That presence of mind and a book of paper matches saved him as he carefully retraced his path using only his sense of touch and lighting matches only when his instincts were at absolute loggerheads with his senses.

Linh held his cigarette between his thumb and fingers and gazed at it. After a few moments, he turned and smiled.

"So, you have nothing to say?"

Military protocol dictated a prisoner of war give only his name, rank, date of birth, and serial number, but it was his rank that had Martin stumped. His captors didn't know he was an officer.

"My name is Martin Shadows, Private First Class, birthdate April 2, 1946, serial number 401-01-9441."

"Why is it that some of you wish to play the role of the patriot for your army, while others share information with us so freely?"

"I don't know what you mean."

"Colonel Nguyen said your comrades Sergeant Kurbo and Private Greyman shared much with him about your operations, but you seem so reluctant. Why is that?"

"They probably believed he was actually a colonel in the South Vietnamese Army and not a spy."

"Aaaahhh! But you *did* suspect him, correct?"

"I had no idea. I only thought it ill-advised to talk about our operations when it wasn't necessary."

"But he was supposed to be a member of the puppet army your government supports."

Martin remained silent.

"So, I will accept that explanation for now, but you seem somewhat, let's say, more refined than the average American soldier, Private Shadows. You perhaps have attended a university, yes?"

Martin inhaled the last of his cigarette and glanced at the ivory ashtray on the desk. It was engraved with the elephant head representing the Hindu god Ganesh.

"May I?" he asked, motioning toward the ashtray. Only an inch of the cigarette remained before the fire would reach his fingers.

Linh's lips tightened into a hard grin.

"And now we reach our first opportunity for negotiation. Perhaps, if I grant you the use of my ashtray you will then answer just one question for me."

Martin remained silent.

"I must warn you. Should you drop your cigarette to the floor, punishment will be swift and severe. Therefore, let me ask you this: your fellow American, Private Greyman, told Colonel Nguyen that he thought you were sent to his unit as a spy. Were you?"

"I'm not sure why Greyman would think that."

"But you have not answered my question."

"Lord Ganesh would not be proud of you, Colonel, using his image for this purpose."

Linh glanced at the ashtray before his brows folded together in anger. Martin maintained his steady gaze and without so much as a blink reached with his left hand and mashed the glowing end of the cigarette between his thumb and index finger. He held it a moment before casually dropping it into his shirt pocket. Linh's eyes glared wide while his face grew into a mask of red rage.

"You are a fool, Shadows! You make light of things for which you have little understanding."

Martin shrugged. After a moment Linh seemed to regather his composure.

"Let me say this. I can help you. Yes, I am commandant and

have final say on matters, but there is a special interrogator here. His name is Mister Cháng, and he is from the People's Republic of China. He has special privileges granted by my government to interrogate highly valued prisoners of war, and I believe you may find his methods much less to your liking than mine. Therefore, let us continue, and we will see if we can avoid a visit with Mister Cháng."

The questions continued, often the same ones repeated in different ways, again and again, but Linh still offered him no water. Martin's lips were beginning to crack, while his tongue enlarged. The interrogation lasted for hours—how many, he wasn't sure. With no clocks and no sense of sunrise or sunset, time was lost, much as it had been that day in the sweat lodge. But he refused to give in.

Sometime later, Linh stood and stared down at him with almost sympathetic eyes. "I have done my best to dissuade you of your stubbornness, Shadows. I am afraid your lack of cooperation will result in unpleasant consequences. You will soon see."

Martin was fading into delirium when the guards finally took him back to his cell. If he wasn't given water soon, he would die. They opened the steel door, and only then did he see the possibility of salvation. The dim light from the outside corridor glistened against something wet on the back wall—or was it simply a product of his delirium, the mirage of an oasis in the desert? The metal door clanked shut behind him.

Crawling forward in the darkness, he felt his way along the floor until his hands found the back wall. He nearly shouted for joy. It was there. The relentless dripping from somewhere below was being fed by this luxurious film of water that he now sucked ravenously from the rock wall. He slurped the moisture until he could stand no more. Afterward, he lay flat on his back and stared up into the darkness.

He remembered when Two Shadows said, ...*fear not the thirst caused by Chanunupa Wakan*... And it seemed another vision had manifested its truth. What else could he have meant, and what more had he said that could relate to Martin's current dilemma? He had to think. He had to go through every aspect of his grandfather's visions and of this place where he was imprisoned. If escape was possible, those words might help him find a way.

As Martin thought about it, he realized escape could happen only while he was outside of the cell—perhaps while going to or from the interrogation room. Getting off the island was another obstacle, and he was rapidly losing weight and weakening. He thought of the skeletal wraith in the adjacent cell and wondered how long before he too looked that way. The situation seemed hopeless—an unbreachable cell, hundred-foot cliffs, shark-infested waters, and perhaps twenty or thirty guards. Yet, there was only one way he could lose. That would be when he stopped fighting.

CHAPTER EIGHTEEN

Martin awakened with no idea how long he had been sleeping. He had dreamt again of hearing the clicking of a rock. At least he thought it was a dream. He had no clue, until an idea came to him. Coming to his knees, he felt his way through the darkness as he crawled across the floor to the back of the cell where he again sucked the life-giving moisture from the wall. Afterward, he began exploring the cell with his fingers. He was searching for something he had found previously.

Establishing a pattern, he made his way back and forth until he found what he was after—a rough place on the floor containing several small rocks. The largest, the size of a silver dollar, was thick enough to have some weight. It would do. After finding the cell door, he reoriented himself and crawled to the wall separating his from the adjoining cell. He tapped the sandstone wall lightly one time. The sound was dull. He tried the floor. The rock there was harder, resulting in a sharper sound.

He waited, and his prayers were answered as there came a light tap from the opposite side. It was followed by a second, noticeably different sound—a sharper tap. The person there was doing the same thing, striking first the wall, then the floor. Martin's mind raced.

That was it. He rapidly tapped the floor three times, the wall a little slower with three more taps, and the floor again with another three rapid taps—Morse Code for SOS, the international distress call. With only a cursory knowledge of the code, he hoped to make sense of the forthcoming message. He waited.

After several seconds there came a flurry of tentative taps. They continued until the question was completed. "W-h-e-r-e y-e-a-r-n-e-d c-o-d-e-?"

Martin thought for a moment before slowly tapping his response, "B-o-y S-c-o-u-t-s."

The taps from the other side came again. "W-h-e-r-e f-r-o-z?"

Again, Martin paused. It had been a long time since he earned his Boy Scout communications merit badge. It was something his father had insisted he do—join the Scouts. The Z must have been an M.

"K-e-n-t-u-c-k-y."

He waited.

"G-r-e-e-n g-r-a-s-s t-h-e-r-e?"

It was a question but more importantly, a test.

"B-l-u-e g-r-a-s-s," he responded.

After several moments, the person on the other side seemed satisfied and began tapping out another message. With no way of making notes, Martin was struggling. The message ended, and he tried to make sense of it.

"F-m-n-d y-o-o-s-e b-y-o-c-k w-a-y-y."

An extended silence ensued, broken only by the dripping water somewhere below. Was it a code within the code? He saw the words clearly in his mind's eye. He had either become confused and made more mistakes, or—. It came to him. It was the M and the Y that were incorrect. "*Find loose block wall.*" That was it, but he had searched the cell, and there was no loose block wall. It made no sense.

A single tap sounded from the opposite side, but this time it was several feet away, back near the rear of the cell. On his knees, Martin worked his way along the wall, searching with his fingers, until he felt the outlines of mortared joints—a place sealed with man-made concrete blocks. This was it.

With his fingers, he traced the lines, and after a few minutes he found a mortarless crack. It followed the shape of a rectangular block. Forcing his fingers into the crevasses on each side, he began pulling. Rocking it back and forth, he was able to slowly ease the block from the wall.

"What's your name?"

The voice was a barely audible whisper coming from the adjacent cell, but it precipitated an instant well of emotion as Martin tried to whisper but choked. After swallowing several times, he tried again. "Martin Shadows."

"Where were you captured?"

"Near FSB Suzy, south of Chu Lai. Who are you?"

"Sergeant Luis Ravera, Second Special Forces. When were you captured?"

"Two or three weeks ago, I think—maybe four. I don't know. I've lost track of time. How about you?"

"What month and year is it?"

"November 1968."

"I've been here nearly a year."

"Where are we?" Martin asked.

"A small island off the coast of North Vietnam. It's a karst formation—full of caves. I've only been outside three times. It's flat on top, maybe fifty or sixty acres, and it's covered with jungle, but there aren't any buildings out there. I think they want the Navy jets to think it's uninhabited."

"Are there more prisoners here?"

"The only other American was my A-team RTO, Sergeant Bob Jenkins, but Cháng claims he killed him a few months back. There are also four Montagnards from my team still here, but I haven't seen them for several weeks."

"You got any ideas how we can get out of here?"

"Not really. There are hundred-foot cliffs all the way around the island, and the water below is filled with rocks. They keep a couple of dogs up there—rottweilers I think. The gooks kill the monkeys to feed them or else let them eat escaped prisoners."

"Why do you think they—"

"Sshshh! Put the block back."

The shuffling sounds of boots came from the outside hallway. Martin pushed the block back into place and ran his hand over the wall to make certain it was flush. Rolling away, he crawled to the center of the cell and waited. A moment later the steel door swung open, and he was again blinded by flashlights.

With his arms cinched over a thick piece of cane across his shoulder blades, Martin felt his shoulder joints were about to rip from their sockets. The interrogation had gone on now for over five hours. His shirt and trousers had been stripped away, and he had been beaten with bamboo until his back was a mass of bleeding welts. Sitting naked on the folding metal chair, he again faced Colonel Linh who wore a mask of smug satisfaction.

"I warned you, Private Shadows, but you refused my help. You left me with no better means to gain your attention, but this is a mere prelude. I am leaving now to enjoy the outside fresh air and have a cup of tea. In a few minutes you will meet my counterpart, an experienced interrogator named Mister Cháng. As I said previously, he is from the People's Republic of China. Perhaps he can help you find the sensibility to answer our questions."

It was known that torture broke everyone at some point, but

Martin found ways to distract his mind from the pain. The cool metal surface of the chair was soothing to the raw skin on his back and buttocks. A few moments later the Chinese interrogator walked in and dropped a black canvas bag on the table. It landed with a thud, while Cháng held his chin arrogantly high and gazed down the bridge of his nose at him. Martin met his gaze with defiance. His assessment was immediate. This was a pompous bastard with no soul. After several long moments, Cháng sighed.

"So, what is it about you that creates such paranoia amongst my Vietnamese comrades? They are a superstitious people with their gods and spirits and such. They fear that which they cannot explain. Are you one of those unexplainable phenomena, or is there some logical reason for their fear? Maybe you really are a spy, right?"

His tone was one of mock-sympathy, but his accent-free speech and perfect grammar sent red flags waving in the back of Martin's mind. He studied this new adversary. Despite a rigid military deportment, Cháng had his hands on his hips—projecting a certain casualness, almost like that of an American.

"I don't know."

"You don't know what—if you are a spy, a spirit, or why you're a suspect? Perhaps you don't know why they are paranoid, right? Come on. Help me out. Help *yourself* out."

"Your question is confusing."

"Ha! Yes, and you seem puzzled about me as well. I see it in your eyes."

This man was clever—too clever—and he possessed a well-above-average grasp of American linguistics. He spoke as if they were old buddies sitting at a bar and having drinks.

"Okay, let me answer your question. Yes, I lived in your country for several years—California, where I attended university in Berkeley as a young man. It is a school that educates future generations in a manner which guarantees a frame of thought that will someday change your country for the better."

It was tempting to argue but Martin held his tongue.

"There are many like me that your foolish government freely invites into their institutions. We drink your wine and learn your ways. You Americans are a weak people who have made Mickey Mouse and Chevrolet your gods. You are easily swayed, and your fascist corporations control you. You cannot see this little war for what it is—a simple military exercise to enrich your military industrial complex. For us in the People's Republic of China, it is an anomaly, a mere bump on our path toward a much greater goal. Regardless of its outcome, we will eventually own you from within. So, why don't you save yourself?"

"From what?"

"So, you don't care about yourself?"

"I am only here to do my duty."

"Ah, what loyalty! And what is this duty you speak of when your own people demonstrate against this war? Why is it so important?"

"I'm not sure, except that I have taken an oath to my country."

"Yes, but if you are not sure, then why is it important?"

"Because no matter what other Americans are saying, I still have one responsibility and that is to my fellow soldiers. Helping them survive this war is my duty and the best thing I can do."

"So, protecting your fellow soldiers is the most important thing?"

"I believe war makes most men think that way."

"Ah, yes. I suppose your friends, Sergeant Kurbo and Private Greyman, must think that way as well."

It was clear that Cháng was well briefed, and Martin was angry with himself. He had let Cháng draw him into a senseless argument.

"Kurbo is dead, and Greyman doesn't speak for most of us."

"I am tired of your word games, Private Shadows. Perhaps this will help you understand the wisdom of cooperation."

The interrogator opened the canvas bag and withdrew two coils of electrical wire. It was jumper cables with alligator clips on the ends. After donning heavy rubber gloves, he attached the cables to a wall box and clamped one of the alligator clips to Martin's chair. The relief he had felt earlier from the chair's cool metal now turned to raw fear. Cháng held the other clip in a gloved hand, raised his eyebrows, and quizzically cocked his head to one side.

"The Vietnamese are like old women with their fears of spirits, ghosts, and enemy soldiers with unexplainable powers, but in your case, I believe there is something to know. One more time I ask you, what is it that makes the Vietnamese suspect you are worthy of special interrogation?"

"I don't know."

Cháng clamped the second alligator clip to the chair and stepped back. Martin's muscles spasmed into vice-like cramps as stars darted before his eyes. His throat locked shut. The single overhead bulb flickered and dimmed. When Cháng removed the clip, Martin fell to the floor.

"Get back in your chair, Private Shadows. We are not yet done."

With his arms still cinched behind his back, Martin couldn't move. Cháng slammed the toe of his boot into his ribs, knocking the breath from his lungs. More stars danced before his eyes.

"Get back in the chair."

Old Two Shadows appeared before him. *Your Lakota blood serves you well, Martin Shadows. You will leave your warrior's mark on your enemies. Mask your pain as you have, and they will fear and respect you.*

Martin's lungs reopened and he sucked in a deep breath. Only with the greatest effort was he able to speak in a calm and metered manner, "Fear of your boot and your electricity do not keep me from the chair, Mister Cháng. My arms are bound, and my muscles are not responding."

With his jaw lying against the floor, Martin cut his eyes up at him. Cháng's lips were parted ever so slightly, but it was his eyes that revealed his incredulity. Cháng barked an order to someone outside the door. Two guards quickly entered, jerked Martin to his feet, and slammed him into the chair. Cháng motioned them out the door again.

"So, young Shadows, you claim yourself a man who stands by his fellow soldiers."

Martin gazed back at his adversary with his best poker face, but it was useless. His was a losing hand, and he wasn't sure how much more he could take.

"Answer my question. Is that not so?"

And it came to him that Cháng had locked in on one thing, a heat-seeking missile with the singular mission of finding its target. He was focused on Martin's loyalty to his fellow soldiers. It was a battle Martin couldn't win, but he wasn't going to simply roll over and die without a fight.

"Tell me something, Cháng, do you fight for your people, or is it for your membership in the ruling class of the proletariat?"

Chang's eyes glared with anger. Martin refused to stop.

"Do you pay honor first to your Communist Party or to your family, friends, and—"

"Silence, you bourgeois ass! Your tongue, even now, proves my point. You must understand that there is something more important than your greed for materialistic things and the approval of your friends. Nothing is more important than the Party."

"And I rest my case. You would sell your own family for this Party."

Cháng stepped forward and swung a gloved fist, striking Martin's jaw. Although stunned, he smiled and forced his eyes to lock with Cháng's.

"Your best?"

"You are pathetic, Shadows. Your defiance is like that of a sniveling rabbit before an eagle."

Cháng grabbed the alligator clip and again touched it to the metal chair. Sparks sprayed across the floor, and the light bulb again flickered. Martin convulsed and tumbled to the floor. Despite the stars in his eyes and his cramping muscles, he climbed back into the chair. His tongue tasted as if it had been shellacked with liquid metal, and the room was filled with the odor of overheated electrical wiring.

Cháng again was clearly rattled by this resistance, but there was no sense in tempting the sadistic bastard further. Martin's body was overruling his mind, telling him to stop being such a stubborn ass. He gazed steadfastly at Cháng—a typical government bureaucrat with too much power and an overwhelming ego.

"You know if you want something, all you have to do is ask," Martin said, "but I have to know what the hell you're talking about."

Cháng sighed deeply and slowly shook his head.

"You are what Americans call a smartass, Shadows. I find this somewhat admirable, given your current condition, but you will soon reveal what I want to know, because I already know what you fear most. I can get the truth from you without this unpleasantness, but I *do* find it somewhat entertaining. Come on now, save yourself the pain. Tell me what it is you are hiding. Tell me why you were at Firebase Suzy, disguised as an enlisted man, *Lieutenant* Martin Shadows."

For the first time, Martin felt the full weight of his adversary's advantage. Cháng had known all along, but how? Was the American military so infiltrated with spies that his mission had been compromised from the start? Some idiot at MAC-V was probably talking to a Vietnamese girlfriend or some ARVN officer who was an An Ninh agent. As a result, he was here now, getting fried in this NVA prison.

"You Americans are so cocky, yet so ignorant. Don't you know we have our people everywhere in your American military installations? We know both you and Sergeant Ravera were trained in your army's intelligence school at Fort Holabird. That is why you are both here at this special prison. We focus on the Holabird alumni. We also have passenger manifests from every flight into Vietnam, and yours listed you as a U.S. Army Lieutenant. So tell me, Lieutenant Shadows, why have you lied to us about your rank?"

Resistance was futile, except for one thing. Telling Cháng the truth might make Martin useless to them. He was not part of a counter-espionage group, and if they truly understood his mission, they would probably throw him in a cell and let him rot. Cháng stepped forward and again touched the metal chair with the alligator clip.

CHAPTER NINETEEN

Once again Martin awoke in darkness. He was back in a familiar place—his cell. The interrogation had lasted for hours, and he'd been subjected to electrical shocks until his mind and body were degrading to a vegetative state. He was sinking fast, and hope was fading as he became lost in a world of hallucinogenic dreams—a tiger leaping out from the flames of a burning jungle, an eagle screaming as it dove earthward, and the rhythmic thump of war drums somewhere in the mountains. He was there. He saw it. He heard it, and it was all very real.

Again they came, and again he sat in the little box of a room and in the same metal chair that was now his enemy. Today—or was it tonight—he no longer had any sense of time—the interrogator was Colonel Linh. The Vietnamese colonel circled the chair as if he were a cat stalking its prey. When Lihn finished his cigarette, he mashed the butt into the ivory ashtray and studied him with cold eyes. Martin waited for the cat to leap.

"What shall we discuss today, Lieutenant Shadows? Perhaps you wonder what has become of Colonel Nguyen, no? I will tell you anyway. He has returned to Quang Ngai Province to interrogate your three comrades who were captured with you."

This was another stunning revelation, but Martin refused to

react as he remained head-down and unmoving. He had thought Lieutenant Jake Randal, Ray Lopez, and Joe Thunders were killed that day in the village. This news instilled in him new and conflicting emotions. That they were alive should have been a good thing, but they were likely being held in some leech-infested cage somewhere deep in the jungle where they were destined to die. Their lot was likely worse than his. At this point, he wasn't certain that death wasn't his best option, except now he had others to consider.

"They're not alive. They were killed when I was captured."

"That is not so, Lieutenant. That is why Colonel Nguyen went back south."

"If they were alive, why didn't Colonel Nguyen bring them here when he brought me?"

"Colonel Nguyen was unsure how many soldiers were with you that day, and his primary intent was to escape. Unlike your wounded comrades, your aggressive behavior made you an opportune target for him to capture."

Linh's motive was clear, whether they were dead or alive, he was using Martin's fellow soldiers as leverage. Martin knew he had screwed up during his first interrogation when he declared his loyalty to them, and the two interrogators were now using that knowledge as they intensified their questioning.

"By now Colonel Nguyen is back in Quang Ngai Province, and Mister Cháng has shown him techniques which he will use to extract any useful information from your friends. If he is successful, we will know what we need to know. Perhaps then we will let you feed my dogs. What do you say to that?"

Martin remained silent.

"Mister Cháng will join us shortly. We are taking you for a walk on the island today. He has a surprise for you."

Exhausted emotionally and physically, Martin expected only

the worst from this latest revelation. Nothing these sadistic bastards offered, surprise or otherwise, would be something good. There could be nothing more they didn't already know about him, and if there was, he couldn't fathom what it might be. A few minutes later he stepped out into the first daylight he had seen in weeks. He could barely crack his eyelids against the blinding sunlight.

Cháng and Linh had donned wire-rimmed aviator sunglasses. Both wore sidearms and both had cigarettes dangling from their lips. Martin would have ridiculed their Hollywood personas, but he was beyond further resistance. He was done. At his first opportunity he was going to escape or die trying.

Deep bellowing barks and growls came from the path up ahead as four men came into view. Two were on either side of a dog, holding the muscular animals between stretched tethers. The dogs lunged and scratched at the rocky path while their mouths dripped saliva and they strained against their leashes.

Linh motioned to the guard behind Martin and pointed to his restraints. The guard quickly cut the ropes from his hobbled legs and his wrists. It made sense. He couldn't outrun the dogs. The freedom to walk unrestrained was an abnormal luxury. Linh stood apart from them and drew his sidearm, holding it at his side.

"Need I explain," he asked, "why any attempt to escape will not end well for you?"

Martin didn't bother to respond as they walked up a slight incline to where a magnificent ocean view appeared beyond the palms. The sparkling blue-green waters of the South China Sea stretched as far as the eye could see—all the way to the horizon. Somewhere out there might be his death, but somewhere out there might also be freedom. He was drawn forward as if something was pulling him toward the ocean. It was beyond rational thought, but he now knew what he would do. He had only to wait for the right moment.

They walked him to the edge of the precipice where he gazed down at the water below. At the base of the cliff, the surf broke among boulders and shards of rock—eons of rubble that built a shallow but craggy ring of talus around the island—except for one place. It was directly below, partially hidden by the outgrowth of vegetation on the cliff-face. The narrow boat channel, likely cleared by prison labor, cut through the jagged piles of rocks. It hugged the base of the cliff before disappearing into the cavern estuary.

"Ah, and now for your surprise, Lieutenant Shadows!" Linh said.

Cháng sucked his cigarette with smiling lips as a guard escorted a ragged and stumbling man up the path to the top of the cliff. It had to be him, Martin's next-door cellmate, and as he drew closer, he saw the recognition in his eyes. It was him, and he was smiling. He even winked. Martin swallowed the lump in his throat. This man had either succumbed to insanity or else was the personification of bravery.

"So," Cháng said, "now you and your friend can talk freely without the use of your little rock tapping codes."

Martin had hidden his emotion well—at least until now. It all gave way in an instant. These bastards knew everything.

"Oh!" Linh said in a mocking voice. "Have we finally convinced you that we are not fools? Tell me, my clever friend."

Martin said nothing while staring at Sergeant Luis Ravera, a proud Army Special Forces Green Beret, now a nearly skeletal ghost of a soldier standing before him.

"Lieutenant Shadows is a brave American army officer who always protects his men," Cháng said. "He has told me as much, Sergeant Ravera. Surely you must find this an admirable trait for one of your officers, yes?"

"He's not an officer," Ravera said. "He's an enlisted man."

"So, he lied to you as well?"

Ravera turned to Martin.

Martin nodded. "Yeah, I already figured they were listening."

Ravera smiled. Martin gazed down at the waves splashing through the rocks below. It was at least a hundred feet or more to the water, and the boat channel was partially obscured by the vegetation on the face of the cliff.

"Here is my offer, Lieutenant Shadows," Linh said. "Tell me everything, and we will not throw the sergeant onto the rocks below. Lie, and his death will be because of you. As you can see, we already know the truth. You have only to verify it in more detail. And if you force us to kill him, we will bring more of your soldiers here to our island and throw them to their deaths, until you see the wisdom in cooperation. Tell me about this spy network you Americans have created to infiltrate the Vietnamese puppet army."

"Tell him nothing!" Ravera shouted. "Those rocks will hurt for only a second, but you might get more men killed if—"

Cháng crashed his fist into Ravera's jaw, dropping him to his knees. "Such bravery, my great Green Beret friend. Now, remain silent and allow your superior officer to speak."

Martin helped him to his feet.

"Very touching, Lieutenant, that you help this lowly enlisted man, but what shall it be? You say your fellow soldiers are the most important thing to you. Show me this."

A strange wailing moan arose from somewhere far back on the island. Linh's eyes grew wide, but it was the guards who seemed suddenly frozen with terror as they gazed into the jungle. It ceased, but a moment later arose again. It was as if the wind was funneling through a narrow tunnel—something Martin had once heard near a cave in Kentucky. And he remembered his grandfather's strange vision when he said: *the rocks there cry, and those who hear their wails believe they come from the spirit world.*

He turned his gaze again to the waters below. The large patrol boat he had seen in the estuary probably drafted five feet or more of water. If the channel was cleared for it, the depth was at least eight or ten feet. Likely it was more, but a feet-first plunge from this height required four meters or more to avoid hitting the bottom. One thing seemed to be working in his favor. The tide was rising.

Martin turned and stared into Linh's eyes. "You can ask your questions, but first you should know that I will never sacrifice a single man for myself, and someday I will kill you and your Chinese lackey."

Clearly rattled by the wailing moans and Martin's lack of fear, Linh's mouth fell open, but Cháng laughed aloud.

"You are a fool, Shadows," he said, but it was the telltale crack in his voice that revealed his amazement.

Martin shrugged. "And that is why you will die."

"Why? Are you saying the reason I will die is because you are a fool?"

"No. You will die because you *believe* I am a fool."

Chang's incredulity morphed to anger as his face reddened and his eyes glared with hatred.

"You truly are a fool, Lieutenant Shadows."

Again, Martin shrugged. "Perhaps so. We will soon see."

He took two quick steps and jumped from the cliff.

CHAPTER TWENTY

It was truly a leap of faith—a faith in his grandfather's visions. Up to this very moment, Martin's doubts remained, but the old man's prognostications, although explainable, had become eerily accurate. His remaining hope was that Two Shadows had made predictions of events yet to occur. Crossing his feet at the ankles, he fought to remain vertical while plummeting through the cliff's outgrowth of vegetation. He lost that fight in a flash.

The gauntlet of limbs and vines caught his feet and sent him tumbling, but it slowed his descent. He drew into a ball to protect his body as he was thrashed and pummeled. A moment later he broke through into clear air. Straightening his body, he extended his arms above his head. The water came up in a rush.

A broken spine or fractured skull on the rocks spelled instantaneous death, but uncontrolled impact with the water could be nearly as bad. He arched his back and his bare feet stung as they broke the surface. An instant later his body thumped the bottom. It was enough to arrest the last of his vertical descent yet leave him relatively unharmed.

He had landed in the channel, but the impact drained his lungs. Fighting to reach the cliff, he burst to the surface after only a few strokes. Martin rolled onto his back and looked up. He'd done it.

The vegetation hid him from those atop the cliff.

Lunging toward the rocky face of the cliff, he swam with nothing but the strength of adrenaline. The tide was rising, and Linh would no doubt order an immediate search for his body. Martin made his way along the base of the cliff for a hundred yards before exhaustion overcame him. Grabbing a vine, he held it as his only lifeline to avoid sinking beneath the raging surf. Already twenty minutes had passed, but he had yet to escape the channel.

The cover of nightfall couldn't come soon enough, and his hopes dimmed as the hum of an outboard motor came from nearby. Martin gazed back down the channel toward the estuary. They were quick—too quick. Already, Linh's men had launched the skiff and were searching for his body. He had no choice but to move. The sound of the seawater gurgling as it rushed into a crevasse came from somewhere further along the cliff—a place where he hoped to hide.

Despite his exhaustion, he released the vine and let the rushing water propel him like so much flotsam toward the sound. The power of the current was overwhelming, and his efforts were weak. The plunge from the cliff and the impact with the water had taken their toll. The rushing tide could take him to hell, but he no longer had the strength to resist.

The hum of the outboard grew louder. They were drawing near, but a huge swell lifted him from the channel, over the rocks and boulders, and sent him tumbling along the cliff wall. Clinging desperately to an outcropping, he watched and waited, but again he was swept away by another massive swell of swirling tidal current. Unable to negotiate these treacherous waters, the skiff would have to remain in the channel. Unseen, he had made good his escape, but Martin's elation was short-lived.

By the time he saw what was coming, it was too late. The rushing current was sucking him downward into a monstrous whirlpool. This was it—the end. Quickly drawn beneath the surface and into total darkness, he was submerged in the tumbling torrent of a raging underground river. Battered and stunned, he fought until the sea water began filling his lungs and stars floated before his eyes.

Knowing he had only seconds remaining, Martin drew his hands along the rocky walls, searching for an air pocket. It seemed futile until he realized the current had abated and the rock walls had disappeared. Lunging upward, he broke the surface, belching sea water and sucking gulps of lifesaving air. He was in total darkness, and his gasping breaths echoed from rock walls. He was in another cavern, now pushed along by a calmer and gentler current as it spun him about in a circle.

With nothing but his hands and ears as guides, he drifted along, searching for some form of refuge, until he found a rock shelf. With his last ounce of strength, he climbed atop the shelf, where he lay coughing more seawater from his lungs. He could scarcely believe he was alive.

———————————

Martin didn't know how long he had been asleep, hours perhaps, but his dreams made him believe there was a caress of warm tropical air flowing across his body. He dreamt he was in a hammock on a tropical island, and there was a brown-eyed maiden feeding him slices of mango. He gazed at her beautiful breasts and knew now that he had died and gone to heaven. Only when he heard water dripping somewhere nearby and the girl disappeared did he realize it was a dream.

Sitting up, he noticed a faint light was coming from somewhere below the rock shelf. He coughed and belched more sea water. It was nasty but on the plus-side it proved he was still alive.

Searching the shadows, he realized the water level had dropped, and he was in a relatively large cavern. The light was coming from the opening where he had been sucked into the cavern at the base of the cliff. The tide had receded, and the air coming from the entrance was flowing past him, but to where? It was a steady breeze going somewhere further back into the cave.

Rolling to his knees, he began feeling his way up a steep incline, climbing deeper into the cavern until he found a smaller opening. The warm air rushed past him into the mouth of this new cave. He crawled inside, keeping the airflow at his back while scratching and clawing his way upward with only the air and his sense of touch as guides. After nearly two hours, he spotted a faint gray light somewhere high above. It had to be the salvation he hoped for—the island surface.

After several false starts, Martin found a scalable section of wall. Wedging himself between the rocks, he climbed until he reached another opening—the place where he could now see the source of the faint light. He was braced between vertical crevasses, but the lighted opening was nearly seven feet away across a pitch-black void. He had no idea how high he had climbed, but he had to jump to the other side.

While positioning himself for the leap, Martin's foot dislodged a small rock. He paused and listened as it fell away into the darkness below. Nearly three seconds elapsed before a faint click came from far down in the abyss. The walls of the cave were slick with moisture. If he failed to reach the other side or slipped, it would be all over.

His mind raced headlong into the possibilities. Dying in this cave thousands of miles from home guaranteed his remains would never be found. And yet it wasn't so much that he was worried about himself as he was for his mother and father who would never know what happened to him. His disappearance would be something worse than death for them, but it was his grandfather's words that again gave him strength. He jumped.

Clearing the abyss with ease, Martin crashed onto the floor of the next opening and threw his head back, searching for the source of the light. He'd done it. At the top of this vertical shaft, nearly fifty feet above was daylight. Wedging himself between the walls, he climbed rapidly toward the surface.

Within minutes he reached the opening and stared out through a jungle of lush green ferns and cords of twisting vines climbing into the trees above. He had reached the top of the island escarpment. The shaft opening, little more than four feet across, was totally hidden by a mass of shoulder-high ferns and tall banyan trees. Crawling out, he rolled on his back and rested until he caught his breath.

The sky was a flaming orange, and the sun was low in the west. He listened. The sounds of roosting birds, insects, and geckos came from the jungle, but rest was not to be his. He had to find food, water, and with luck, a weapon. This would require finding the prison entrance. Martin had only his internal compass and a Scientific Wild Ass Guess, as the snipers called it, to determine which direction he should go. Taking a SWAG, he struck out toward the southeast.

Going back into the prison was another questionable choice, but it was his only option if he was to get the supplies he needed. Pushing forward, he'd gone only a couple hundred feet when he stumbled onto a well-worn footpath. It would likely take him where he needed to go. Barefooted, he moved silently in the dusky shadows, up the narrow trail, until he spotted a sentry sitting on a rock.

After studying the guard and his surroundings for several minutes, Martin determined he was at the main prison entrance. The guard stared blankly into the jungle with unfocused eyes, and his weapon lay across his lap. Remaining in the shadows, Martin found a grapefruit-size rock and eased closer. The guard's head was now drooping, and Martin realized he had removed his pith helmet—a stroke of luck. Stepping forward, he drove the rock downward into the man's skull. Death was instantaneous, and there was minimal blood.

Grabbing the soldier's AK-47 and helmet, he lifted the body over his shoulder and glanced about. With no blood, there was no evidence of foul play. The guard would simply disappear. He carried the body up the trail toward the cliff. The soldier had little else besides his weapon and several magazines of ammo. Setting those aside, Martin heaved the body over the cliff, watching as it tumbled into the surf below.

Returning to where the sentry had stood guard, he paused and studied his surroundings. Martin now had a weapon, but his only hope of surviving hinged on finding food and water. It remained quiet as he crept inside and followed the long tunnel leading down to the center of the prison complex. This was the same corridor used when they took him up to the cliffs. As with the others, lightbulbs were strung along the ceiling, and there were stairways—some cut into the cavern floor and others made of wood.

His heavy breathing was amplified by the rock walls, and he couldn't help but second-guess himself. Perhaps re-entering the prison was a mistake. It would have been easier to simply steal a boat, to leave the island and strike out for the mainland, but that meant leaving Sergeant Ravera behind. He couldn't do that.

After a few hundred feet, the corridor opened into the enormous underground prison complex, the one where they had taken him for interrogation. He again stood in awe of the gallery of terraced wooden balconies, stairways, and doors. A couple hundred feet across the way, he spotted the corridor that led to the prison cells. Only now did he hear again the barely audible hum of a generator as he studied the cathedral-like room for several minutes. No sentries were evident. Easing forward on the raised walkway, he made his way into the giant room.

Martin walked only a few steps before spotting stacks of wooden crates near an open door. This had to be it—the supply room. He glanced around before stepping inside. The room was packed with boxes, drums, and more crates, along with shelves of supplies. A quick assessment revealed ammunition, coils of rope, squares of C-4 explosive, cases of American C-rations, canned water, and even several pairs of worn jungle boots, along with canteens and an American M-7 bayonet. It was even more than he had hoped for.

Stamped lettering on one of the crates caught his eye: Grenade, Frag, M-67. American fragmentation grenades were much more dependable than their Chi-Com counterparts. It was a motherlode find, but the thing he needed most, a flashlight with batteries, was nowhere to be found. After donning a pair of the jungle boots, he rummaged around till he found a sun-faded rucksack—something he needed to carry the rope, the C-4 explosive, grenades, canteens, C-rations, and ammo—everything he needed to bring the *havoc* his grandfather had foreseen.

For now, these would suffice. He shoved the bayonet under his belt and peeked out the door. Just before stepping out, he spotted a man on a walkway far above. He was smoking a cigarette and relieving himself. Jerking his head back, Martin waited. After a couple minutes, with one eye barely beyond the edge of the doorway, he looked again. The soldier was gone and there was no sign of movement.

Martin threw the rucksack over his shoulder and hurried down the walkway and up through the tunnel corridor to the surface. Returning to his little cavern entrance amongst the ferns seemed the obvious choice, but he paused. He had been lucky so far, but with no flashlight it would be another risky climb back down to his underground hiding place. The gunboat in the estuary was the answer. There would be more supplies there. Turning about, he backtracked up the trail to the cliff.

A fat yellow moon had risen, casting its luminous glow across the tropical ocean. Soft shafts of moonlight penetrated the palm trees. Martin paused. The salty odor of the sea, a warm night breeze, and the moonlit sky were a relief from the cold, wet caverns below. It was a mesmerizing feeling not unlike that of a jungle paradise, but this wasn't paradise. It was hell. Never had he realized hell could be so beautiful. He had to force himself to remain focused.

While gazing into the foamy surf far below, he formulated a plan. It was risky, but not as risky as the cave. With his rucksack and the AK-47 slung across his back, he slipped over the edge of the cliff and began climbing down through the outgrowth of vines and roots. Carefully, he clung to precarious handholds, lowering himself until the vegetation played out. The soft glow of the moonlight revealed the foaming white surf, still fifty feet below. Jumping with the rifle and rucksack was out of the question. They would take him straight to the bottom of the channel where he would lose everything.

Uncoiling the rope, he tied it off to a protruding rock before letting it drop. If he figured correctly, he was somewhere close to the mouth of the underground estuary where the boats were hidden. He didn't hesitate as he descended hand over hand until reaching the water, where he clung to the rock face. The surf was light, but the heavy rucksack weighed him down as he struggled handhold to handhold along the cliff toward the cavern entrance.

CHAPTER TWENTY-ONE

Colonel Linh awakened to someone knocking incessantly at his door. From outside came the voice of his lieutenant calling his name. He sighed. After the prisoner committed suicide by jumping from the cliff, the entire prison cadre had become akin to a troop of spooked monkeys. It was indeed a bad omen, but he couldn't allow himself to think like his men. He rubbed the sleep from his eyes, yet his first thought was that the old Green Beret, Ravera, had also committed suicide. He buttoned his shirt and opened the door.

"What is it, lieutenant?"

"Colonel Linh, I am sorry to disturb you, but our sentry at the upper entrance is missing. We have searched the island for several hours, but he is nowhere to be found."

Linh glanced at his watch. It was after midnight.

"Post another guard. We will search for him again in the morning."

"But Colonel—"

"Post another sentry. We will deal with it in the morning."

There was no sense in plunging into the island jungle at night. The young lieutenant stared back at him with wide-eyed uncertainty.

"Go. Go now, and do not worry. We will find him."

The lieutenant delivered a half-hearted salute and backed away from the door. Linh gave him a reassuring nod. The men did this every time something of this sort happened. No doubt the sentry had wondered off somewhere and gotten lost. Hopefully, he hadn't fallen from one of the cliffs. He wouldn't be the first. Linh sat on his cot and sipped water from his bedside cup. He had lost two men in the two years since he arrived here, neither of whom was ever found. He often wondered if they were deserters, or had fallen from the cliffs, or perhaps there was another cause—something his men insisted had happened.

They explained how their ancient beliefs of the specter— Bóng Ma—foretold these things. They insisted that *Con Ma Lang Thang*, the wandering ghost of the dead, had taken these men. Others said there was a tiger on the island, while others said it was the spirit Ma Trành, the tiger demon. It would have been easy to explain it all as superstition, but Linh's parents and many of his recent ancestors had spoken of their experiences with such spirits.

He had never seen such a thing for himself. It was much the same with the god of the French Catholics, and for that matter the gods of any of them, be they Buddhist, Hindu, Catholic, or any of the religions. He had always wanted a sign from one—any one of them, but there were only these stories of spirits—ghosts, saints, and devils, and shadows of the night. The Chinese interrogator, Cháng, had scolded his men when they talked of such spirits, but Linh remained silent. He wasn't so sure.

It made sense that this American, Lieutenant Shadows, could become one of those wandering ghosts. After all, he was markedly different from most Americans he had met. There was something that set him apart, but Linh wasn't sure what it was. Nearly six months had passed since the last man disappeared from the island, and it had coincided with the death of the first American Special Forces prisoner—the man Cháng had killed. Now another guard was gone the same day as Shadows's suicide. Linh lay back on his cot. If his men were to be believed, Bóng Ma was the reason. Only time would tell. He dropped into a restless sleep.

Linh awakened already tired, but according to his watch, it was morning. Using his towel, he wiped the night sweat from his body and used the water in the bedside porcelain basin to rinse his face. After donning his uniform, he made his way to the main communications office where the lieutenant sprang to his feet. Linh gave a cursory wave with the back of his hand toward the young officer.

"Have you found the missing man?"

The lieutenant appeared fearful, almost as if he were facing execution.

"I am sorry, Colonel Linh, but we have not. I have ordered a search party. They departed at first light."

"And why are you not with them?"

Linh already knew the answer.

"Someone needed to stay here to monitor the radios and keep you informed."

Linh rubbed his forehead. There were capable men available to monitor the radios. The lieutenant had already proven his bravery on the battlefield, yet he was frightened by something he feared more than death—Bong Ma.

Cháng hadn't come from his room since Shadows leapt from the cliff, but he needed to be informed of the missing sentry. A stubborn subscriber to simple answers, the Chinaman would likely call the guard a deserter, but then, Cháng was an idiot. His heart and mind belonged to the Chinese Communist Party where there was no nuance of spiritual belief outside of its own rigid secular orthodoxy. And perhaps he was right. There was probably some logical explanation—the guard was a deserter, or he had simply wandered off and become lost.

Colonel Linh lit the last one of his Chesterfields and walked out to the nearby palm grove where he normally took breakfast. The sun was about to rise, and the air was refreshing. Life in the underground prison gnawed at a man's psyche. He hated it, but his orders were strict—minimal above-ground activity was required to avoid possible discovery by passing American aircraft. Even the sentries, other than those in the estuary, weren't allowed flashlights. He had finished his cigarette when Cháng walked into the grove.

"I sense something has occurred, Colonel. What is it?"

Linh truly despised this man. His Chinese counterpart seldom missed anything, yet he had not the courtesy to at least offer a morning greeting before beginning his interrogation.

"I am happy you could finally join me this morning, Mister Cháng. The sentry there at the main entrance wandered off during the night, and I have a party out searching for him."

Cháng's face became stony. He didn't bother with the amber holder as he lit a cigarette and sucked furiously.

"And why would your man wander off this way?"

"I am not certain. Since the American killed himself yesterday, my men have been quite unsettled. It is a bad omen, and they fear his spirit."

"Serious soldiers in the Peoples' Army have no room for culturally backward and morally corrupt superstitions, Colonel. Why do you tolerate this ridiculous behavior?"

"I am reluctant to describe a man's personal beliefs of the

afterlife or of Con Ma Lang as ridiculous, especially when I have no evidence to the contrary. I respect a person's religious beliefs, even if some may seem like superstition."

"Oh, and what is the difference between religion and superstition?"

"There is much, but that is an answer you must find for yourself."

"You seem so certain; therefore, you must have the truth. Tell me the answer."

"I cannot tell you my answer because that is *my* truth, and I cannot force it upon you. When you find it for yourself, it then becomes *your* truth."

"Oh, great philosopher, you make me tired with your babble."

"And I find your acerbic wit a cousin to your sophomoric wisdom."

"Colonel, I have little patience for these things, so spare me further argument. Please inform me when your man is found. And you may consider now as an opportune time to press our other prisoner for more information. Our Green Beret seemed equally dismayed by his comrade's suicide, and we should take advantage of this new vulnerability."

"You may want to avoid leaving the interior complex today," Linh said. "I have ordered the dogs released when my men return. If there is anyone on the island, we will soon know. Perhaps the dogs will prove you correct."

"Ah, so you *do* believe there may be a rational explanation. What if they find nothing?"

Linh despised Cháng's arrogance but refused to be baited into his trap.

"We will continue to remain alert. In the meantime, we will question the other prisoner."

The Green Beret's face revealed, as Cháng described it, *a renewed vulnerability*. Ravera's eyes had returned to the same unfocused stare he possessed when he first arrived at the prison. Linh felt a degree of sympathy for him as the guards tied the sergeant to the metal chair. Lighting a cigarette, he casually circled behind him while contemplating how best to begin his questioning.

"So, Sergeant Ravera, you and your four tribesmen are once again alone here on our island."

"Possibly," Ravera answered.

"Possibly?"

"Your men who escorted me here—their eyes tell me otherwise."

The Green Beret was a cagey bastard. Linh already knew this from previous interrogations. Ravera had misled them with his false allegiance and bogus information, but this was a different ploy. Linh decided to move slowly.

"Oh, and what is it their eyes tell you?"

"They are frightened, and the only thing I can think is that you didn't find his body. Is that it?"

"You are full of foolish hope, Sergeant."

"Then what is it you and your men fear?"

"I fear nothing," Linh shouted. "My men, they are only unsettled by your comrade's suicide. That is all."

"I've served several tours here in Vietnam, and I overheard your men discussing Con Ma Lang Thang and Ma Trành. Your men are more than unsettled. They fear these spirits. And you, do you fear them?"

Linh couldn't believe his ears. This American knew more about his culture than he had ever imagined. He stabbed his half-smoked cigarette into the ivory ashtray. The prisoner smiled.

"My men fear nothing. Your comrade is dead, and that is the end of it. If you do not wish to join him, I suggest you begin talking."

"About what? I have no idea who he was other than his name and rank."

The prisoner was already ahead of him. Linh realized he had lost his advantage. He shouted for the guards.

"Consider yourself fortunate that I am in no mood for your foolishness. I have other more important matters to which I must attend. We will talk more about this later. In the meantime, if Ma Trành should devour one of my men, I will be the first to inform you."

CHAPTER TWENTY-TWO

After descending the face of the cliff, Martin worked his way along the channel toward the estuary. Even at low tide the channel was still deep, and the weight of the rucksack forced him to cling to the rocky ledges. Behind him, the night sky was graying with the dawn, and the waves gurgled among the rocks as he entered the cavern. The only light—a rippling dull sparkle on the water—came from the bulbs burning on the stairway high above.

The wooden junk, the small run-about, and the patrol boat were still there, tethered to the rock shelf and floating quietly. Ghostly shadows concealed much of the estuary's detail, but a single sentry was visible, sitting on a fuel drum near the back wall. His weapon lay on an adjacent drum along with his pith helmet. With his arms wrapped around his knees, he stared into the darkness.

Martin used the shadows to his advantage as he slid his rucksack atop a ledge and climbed out, but the water dripping from his clothes broke the silence. He froze, momentarily un-nerved. The sentry didn't move, and after a few seconds the silence returned. It made sense. Dripping water probably wasn't that unusual. Martin exhaled. He had to determine if the guard had a routine or if there were more of them about. Crawling further back into the shadows of the ledge, he waited and watched.

He waited for nearly an hour, but only once did the guard stretch, pick up his weapon, and walk across the rock shelf to the boats. After a few minutes spent staring out at the cavern entrance and the morning daylight, he returned to his perch atop the drum. There were apparently no other sentries.

Martin's plan was to sneak aboard the patrol boat and search for a flashlight, batteries, and any other useful supplies, but with the boat's gangway in plain view of the guard, he was forced to swim to the stern and climb aboard there. After slipping off the ledge into the water, he had made his way to the rear of the boat, when there came a shout from above. He froze in fear. If discovered, he'd likely be shot.

A soldier peered down from the stairway platform sixty feet above. Again he called out. The guard sitting on the drum grabbed his helmet and weapon and stumbled out to where he could be seen. The man at the top of the stairway gestured wildly as he shouted at the sentry. Martin understood little that was said but enough to understand the sentry was getting an ass-chewing and being told to stay alert.

Exhaling, Martin waited until the silence returned before climbing over the stern of the patrol boat. Once on board, he entered a small cabin beneath the foredeck. It was enveloped in total darkness. Running his fingers along walls and through cabinets, he searched, almost to the point of frustration before feeling a cylindrical object. Picking it up, he ran his fingers over its surface. It was a flashlight. He began pushing buttons until a bright light flooded the cabin.

A treasure trove of supplies surrounded him—everything from extra batteries and signal flares to flotation devices. After stuffing his pockets, he donned a flotation jacket and extinguished the light. Quietly he climbed back to the upper deck and peeked over the transom. The sentry was still on the drum, but his head had nodded. Martin slipped over the stern and swam back to the ledge where the rest of his booty was stored. He had to hurry to reach his cavern sanctuary before the tide rose again.

After leaving the estuary, Martin made his way along the face of the cliff, and once again he swam beneath the ceiling of the cave where he had been sucked under during a rising tide. This time, there was no whirlpool, and low tide made the entrance somewhat more hospitable. As he made his way inside, the flashlight enabled him to better assess the hidden cavern.

It was much larger than he thought, but he quickly found the tunnel that had led him to the surface the previous day. There were several other openings, but one in particular caught his eye. It was below the rock shelf, and the low tide had only now revealed it. It stood out because there was a small but steady stream of water trickling from it.

Martin sat and studied the opening while repeatedly pulling the M-7 bayonet across a sandstone outcropping. He pulled the blade first on one edge then the other for nearly an hour before scraping it gently against his forearm. It shaved the hair, but he wasn't quite satisfied. He continued until it had a straight-razor edge on both sides. Tossing the metal sheath into the water below, he cut a pouch from the rucksack and fashioned his own sheath— one from which the bayonet could be drawn without the metal-on-metal sound. When he was done, he secured it beneath his belt.

It was time to inspect the opening from which the water trickled. He thought about the constant dripping sound he had heard from his cell, and he wondered. The opening was barely large enough for a man to crawl into, but he was curious. It might lead to the cavern where the prisoner cells were located. It was a long shot, but he wasn't going to leave Sergeant Ravera behind.

After pocketing extra batteries for the flashlight, he stored his other supplies on the ledge and crawled down to the small hole. It was indeed tiny, but he squeezed inside as the passageway narrowed even further. He was forced to push his head and shoulders deeper between rock crevices while squirming his way upward. With each forced passage he recalled the tales of lost cave explorers back home in Kentucky—spelunkers whose skeletons were sometimes found decades later wedged in tiny crevices where they had become stuck and died. True or not, he refused to stop.

After nearly an hour, a familiar sound came from the darkness—the dripping of water somewhere in the rocks above. And it wasn't simply the dripping sound, but the same incessant pattern that matched the one he had listened to while in his cell, drip-drip…drip, a pause, drip- drip…drip. By now his body was a mass of abrasions and bruises, but he squeezed and pulled himself upward until finally reaching a larger cavern where he could stand upright. A shallow pool of water covered the rocky floor.

Sloshing through it, he pointed his flashlight at the ceiling until he saw two drops of water fall from a narrow crevice. There was a pause and a third drop fell, followed by another pause. This was it—his "drip-drip…drip" timekeeper. He was just below the prison cells.

The crack widened as it ran along the cave's ceiling. Following it, he found where it spread into an even wider gap. If he figured right, he was directly below Sergeant Ravera's cell. Shoving his hand into the crevice, Martin scaled the wall, pointing his flashlight into what was little more than a six-inch gap in the stone.

"Who's there?" came a voice.

"It's me, Lieutenant Shadows."

There was a long pause.

"It's me, Sarge. I survived the jump. The brush broke my fall, and I landed in the canal."

"Madre Santa! Dime qué creer!" It came as a ragged whisper from only two feet above.

Martin didn't understand.

"What?"

"Never mind. She has answered my prayers. Why are you down there?"

"I came to get you."

"Forget it. The stone between us is at least two feet thick. Get the hell off this island while you can. You can tell them where I am when you get back to our people."

"Never happen, Sarge. A good officer doesn't abandon his men."

"Oh, for the love of Christ, save that high-falutin' bullshit for your fairy godmother. Get the hell out of here while you can. Go! Go now."

"Stay strong, Sarge. I've already killed one guard, and I'm not stopping till I get you out of here."

"Wait. What did you say?"

"Yeah. I killed the sentry at the outside entrance. I made him disappear and took his gear."

Several seconds passed in silence, broken only by the dripping water.

"That's gotta be it."

"Gotta be what, Sarge?"

"Colonel Linh's men are scared shitless. I knew something was wrong when he tried to interrogate me earlier. He said it was because you jumped off the cliff, but it was the guard you killed, and the wailing sound that came just before you jumped."

"So, what are they scared of?"

"These people are superstitious as hell. I've heard them talk before about the island being haunted. They think it's your spirit come back to haunt them. I believe it's messed with Linh's head, too."

Martin paused as he thought about it.

"Well, I'm not a spirit—leastwise not yet, but what was that sound anyway? It *was* sort of spooky."

"I have my theory on it. I'll tell you later, but you need to listen to me now. I've worked with the Vietnamese for three years, and I'm telling you they are very superstitious. This might be your ticket out of this hell hole. Do what you can to spook them some more. Try to scare the hell out of them. They're already skittish, and you might just push them over the edge. It might give you the chance to steal a boat and get off the island."

Martin paused. The Green Berets worked closely with native populations, embedding with them, learning their ways, and influencing them to fight against those who would oppress them. What Ravera said made sense, if only there was a way to make it happen.

"Okay, Sarge. Let me see what I can come up with."

There was only silence in return. Martin freed his now aching hand from the crevice and dropped to the floor with a splash. More determined than ever, he snaked his way back into the narrow crevice and worked his way down to the hidden cavern.

While eating one of his C-ration meals, he worked the bayonet's blade to an even keener edge. Nearly twelve inches overall, it had an eight-inch blade, now razor sharp on both sides. It was the perfect weapon where stealth was needed. After all, the only way he was going to free Ravera was by going silently into the main cavern and opening his cell door—a problematic idea if he was forced to use the rifle but a possible one if he used the bayonet instead.

First, he had to determine where all the sentries were located and how many were on the island. If a few more of them disappeared, Ravera's idea to scare them might work. More ideas came to him. Perhaps, packets of the C-4 explosive set somewhere on the island with a slow fuse would create a distraction—the one he needed to commandeer one of the boats. Martin made up his mind. A recon of the entire island was needed. It would be his next step.

He thought of Jake Randal, Joe Thunders, and Ray Lopez. If they really were prisoners somewhere down there in the highlands near Chu Lai, the longer he stayed here on this island, the more likely they would die or disappear forever. First, he had to free Sergeant Ravera, but it had to be done quickly. Then he would head south to search for his men. He would search the highlands for as long as it took to find them.

Martin climbed to the surface and emerged from the shaft entrance among the ferns and banyan trees, but after walking only a few yards he heard the bellowing of the dogs. Quickly, he jumped atop a boulder and gazed up the trail. The massive animals were running free, coming his way, apparently having scented his presence. His planned island reconnaissance was going to hell in a hurry.

Springing from the boulder, he sprinted toward the tunnel opening, but it was too late. The dogs were nearly upon him. Catching an overhead limb, he swung upward into a banyan tree, as the animals skidded into the cluster of ferns below. Snapping and snarling, they leapt wildly as he climbed higher.

The dogs' jaws barely missed his feet, before they tumbled back to the ground. His only way to escape was to reach the vertical shaft entrance—an open hole in the ferns that remained fifteen feet away, but it might as soon be a mile. The muscular animals continued leaping and snapping at his legs, missing by mere inches. He glanced up the trail. The handlers probably weren't far behind.

The limbs of the tree spread like an umbrella frame in a wide circle. One branch, although not very thick, extended outward over the tunnel entrance. It was risky, but his only option. Working his way around the tree, he shinnied outward as the limb sagged and the dogs whined while following his progress with studied curiosity.

Martin's only hope for escape required a split-second leap into the shaft entrance, but he had to catch himself before plummeting to the bottom. It was a perfectly vertical shaft, and too much momentum would cause him to fall fifty feet to certain death. Too little and the dogs would be on him in an instant. He'd be ripped to shreds.

The animals sensed his dilemma and again began leaping and bellowing, their snapping jaws now reaching the limb as it sagged further. From nearby came the nasally voices of the approaching soldiers. Martin had to act quickly. Positioning himself above the hole, he prepared to jump as one of the dogs leapt and fell back, but this time it tumbled into the shaft entrance. After a brief yelp, it disappeared.

The remaining dog, seemingly oblivious to the other's fate, lunged again—its teeth tearing his trousers. Desperate, Martin danced on the sagging limb, but this time the second animal also tumbled into the shaft. Catching itself at the edge, it clawed desperately, but Martin dropped from the tree and gave it a quick nudge with his boot. There was a brief squeal, another yelp, and a moment later a thud from the bottom of the shaft far below.

With the soldiers now drawing closer, he braced himself on either side of the shaft while pulling the surrounding ferns back into place. When he was done, he carefully inched his way fifty feet to the bottom. There he found the two broken corpses of the animals lying in a heap.

His first thought was to shove them deeper into the adjacent abyss, but he paused when he thought of Sergeant Ravera's idea. If the soldiers failed to find the shaft's entrance, they would likely retreat to the safety of the prison before nightfall. The disappearing dogs would leave them baffled, maybe even a little spooked, but there would be another search party the next day. His imagination ran wild as Martin formulated a plan. He waited several hours until the light at the top of the shaft began fading. Nightfall was approaching.

After securing one of the dead animals with the parachute cord, he began the laborious climb back up the shaft. The stars were shining in the night sky by the time he reached the surface. For nearly an hour, he lay quietly among the ferns and listened, and when he was certain there was no one around, he began drawing the rope hand-over-hand pulling the dog's corpse upward. When that was done, he again crawled down, tied the next one, and drew it to the surface as well.

CHAPTER TWENTY-THREE

M artin had worked through the night and was weary but prepared as he waited for daylight. After weighing his options, he realized Sergeant Ravera's suggestion might actually work, and it certainly fit Two Shadows's vision of bringing havoc to his enemies. By his calculation, there were at least twenty-five soldiers on the island, but if Ravera was right about Vietnamese superstition, creating panic might even the odds.

That evening after pulling the dogs' corpses back to the surface, he had placed each in small jungle clearings staggered on opposite sides of the trail. Using the parachute cord, he suspended them with their legs dangling and heads erect such that they swayed gently with the breeze. He pried open their eyes and pulled their lips apart, exposing long white canines. Stepping back, he admired his handiwork. The dogs appeared terrifyingly alive.

When he was done, he crept up the trail to the main prison entrance, where he found not one but two sentries now standing guard. He was beginning to think himself crazed because his first thought was that this was a good thing. It enabled him to get two of them at once. With the razor-edged bayonet in hand, he eased toward the sentries. One slept soundly, while the other stood gazing out at the jungle.

Using the darkness for cover, Martin crept behind the first guard and slit his throat. The second guard never fully awakened, and he too was dispatched in seconds, but Martin now faced a dilemma. For their disappearance to have its full effect, he had to remove all evidence of the struggle, and the ground was soaked with his victims' blood. He had to move quickly.

After carrying the bodies into the jungle and placing one under the feet of each dog, he returned to the prison entrance. There he scraped away the blood-soaked dirt, tracks, and every remnant of evidence that pointed to anything other than a ghostly disappearance. After nearly an hour the task was complete, but his imagination had run amok, and there was more yet to be done.

Returning to the jungle, he stripped naked and coated his body with sandy red mud. The night sky had begun displaying a hint of orange in the east, as he added the final touches to his creations. Pulling the pins from two grenades, he carefully secured the spoons as he wedged one beneath each of the bodies. He then placed several blocks of C-4 around each grenade—perfect booby traps with enough explosive to vaporize everything into a fine red mist.

Satisfied with his work, he laid the AK-47 across his lap and held the bayonet in his hand as he rested against a tree and waited. It was now approaching daylight.

Earlier that evening when Colonel Linh's men returned to tell him about the dogs' mysterious disappearance, they had been terrified as they explained how the animals had simply vanished into thin air. Now, Chang and Linh stood together, leaning against a railing on one of the wooden walkways, as they discussed the situation.

"There *is* a logical explanation for the dogs running away," Cháng said, "and this childish prattle of spirits and ghosts has likely caused your sentry to flee somewhere and hide."

Despite his attempts at logic, Cháng's voice had morphed from its usual sarcastic tone to one with an edge of uncertainty. Linh was happy to see his Chinese counterpart now sharing in his misery. To dismiss spirits so quickly was foolish. There was something strange afoot—something perhaps explainable in Cháng's world, but things didn't always have such explanations in the spirit world, and for the moment, this was where the minds of Linh's men resided. With the disappearance of the sentry, and now the dogs gone as well, their paranoia had increased to something bordering on panic.

"My men found no trace," Linh said. "The dogs were there somewhere just ahead, and they simply vanished. What do you suggest may have happened to them?"

"How should I know? I will go with you tomorrow. We will find them. However, until we solve this little puzzle, I might suggest that you double the guard at the main entrance."

Linh nodded with satisfaction. Cháng was beginning to experience the fear of the unknown.

"That task has already been completed, Mister Cháng. I doubled the guard at the entrance as soon as my men returned today. I also posted two sentries with the boats as well. In the morning we will take every available man to search the island. Now it is late, and I must get some sleep."

———————

Linh awakened with a start and glanced at his watch. It was 06:00 a.m. On the island above it would be barely dawn, and the sun would not yet have risen, but his lieutenant was again pounding at his door. Apparently, there was yet another crisis, and he almost didn't want to know what it might be, but the lieutenant's knocking was relentless.

"I am coming," Linh shouted.

He yanked the door open to find the wide-eyed lieutenant wearing a fine sheen of sweat on his face.

"Colonel, it…they are gone. It is…him. What should we do?"

"Calm yourself, Lieutenant. Now, speak clearly. Who is it that have gone?"

"The guards. They are gone."

"Those we placed at the upper entrance?"

"Yes! They are both gone."

"Have you assembled the troops?"

"I have notified them. They are preparing."

"You must regain your composure."

"But how can we fight a ghost?"

"Let's not make assumptions too quickly."

"But Colonel Linh, my men all say it is Ma Da, and he has come to seek revenge for the—"

"Think, Lieutenant! Ma Da is the spirit of the drowned. How can that be?"

The young lieutenant's face was sweaty and twisted with fear. "Don't you see, Colonel? He leapt from the cliff into the ocean."

"But it is the rocks below that likely killed him, not the ocean."

The lieutenant paused while his eyes became unfocused orbs darting about in search of some fleeting sense of logic. He was no doubt fighting an inner battle with an unsolvable psychological conundrum.

"Now calm yourself, Lieutenant. You must show the men you are their leader. Gather them at the main entrance. Mister Cháng and I will join you shortly."

After donning his uniform, Linh followed the wooden walkway around the giant cavern to Cháng's room where he knocked quietly. The same unchanging vanilla light lit the cavern the same monotonous way twenty-four hours a day. Cháng had described the American city of Los Angeles as being this way—a city with the same temperature, the same smoggy sky, and the same yellow sun every day. A slight shuffling came from inside as a sleepy-eyed Cháng opened the door.

"You are anxious to get started this morning, Colonel. I thought your fear of ghosts would cause you to wait for the sun to rise."

Linh gritted his teeth—quelling his anger. Even now while still drowsy this despicable son of a Con rắn spewed his venom.

"The sun will rise soon, and my lieutenant reports the two sentries at the upper entrance are now also missing."

Cháng's sarcastic smirk faded.

"We will gather there in a quarter-hour," Linh said. "Perhaps you will see fit to join us."

Fifteen minutes later the two men walked the corridor together up to the surface entrance.

"So, Colonel, what is your plan?"

"We will go to the area where the dogs were last heard and divide the men into groups to begin our search."

"And that failing to produce results, what then?"

"We will begin a systematic search of the entire island. We will turn every leaf and every stone. It is not that large, and we should complete the search before nightfall."

As they approached the outside entrance, Linh smelled smoke. He quickened his pace. The men had been warned to never make fires because enemy planes could spot the smoke during the day and the flames at night. He stepped into the early morning sunshine to find the men clustered about, fanning several small fires.

"What is this?" Linh shouted. "Have you lost your minds?"

He cast a nervous eye skyward and listened for the possible

sound of American jets high overhead.

"It is đốt vía," one of the men called out.

"Extinguish these fires immediately. Hurry!"

"What is it?" Cháng asked. "Why have they made the fires?"

Linh knew the reason and didn't want to invite more of Cháng's ridicule, but it was useless to lie.

"My men believe the smoke will keep away the bad spirits."

"And this is something you have taught them?"

"No, Mister Cháng. It is something that comes from ancient beliefs passed to them from their ancestors."

Cháng cast a wary glance skyward.

"If the American jets see this smoke, your men may not have the opportunity to pass their superstitions to the next generation."

"I find your ridicule a tiresome thing, Mister Cháng. I did not make this world to my own design, but I must live in it and tolerate what I cannot change. Perhaps, we could do better if you did the same."

For once, Cháng remained silent as the fires were doused and the smoke faded into the jungle. After the lieutenant formed the men into a patrol column, they moved down the trail into the shadowy jungle. Given the combination of raw nerves and automatic weapons, Linh decided the rear of the column was the safest place to walk. For once the ever-argumentative Cháng found the logic in his suggestion and joined him there.

CHAPTER TWENTY-FOUR

L   inh stopped to light a cigarette as the column ahead
     stretched up the trail, the lead elements disappearing around
     the bend. A cold sweat soaked his back as golden shafts of
misty morning sunlight angled through the treetops and the gentle
ocean breeze stirred the leaves. The tension was reminiscent of
the times he led patrols in search of the French. Cháng stopped
beside him smiling as if they were on a nonchalant morning walk.
Linh shook his head in resignation. Cháng was a fool. Whoever or
whatever had caused the sentries to disappear was nearby.

A nerve-shattering scream exploded in the jungle up ahead.
Drawing his sidearm, Linh ran past several men cowering beside
the trail only to collide with others coming in the opposite direction.
The fleeing soldiers knocked him to the ground as others sprang to
their feet to join them in flight. Linh stumbled to his feet and fired
his pistol into the air.

"Tạm dừng lại!" he shouted.

Cháng stepped up beside him—his sidearm also drawn. "Your
men flee like schoolgirls who have seen Ông Ba Bị."

Despite his cocky words, Cháng's peeling façade revealed his
fear. The Chinaman's pragmatism was rapidly fading under the
scorching light of a new and unexplainable reality.

"I have heard enough, Mister Cháng. If you too aren't compelled to flee, then stay here and do not allow any more of them to run away while I go ahead."

Cháng remained silent while his eyes darted about, searching the surrounding jungle. Linh walked up the trail until he spotted the lieutenant up ahead standing with two men. With their backs to him, they seemed mesmerized as they stared at something out in the jungle. He approached carefully, until the lieutenant heard him and turned. His face was drained of color and his movements resembled those of a failing automaton.

"Where are the rest of our men?" Linh asked.

"They have fled into the jungle, Colonel."

The young officer's eyes were white orbs bulging from his face.

"What frightened them?"

The lieutenant turned stiffly and pointed with a quivering finger to a clearing a hundred feet away where one of the dogs stood, staring at him. The dog was standing over one of the missing sentries. Linh's throat constricted as he raised his pistol and fired, but the animal didn't move. He fired again. Still the dog, the thing, whatever it was, did not move.

He emptied the pistol. The shots echoed into silence, and a light mist drifted across the jungle opening, as his heart thudded in his chest. A visceral horror gripped him, and he wanted to run, but he was their leader, and his men mustn't see his fear. He fought to maintain his composure. This thing out there had to be a mirage. That was the only explanation.

"It is not real," he said, his voice breaking. "Go. Walk to it. Take these two men with you and it will go away."

The lieutenant remained frozen in place, staring instead at the ghostly hallucination which refused to leave the misty jungle clearing.

"Go!" Linh shouted. "You will see that I am right. Go now!"

The lieutenant with the two soldiers at his side reluctantly started forward one step at a time. The three men held their weapons high and extended at arm's length. Linh stood watching as they entered the clearing and stopped, but the mirage remained before them, floating in the mist. The lieutenant glanced back, and Linh nodded, motioning him forward with his pistol. Leaning forward and bending at the waist, the young officer reached out and grasped one of the dead soldier's boots. He tugged at it lightly as he held his pistol at the ready. It seemed real. The lieutenant began pulling it away from the dog.

A massive explosion drove Linh backward, sending him reeling as limbs, leaves, and other debris rained down around him. Despite the stunning blast, his years of combat and military training took charge as he quickly regained his feet. The explosion had vaporized the mirage and his men. The jungle clearing was now shrouded with a light pink mist drifting through the shafts of sunlight. He shuddered at the realization of what he was seeing.

Linh spun about to flee but stopped when he spotted something else further ahead. The mirage had reappeared—this time on the opposite side of the trail. The dog was again standing over the dead soldier, except there was now a figure standing beside it, Quỷ Nhập Tràng. It was a man-like figure that resembled the dead American. It was him or an apparition of his spirit, but it was made of mud and stood staring at him while nonchalantly petting the dog's head. Linh now feared he too was dead—already a member of this spirit world—but he realized he still held his pistol in his hand.

The spirit turned as if to walk away, but Linh would have none of that. Raising the gun, he squeezed the trigger. Nothing happened. Clenching the pistol, he jerked the trigger again and again, but it didn't fire. It was empty. The figure disappeared into the jungle mist, and he could stand no more. Turning, he fled back to where he had left Cháng. The Chinaman was there, standing calmly. Linh stopped—panting and fighting to regain his senses. He was met by the stonewall of his own pride while facing the reality of what he had just witnessed.

"Your men fled when they heard the explosion, Colonel Linh. They refused to heed my threats."

Linh scarcely heard him as he closed his eyes and fought back his panic. Allowing this ignorant Chinaman the satisfaction of seeing him in fear was out of the question, but how could he make this blind man see what he had just witnessed?

"And what was it that exploded?" Cháng asked.

Linh looked down at his hand. He still held his pistol. Drawing a calming breath, he pulled a loaded magazine from his pocket.

"Allow me to reload my pistol, and I will show you."

It was the dangerous product of pride, but he was determined to show this foolish Chinaman that the spirits were as real as the sun and the moon. After steadying his nerve and drawing another deep breath, Linh started back up the trail. Cháng followed. When they arrived, Linh glanced first one way, then the other. Nothing remained in either clearing. It was gone—all of it. His mouth was dry with the metallic taste of fear, a fear worse than any he had experienced, even years ago during the enemy napalm attacks.

"They—it—there was one of the guard dogs. It was there, standing over one of the missing sentries."

He pointed toward the clearing.

"I sent the lieutenant to it, but—"

"And where is it now, Colonel Linh?"

"I do not know. It was as if it exploded and disappeared, but then it appeared again over there." He turned and pointed ahead on the opposite side of the trail but couldn't bring himself to tell Cháng about the man-like figure he had seen.

"I believe we have saboteurs here on the island—most likely American Special Forces," Cháng said.

Linh stared out into the jungle. In the face of all that happened, Cháng was still clinging to his notion of invincible human logic. If only it could be true—he wished it were, but Chang was a myopic fool who refused to see the truth.

"If they are here, then why haven't they simply overwhelmed us? And where are they? Why haven't we seen them?"

"I believe we should go back and radio the mainland for additional troops," Cháng said.

Knowing it was a useless gesture, Linh shook his head. "I have asked many times for more men, but they say I have too many already. They say men are needed for the war against the Americans."

"Perhaps, then we should go back and secure the prison against whoever is doing this. We can then contact Hanoi and tell them we are under attack."

Cháng was correct. They could retreat to the prison caverns, contact Hanoi, and wait. It was their only hope.

Martin now thought of something he should have already done. When the NVA soldiers scattered into the jungle he had silently overwhelmed and killed several of them one by one. By his account, he had eliminated nine men since killing the first sentry the night before. Now, he had one more task to complete before returning to his underground lair.

He followed Linh and Cháng, and when they disappeared into the prison, he quickly found what he sought—the wire leading to the radio antenna. It was mounted in a towering tree above the prison entrance. After whacking out a section of the wire with the bayonet, he hid his work and retreated down the trail to his shaft entrance among the ferns. There was more yet to be done.

CHAPTER TWENTY-FIVE

With his daily situation report well overdue, Linh keyed the microphone to contact the mainland, but nothing happened. He tried repeatedly, but there was only a static hiss coming from the speaker. Cháng paced the floor behind him. Linh would not allow himself to become like the Chinaman by resorting to verbal insults, but it was good the fool finally seemed aware they were facing something neither of them understood. Both men sucked furiously on cigarettes while staring at one another.

"I believe we should go back and find the rest of your men," Cháng said.

Linh contemplated the options.

"Perhaps you are right, but I also feel we should take the patrol boat and return to the mainland."

"I am inclined to agree to that also. Can you operate the boat?"

Linh shrugged. "I have been on it but twice. Perhaps we can find some of the boat's crew, but we must hurry. We will need the coming high tide to navigate through the canal."

After arming themselves with AK-47s and grenades, the two men hurried up the corridor toward the main entrance. The sun shone brightly up ahead, but there was something large hanging near the opening. They slowed their pace and eased closer. It was the body of yet another one of the men. It was suspended by the feet from a rope above the entrance. Linh glanced about. It was eerily quiet. Nothing moved. Again, he found his heart in his throat.

Wordlessly, he and Cháng eased closer and studied the corpse for several seconds. Neither man dared touch it. It was the body of one of the patrol boat's crew. Fully clothed, it hung with wide-open eyes, mouth agape, but without so much as a scratch or scrape. Cháng studied the neck carefully, apparently searching for evidence of strangulation. There was none.

"How do you think this man died?" he asked.

Cháng's voice was barely audible, and Linh, despite his fright, found the temptation too great.

"I am not going to speculate for you, Mister Cháng. I would think a man who believes there are answers for everything could supply one now."

Cháng's face twisted with anger, but Linh's well-placed jab left him momentarily speechless. He finally sighed in resignation.

"I have no answer."

Linh would have relished his victory, but their battle of wills no longer mattered. He was ready to leave the island—to get as far away from it as possible.

"Let's forego our search and get to the patrol boat. We will take the Green Beret prisoner and try to operate the boat ourselves. Barring that, I know the junk well, and it has enough fuel to reach the mainland."

"What will you do about your Bru prisoners?" Cháng asked.

"We will leave them in the cells. They will not last long. The only one sent here for his value is the American."

"I believe we should take the tribesmen as well," Chang said. "The American is more likely to talk if we use them to barter."

Cháng was right. The người Thượng, or Montagnards as the Americans called them, were captured with the Green Beret. They were his men, and he was quite loyal to them.

"Perhaps you are right. We will take them, but let's be quick."

After tossing the corpses from the cliffs, Martin had returned to the hidden shaft entrance in the ferns and made his way down into the cavern below where his supplies were stashed. Pointing the flashlight down at the water, he realized the tide would soon surge again, blocking his escape to the estuary. He had to move quickly.

He stuffed the rucksack with the supplies, tied it to the flotation jacket, and slid into the water. The water was not yet waist-deep, and the current was minimal. He pushed out through the entrance, where he was met with glaring sunlight and a pounding surf breaking on the rocks. Working his way along the base of the cliff, he climbed over the rocks and boulders until he reached the channel and made his way toward the estuary.

When he finally swam into the cavern entrance, he stopped in the shadows and treaded water while studying his surroundings. The dim light of the amber bulbs reflected across the surface just ahead. Although the estuary was quiet, he refused to become careless. On the rock shelf where the boats were moored, there were now two sentries. Apparently unaware of what was happening on the island above, they sat side by side sleeping soundly. He pushed the rucksack ahead as he swam slowly toward the rock shelf.

After stashing the supplies, Martin made quick work of the two guards. He hid the bodies and climbed aboard the junk. Several gas cans lined the deck, along with various crates and ropes. The old engine in a deck house at the stern sat in a puddle of blackened oil and reeked of leaking gasoline. If it worked, this boat would be his means of escape. A switch and wire led to an old car battery. Martin pulled what appeared to be a choke and hit the switch. The ancient engine coughed, belched a cloud of white smoke, and immediately grumbled to life.

The motor's steady rumble echoed loudly from the surrounding rock walls. Satisfied it was in working order, he quickly killed it. He had to preserve the fuel because he sure as hell didn't know anything about sailboats. The silence returned, and Martin hid his rucksack and supplies inside the compartment below the foredeck.

Leaping back onto the dock, he hurried to the patrol boat, and went to work with the bayonet, ripping wires, cutting hoses, and opening the bilge. The water rushed in, but it would probably take hours for the boat to sink. He went to work disabling the engine. After it was rendered useless, there was but one thing left to do. He had to free Sergeant Ravera.

Leaping up the zig-zagging stairway, he reached the corridor at the top but stopped and backed against the wall. There were two men standing with rifles a couple hundred feet away. It was Linh and Cháng pointing their weapons through an open cell door. Surely, they weren't going to kill the prisoners. Martin raised his AK-47 and waited.

Linh's voice echoed in the cavern hallway as Sergeant Ravera and the four Montagnard prisoners were ordered from their cells. They had been tied together. Martin was about to shoot when he realized Linh and Cháng were pushing the prisoners ahead and coming his way. He eased back into the shadows. Another quick glance confirmed his suspicions. They were coming toward the boats, and they were taking Ravera and the Montagnards with them to escape the island.

Leaping down the stairs, he reached the floor and sprinted to the junk where he crawled into the cramped compartment below the foredeck. After pulling the hatch closed, he burrowed forward, pulling nets and ropes around him before positioning himself at the ready with his AK-47. Murphy's law was the bane of every soldier's existence, but Martin was beginning to think it was tattooed on his back.

He listened, and a few minutes later he heard Linh's and Cháng's curses of frustration. They had found the sabotage of the patrol boat. Moments later, footfalls on the deck above indicated the men were boarding the junk. Linh's voice shouted commands, and Martin realized they were aimed at Ravera and the Montagnards. Their footsteps pounded the wooden deck above but faded as the engine rumbled to life. Martin felt the gentle sway of motion beneath the hull as they began moving, but a new fear arose. If they tried to run the channel at low tide, the boat was certain to founder on the rocks and sink.

———————

The old wooden junk glided from the estuary, but Colonel Linh knew he was far from safe. The tide was not yet in, and there was no choice but to wait until they could safely navigate the canal. The boat sat idle in the water while he studied the cliffs above. He was thankful to have survived whatever was on the island, be it spirit or otherwise, but he was anxious to get as far away as soon as possible. His Chinese counterpart stood on the bow, also staring up at the cliffs.

Cháng, who seemed now to have become a believer, also cast a wary eye toward the estuary entrance. With the sun about to set, it would be dark soon. Linh killed the idling engine and the men used bamboo poles to avoid the rocks while they awaited the rising tide. The surf thundered as the jagged boulders were slowly inundated by the swells.

After a while, the rocks disappeared beneath the surface and only the lapping of the waves against the cliffs remained. The sounds of lizards and insects came from the island's cliff walls, now glowing with the eerie orange of the sinking sun. Linh began poling the boat gently toward open water. He breathed deeply. They were leaving the horror behind and only now was he beginning to relax.

They would soon reach open water and likely arrive on the mainland before daylight. But there came a sound. Linh stopped poling the boat and stared back at the towering rock wall. It began as a quiet but extended moan from back beyond the cliffs. As it grew in volume, he recognized again the distant moaning wails of the island spirits. It lasted several seconds before fading into silence. The spirits were pained and angry. Cháng looked his way, but Linh's throat was constricted, and he was unable to speak. He could take no more.

Tossing the pole aside, he scrambled to the stern and cranked the engine. A smoky cloud of exhaust drifted across the water as he pushed the tiller arm and turned the boat westward toward the mainland. He gazed at Cháng sitting at the bow. The Chinaman was looking back at the island with the battle-weary eyes of a soldier who had stared into the abyss. If not yet a true believer of the spirits, his steadfast pragmatism was at the least deeply shaken.

They had been underway for a while, and as the island grew more distant, Linh again breathed a sigh of relief. Cháng had curled up on the lower deck near the bow and gone to sleep. The smoky old motor chugged reliably onward as nightfall approached. The western sky ahead was aglow with the luminescent afterglow of the sun and bespeckled with the first stars of night.

Now that he had escaped the island, Linh began to worry about something else. He would have to explain all of this to his leaders, and most of them were like Cháng—loyal party members with no souls, or at the least without the courage to admit it if they had one. Yet, he would rather face them than return to whatever was on the island.

He had often wondered if the Party would destroy his soul. And he wondered about the American Green Beret, sitting there on the deck before him, tied to the mast. Did he have a soul? How could he? Americans were all soulless. And what about the four Bru tribesmen who were also tied there beside him. The Vietnamese considered them near animals, but what was it that made them follow this Green Beret and fight so ferociously for his mindless government—one that so cruelly crushed its own proletariat and sought to rule other nations the same way?

He rested his hand on the tiller arm and maintained the westerly heading. The gentle ocean waters soothed his nerves. His heart had now settled back into a peaceful place, and no longer thudded in his ears. With this fiasco, his duty at the prison would likely end in embarrassment—if not something worse. He had always considered the assignment a dubious reward for his noble service against the French—a time when nearly his entire command was wiped out. He still wore the scars—both physical and mental.

That had been an especially trying time, and his leaders recognized his need for a respite. Becoming the commandant of this secret prison, where highly valued prisoners were subjected to special interrogation, was not something he would have chosen. Yet, he had remained for two long years. He now hoped no further such rewards came his way—only an early retirement to his home in the North.

Closing his eyes for a moment, he drew a deep invigorating breath of the fresh ocean air. It was good to be out of the cave complex and off that island. He gazed up at the fading afterglow, but something strange—a stark shadow, seemingly risen from the ocean, had appeared there. It was the silhouette of a man-like creature brandishing a bayonet and standing at the bow of the boat, legs apart, its eyes glowing as hot coals, staring back at him.

He squeezed his eyes shut and reopened them. The shadow had disappeared. An involuntary shudder wracked his body as he drew a deep breath and exhaled. The spirit refused to surrender, but the island was its home. To escape, he had only to get as far away as possible, but he felt something—a presence. It had reappeared and was now standing directly over him, its eyes glowing as a creature risen from the depths of hell.

CHAPTER TWENTY-SIX

When Martin pushed the hatch door open, a man was there curled on the deck. Crawling from his hiding place, he stood over him, clenching his bayonet. It was the Chinese interrogator Cháng lying there at his feet, breathing heavily in a deep sleep. Cháng's AK-47 lay beside him. A few feet beyond, tied to the mast, were Sergeant Ravera and the Montagnard tribesmen staring bug-eyed at him.

Their eyes followed him as Martin stood over the comatose Cháng. Killing him 98instantly was his first thought, but another idea came to him. He took Cháng's AK-47 and stepped lightly past him. After cutting Ravera and the Montagnards free, he gave Ravera Cháng's AK-47 and walked to the stern where Colonel Linh clung to the boat's tiller arm. The colonel's eyes, wide and white in the afterglow of the sunset, were fixed on him, and his mouth was seemingly stuck agape in a silent scream.

Cháng was now awake and sat in stunned silence as Martin stood poised over Linh with the bayonet. After a moment Linh found his voice with an extended, high-pitched, shrieking scream. The scream lasted until his lungs had emptied, yet his mouth remained agape, while his glazed eyes glowed with the reflection of unbridled terror.

"What is it you fear most, Colonel?" Martin asked.

Linh's face, now starved for oxygen, was a pallid gray.

"Could it be that you fear the men you have murdered have come visiting from the spirit world?"

There was still no response. Martin detected a strange odor and glanced down at the colonel's feet. He realized it was the odor of urine.

"Stand up, Colonel Linh."

Linh sprang to his feet. The colonel's trousers were wet, and a yellow puddle had formed around his shoes. Martin recalled when Linh said, *I fear drowning in water because I have never learned to swim.*

"I see only one way for you to escape."

Martin pointed the bayonet toward the water, and without hesitation the colonel leapt headfirst over the side of the boat. The ocean swallowed him as white bubbles rose to the surface. They were all that remained as he disappeared into the dark water. Turning, Martin found one of the Montagnards holding the AK-47 on Cháng while Sergeant Ravera tied him with rope.

Martin gazed skyward at the stars as he found himself again recalling that day in his grandfather's lodge, *...you found a friend in a dark place...but something happened, and you left with your friend on a boat.*

Whatever it was that gave old Two Shadows such powers, Martin, like Cháng, was now a believer. After gaining his bearings, he grabbed the tiller arm and turned the boat southwestward. The boat chugged slowly down the coast while Ravera and the Montagnards fed ravenously on C-rations. Martin sat at the tiller arm, contemplating his next move.

It was a long shot, but if Linh hadn't drowned or been eaten by sharks, there was a chance he could make it back to shore. That would no doubt ignite a frantic search by enemy patrol boats.

Regardless, there was still the possibility of being spotted and randomly searched. After a while, Sergeant Ravera came to the stern and sat beside him.

"Tell me something, Lieutenant. Who the hell do you work for?"

"MAC-V Intelligence."

"Yeah, but what unit are you with? Are you with SOG?"

"I report directly to MAC-V."

"No shit?"

"I was on a special assignment at an army fire support base south of Chu Lai when I was wounded and captured."

"What the hell were you doing?"

"It's classified."

The still frail Ravera gave him a knowing nod.

"What are we going to do with that bastard?" Ravera motioned with is chin toward Cháng.

"I thought maybe you could take him back for questioning."

"That bastard murdered my teammate Bob Jenkins, and he's a Chinese national captured in North Vietnam. The bureaucrats are liable to get cold feet and send him home to China scot-free."

"Sergeant Jenkins died from natural causes," Cháng muttered.

"Shut the fuck up!" Ravera shouted. "Shut the fuck up before I come up there and kill you now, myself."

Despite his debilitated condition, Ravera's trembling red rage would no doubt give him the strength to do just that. Martin placed his hand on the sergeant's shoulder.

"It's okay, brother. Let me handle this."

Ravera sat down hard on the deck and stared off into space, his bloodshot eyes wet and unfocused.

"So, tell me, Mister Cháng," Martin said. "Were those natural causes the electrical shocks you gave him?"

"It was an accident," Cháng said.

"I am sure the shocks you gave me were accidents, too,"

Martin said, "but you seemed to take great pleasure in your work. I believe you said as much."

Cháng remained silent, and Martin noticed the Montagnards staring hard at him. Their eyes reflected the same blood revenge Ravera had threatened—something indicating they too had been subjected to Cháng's torture.

"What are you going to do with him?" Ravera asked.

"I'm going to let your Montagnards decide how to handle it."

One of the Montagnards cast a glance at Ravera. Cháng squirmed as he fought against his restraints.

"The Geneva Conventions are something you Americans always want to—"

"Shut up, bastard!" Ravera shouted. "You can discuss Geneva with them."

The Yards watched Ravera intently for a signal. He gave a slight nod and tilted his head toward Cháng. The little men didn't hesitate as they dragged him onto the bow of the boat.

"Take your time," Ravera muttered. "I want him to enjoy it as much as we did."

Cháng mumbled something, and one of the Montagnards slapped him. Martin looked away. Ravera would do whatever he ordered but stopping the Montagnards might be difficult. He wondered how he would explain this in his After-Action Report. The stars overhead no longer had any beauty. They were mere fillers in the black abyss above, and his soul was lost somewhere beyond their light.

Martin could see little of what was occurring at the bow, but the Montagnards moved slowly, and it seemed a ritual of sorts as they took their time with Cháng. His guttural screams pierced the darkness, but there was no echo, no return from the ocean waters—only blunt silence.

"Kill me now, you cowards!" Cháng screamed.

The hours passed slowly, and the motor chugged relentlessly into the night.

"Lieutenant Shadows," Cháng shouted, but his voice became drowned in gurgling gasps, and Martin realized one of the Montagnards was slowly pouring a bucket of water over his face.

He now began wondering if it was even possible to return to his role as an army officer. He wondered if he could return to a civilized existence. The torture seemed never-ending, but Cháng was apparently still alive as the stars began fading with the gray light of dawn. The Montagnards would likely keep him alive for days, but Martin could stand no more. He turned the boat toward the coastline and nudged Ravera awake.

"Go up there and see what they're doing," he said. "It'll be daylight soon, and we're almost out of fuel. I'm going to take us in close to shore in case a patrol boat shows up."

A few minutes later Ravera returned from the bow. He sat on the transom with a grim countenance and slowly shook his head, but he said nothing.

"Is he dead?"

"He's still alive, but it's pretty ugly up there. They've poured seawater in him till his belly looks like a watermelon, and I won't trouble you with what else they've done except to say it reminds me of the stories my Mexican grandfather used to tell us about the Apache torturing their prisoners. My little Yards must be relatives of those redskin bastards."

Martin cut his eyes toward the little Hispanic Green Beret. The sergeant was clueless.

"The propensity for torture seems to be a universal human trait, Sergeant. But I have to warn you, I'm half Lakota Sioux."

"Oh, shit! Just my luck."

It was the first time Martin had seen Ravera smile.

"Does this mean I'm gonna wake up scalped tomorrow?"

"Maybe."

Ravera laughed and pointed past Martin.

"Well, you better hurry up, because I think we have company coming."

Martin looked over his shoulder. Far out on the horizon was an approaching patrol boat, its foaming wake sparkling white in the first rays of morning sunlight.

"Give each of your men one of the grenades and send one of them back here to take the tiller. You take one of the AKs and get under that tarp up front with Cháng. I'll take one and hide under the rear deck. Tell your men to wave and smile, but if they try to board us we'll have to fight."

Fifteen tense minutes passed while Martin sat below deck beside the smoky gasoline engine. Sweat dripped from his face while he squinted through a crack in the housing and watched the approach of the patrol boat. It was flying the North Vietnamese red flag with a yellow star as it slowed and paralleled them sixty or seventy meters off the port side. Ravera's four Montagnards lined the junk's deck, giving their best imitation of a Mardi Gras parade—smiling and waving wildly.

A helmeted soldier manned a .51 caliber machinegun on the bow of the boat. He stared down the sights of his weapon. The big machinegun would make kindling wood of the junk in a matter of seconds, and several more of them were armed with AK-47s and lining the starboard side. One, apparently an officer, studied the junk through binoculars.

The exhaust fumes from the ancient engine filled the hold as Martin became light-headed. After a few moments, the Vietnamese officer lowered his binoculars and stared with his naked eyes. Martin edged closer to the open hatch. He had to have fresh air.

If something didn't give soon, he would pass out. He continued watching the Montagnards out on the deck.

One was standing at the mast motioning for the patrol boat to come closer. He pointed his fingers at his open mouth and rubbed his belly as if he were hungry. These little men may have been from a primitive culture, but they were by no means stupid. He was using reverse psychology—or was he? Perhaps he really did want them to come closer. After all, his people held a deep hatred for what the Communists had done to their families.

The officer turned to speak to a man sitting beside him—one Martin hadn't noticed until now. The officer pointed at his passenger and back at the junk. That was when Martin recognized him. It was Colonel Linh. He eased the safety off his weapon. Linh gazed up at the officer and back at the junk. A moment later he wagged his head emphatically, but Martin saw it in his eyes. Linh knew full well who they were. Yet, he was denying it.

A moment later the patrol boat made a rapid turn and gunned its engine as it headed back out to sea. Martin exhaled as the wake of the rapidly departing boat rocked the junk back and forth. Sergeant Ravera emerged from beneath the tarp and Martin crawled out from the rear deck compartment. The fresh air cleared his head, and he turned toward the morning sun. Now a giant orange sphere, it cast its sparkling fire across the water.

"Did you see him?" Martin asked.

"See who?"

"Linh. He was on that patrol boat."

Ravera squinted. "You sure?"

"Positive, and he told the boat's captain that this wasn't his boat."

"Why would the bastard do that?"

"Maybe the commie bastard finally realized there's a higher power than the Party."

A brisk breeze rose out of the northeast. It was going to be a good morning, or so it seemed until Martin thought of Cháng. He'd completely forgotten about him.

"Where's Cháng?"

Ravera motioned with his head toward the bow. "He's under the tarp, but you won't have to worry about him anymore. The men stuffed a rag in his mouth, but the bastard heard the patrol boat and started gruntin' and kickin'. I did what I had to do."

Ravera motioned toward one of the Montagnards. "Khonu, dump him overboard."

The mangled body floated away, and Martin wasn't sure if he was revulsed, satisfied, or simply sad—or perhaps he no longer cared. He no longer knew his own mind. A while later the motor chugged its last and went silent. Martin was certain his soul had done the same. Cháng's body had disappeared in the wake, and he could no longer find an emotion to cling to for asylum.

"What's wrong with it?" Ravera asked.

Martin snapped back into the moment, realizing the sergeant had asked him a question.

"Wrong with what?"

"What's wrong with the motor?"

"Oh. It's out of gas," he said. He gazed at the batten sail piled below the mast. "You know anything about sailing?"

"Hell, Lieutenant! I'm from the brush country of south Texas. I ain't never seen a sailboat before I got to Nam."

Martin cast a quick glance toward the shore. It was no more than a thousand yards away. The grasses and palms there were dark and shadowy.

"Well, we need to do something. Let's see if we can get this sail rigged and beach the boat before we end up somewhere in the middle of the Pacific."

CHAPTER TWENTY-SEVEN

After an hour wrestling with the bamboo braced sail, Ravera and his Montagnard crew had raised it, while Martin steered with the tiller and the boat glided southwestward. They were actually moving faster than they had with the gasoline engine. Martin stood at the stern, studying the horizon. Beside a few cottony patches of clouds, the sky was clear and the breeze strong. His heart should have been soaring, but he was thinking of what to do next.

He could give himself up to the first Americans they met—as Sergeant Ravera planned to do—or he could take care of unfinished business. The war was no longer relevant to him in his role as an army officer. It had become more. It had become something personal—something that demanded he verify his statements to Cháng, Linh, and most of all himself that his men came first. If Jake, Joe, and Ray were still out there, he would not leave them behind. He had to search for them now, before he lost the opportunity.

If as Colonel Linh claimed, they were prisoners of the Viet Cong, finding them in the highlands of Quảng Ngai Province would be a long shot at best. But returning to MAC-V would almost certainly end his search. The army might make attempts to find them, but only so much time and resources would be spent before they gave up, and the lost soldiers' status would remain MIA. He, on the other hand, was also listed as MIA and the status left him free to search for as long as it took.

The coast slipped by on the starboard side less than a quarter mile away, and by late afternoon billowing nimbus clouds were piling high all around. They had passed several villages and numerous fishing boats, but no one paid them much notice. Far out on the horizon, the deep purple undersides of the clouds squatted against the sea, but it was from somewhere onshore that there came the distant rumble of thunder. More storms perhaps, or so Martin thought, until the quiet rumbles came again. This time they were slightly more distinct, and the rhythms didn't match those of a storm. He cocked his head and listened.

Ravera stood up at the bow and shaded his eyes as he gazed westward. The thunder stopped. After a moment he turned and looked back at Martin. "Did you hear that?"

"Yeah. What do you think?"

"I think it was artillery," the sergeant said. "We must be near the DMZ."

"Maybe. Let's keep going till the rain starts. We'll head into shore then."

Ravera nodded, but the seas were already growing choppy as the clouds thickened. An hour later, huge thunderheads surrounded them, and a sudden gust of cold wind tipped the boat precariously as the men cast fearful glances back at Martin. Their fate was in his hands. To lose everything now would be the ultimate irony. Pushing the tiller arm hard to the left, he turned toward shore.

"Trim the sail so it takes us in," he shouted.

The boat ran aground in the surf as the men gathered their gear and leapt overboard. Running across a narrow beach, they made their way into an undergrowth of palms as the sky opened with a torrential downpour. Spreading the tarp, they huddled beneath it, and swatted at the clouds of mosquitoes. Ravera cast a questioning glance at Martin.

"What's the plan?"

"Sarge, when this storm passes, if you think you're up to it, I want you to take your men and the weapons and head inland. Try to make your way to an American installation."

"I can do that. And you, what are you going to do?"

"I'm doing the same, but we'll go our separate ways. If you haven't heard from me in three months, tell the army I was with you, but not until then."

"But what about your family? You're probably reported MIA."

Martin gazed down at the ground. His mother and father were no doubt clinging to the hope that their son's MIA status meant he was still alive. He wanted to tell them as much, but that meant leaving behind any hope of finding his three partners.

"Yeah, I know. I wish I could get word to them, but that would mean giving up on finding my men."

"So, you're going down there with what—that bayonet?"

"If I get myself into a situation where I need an AK, I'm probably gonna get killed anyway. You and your Yards need the three AKs if you want any chance of getting back safely. Besides, I'm pretty confident I can get another weapon."

"You are one spooky dude, Shadows—I mean, sir, I mean—"

"I didn't have a rifle before I escaped, and now we have three, right? I'll get another one pretty soon."

"Like I said, you're just plain old spooky."

"Speaking of spooky," Martin said, "what were those weird wailing sounds we heard back on the island?"

"Oh yeah. Well, I'm not certain, but I have an idea. At first, I thought it was the wind, but sometimes the sounds happened even when the wind was dead calm—leastwise that's what a guard told me. One guard talked to me quite a bit. He always warned me when the spirits were restless—the wailing.

"I could also tell when the tide was high because the air inside my cell grew thicker, warmer, and wetter, and there was no draft at all. I finally realized the guard's warnings about the spirits coincided with a rising tide. I believe the tide compressed the air in one of the underwater caves somewhere and it was being released through smaller openings or fissures somewhere on the surface of the island. That's the best I could figure."

"Do you believe in spirits or things with no natural explanations?" Martin asked.

"I suppose so. Why?"

"I do. I've seen too much to believe otherwise."

"Well, it was only a theory. I mean if you believe it was spirits or s—"

"Oh, no! I think your explanation makes perfect sense, and you're probably right. I'm just saying that I've experienced things that have no natural explanations. We can talk about them another time. Just get yourself and your men home safely."

"Oh, I can do that. That's what we did in Laos—well, except for that last mission. It was a snafu from the git-go."

"Good luck, Sergeant. I hope we meet again someday."

"I look forward to it, Lieutenant. I'll buy you a beer."

"I'll accept, but only if it's with a shot of Four Roses."

"Four Roses?"

"Yeah. That's my father's favorite Kentucky Bourbon."

"You got it."

The rain ended before daylight the next morning, and Martin watched as the ghostly figures of Ravera and his Montagnards disappeared into the early morning mist. Further inland, the thunder of artillery had echoed several times during the night, but he had no intention of heading that way. He was going to the highlands south of Chu Lai.

For two days Martin waded muddy rivers and circumvented the villages as he made his way southward amidst the sputter of occasional firefights—often punctuated by artillery and sometimes the subtle roar of fighter jets high overhead. Progress was slow as he turned, circled, and occasionally backtracked to avoid these small battles, but a particularly intense fight broke out somewhere just ahead that day—probably less than four hundred meters away.

After hiding his rucksack beside the trail, Martin climbed into a tree for a better view, but the firefight ended as abruptly as it had begun, and there remained only the silence. Nothing but sandy, brush-covered hills were visible up ahead. He waited, expecting helicopters or perhaps artillery, but there was none—only the quiet whispers of the wind in the surrounding trees. He tried to envision what had happened, but it made little sense. He would have to again change direction.

Grasping a tree limb, he was about to drop to the ground when he spotted a line of soldiers coming his way. They were close and approaching on the trail directly to his front. He suddenly wished he hadn't given Ravera all three AK-47s. Partially hidden by the surrounding grass and brush, the column was winding its way up a gentle slope. Flattening his body atop a wide tree limb, Martin drew his bayonet.

At first it was puzzling, because some of the soldiers were white men, but there were also North Vietnamese soldiers wearing pith helmets. Only when they walked directly beneath him, did Martin realize four North Vietnamese soldiers were escorting four

American Marine POWs. Two of the Marines were drenched with blood, and all were covered with red dust and had parachute cord tied around their necks.

One enemy soldier led the column while three others followed at the rear. All were loaded down with captured weapons and gear. Motionless, Martin waited while they hurried by beneath him. After the last one passed, he dropped silently to the ground and squatted on the trail. They were clueless, and with cat-like stealth he quickly caught up with the last man in the line. Slapping his palm over his mouth, he pulled the bayonet across the soldier's throat.

Lowering the lifeless body to the ground, he grabbed the soldier's AK-47 and slung it over his shoulder. The next man in the column continued up the trail, oblivious to his comrade's fate. Again, Martin caught up and clamped his hand over the soldier's mouth. A quick swipe with the bayonet sent blood spurting, but a struggle ensued, alerting the others as weapons and gear clattered to the ground.

"Get down!" Martin shouted.

Their training was evident as the Marines dropped instantly to the ground. Firing the AK-47 point-blank, he killed the third enemy soldier, but the remaining one at the head of the column had disappeared. Martin ran forward, but the enemy point man was no longer in sight.

…you sprang like the cougar from a tree to kill your enemy with your knife.

"Shit," he muttered.

His grandfather's words were as real as the wide-eyed Marines now staring at him in stunned silence.

"Get your weapons. Make sure they're loaded."

The men cast bewildered glances at one another.

"Who the hell are you?" one of them asked. The Marine wore sergeant's stripes.

"I'm the man who just gave you a second chance. Now, do as I said, get your weapons and gear and follow me. We need to get off this trail."

Twenty minutes later Martin led them into a thicket of scrub grass and palms beside a muddy river.

"Okay, let's get a look at those wounds. How'd you guys get captured?"

Fresh blood trickled down their backs as they removed their fatigue shirts. One Marine had a jagged gash exposing the bone on his shoulder. The other had what appeared to be a grazing bullet wound across his back. Both were serious, but not necessarily fatal if they received medical care soon.

"We were busy trying to get these guys patched up when thirty of them flanked us from behind," the sergeant said. "They were all over us before we knew they were there."

"Where are the rest of your men?"

"Probably dead. We got ambushed by a company of NVA regulars, and there weren't but twelve of us to begin with."

"Where are we?" Martin asked.

Wrinkled brows and questioning stares were their only responses.

"Where is your base?"

"Dong Ha. We're recon. They choppered us over here to find those gooks, but I suppose they found us first. Now, we ain't got a radio, and there's at least a company of those bastards between us and home."

"How many clicks to the highway?"

"Not sure, but like I said, there's a whole damned NVA company out there between us and the highway."

"Okay, we'll just have to move slow and pay attention. You guys are Marine Recon, right?"

"Damned right, we are, but who the hell are *you*?"

The Marine glared at Martin, whose fatigue shirt and trousers were tattered remnants. And having not shaved in well over a month, he was sporting a beard of sorts—as much as his Lakota blood allowed.

"I'm an army lieutenant. Let's get moving."

"What the fuck are you doing this far up in I-Corps?"

"I was a POW for a while. Now, I'm hunting Charlie."

"You just killed two gooks with a bayonet. You're skinny as hell, and you got a beard. You're a spooky sonofabitch. You know that?"

"So, I've been told. Do you want to go with me or not?" Martin turned and began walking away. "I'm heading out."

"Why are you going north? The DMZ is up that way."

He stopped and looked back.

"You just said there's an NVA company south of here. Look, I'm done talking. Come with me if you want. I'm leaving."

For several seconds they exchanged angry glares before the sergeant nodded and snatched up his rifle.

"Lead the way, Lieutenant."

CHAPTER TWENTY-EIGHT

Eventually, Martin circled westward, avoiding the villages and roads as the terrain began to change. By midafternoon they reached an area of gently rolling hills covered with yellow grass and scrub brush. The two wounded were now struggling to keep up, while the others did their best to support them. They needed a breather, and Martin had signaled for a halt when there came the distant roar of diesel engines.

"Do you hear that?" one Marine asked.

Martin cocked his head and listened. "Yeah."

"Do you have any smoke or flares?" the gunnery sergeant asked.

"Yeah, but we need to make sure they're ours first," Martin said.

He dug into his backpack and found the flare gun he'd taken from the patrol boat.

"Okay, let's move out. When we're sure they're our people, I'll send up a flare."

Martin led the way until they spotted the trucks seven or eight hundred meters away.

"Hey, those are ours!" one of the Marines shouted.

He began waving his arms.

"Stop!" Martin shouted. "Get down."

"Why? We've got to stop them."

"We need to get closer. If they mistake us for NVA, they'll light us up."

He turned to the gunnery sergeant. "When we get close, I'm going to shoot a flare. You lead the way, and let's try to catch them before they're gone."

Within minutes the convoy was passing by two hundred meters away as Martin shot a flare skyward. The two Marines that weren't wounded shouted and waved their arms over their heads as the trucks ground to a halt and a platoon of Marines spilled out along the road. Recognition came quickly and a lieutenant motioned them forward.

An RTO radioed for a medevac, while a corpsman hooked the two wounded men to plasma bottles and hit them with morphine surettes. The young officer eyed Martin with suspicious eyes while peppering the other two Marines with questions.

"And you say this guy freed you with just a bayonet?" the lieutenant said.

The sergeant nodded while the Marine lieutenant gazed steadily at Martin.

"Well, it's pretty obvious you're a U.S. soldier, but who the hell are you, mister fuzzy face, and why are you out here in the boonies?"

"Lieutenant, I can't—"

"Whoa!" the lieutenant said. "You'll address me as 'sir.' Understood?"

"Sir," Martin said in a soothing voice, "my name is not fuzzy face, and if you don't show me some respect, I'm going to kick your pompous ass right here before God and all your men."

Martin suddenly realized he had changed—and not for the better. This wasn't who he was, but it was *who he had become*. The lieutenant's face drained of color as he stood rigid and unresponsive. Several battle-hardened Marines glanced around at one another with raised eyebrows.

"Now, as a fellow officer, I am sure you must carry a shaving kit, so if you will be so kind as to loan me yours along with some water, I'll clean up your fuzzy-face problem. In the meantime, my reason for being here is classified."

The lieutenant cast a puzzled glance at Martin. "You're part of SOG, aren't you?"

"That's right, Lieutenant, but I can't tell you anything more. I am sorry for losing my temper, and I will appreciate your help."

An hour later, Martin was freshly shaved and on board a Sikorsky medevac chopper with the wounded Marines. Several other wounded were already on the helicopter along with a navy corpsman.

"Where are we headed?" Martin asked the crew chief.

"We *were* enroute to the hospital down at Da Nang—transferring these guys down there from Charlie-Med when we got the call to pick up you guys. They said it was a cold LZ and your wounded were urgent, so we came in. Problem now is we've got mechanical problems. We may have to divert."

Martin gazed out the plexiglass window. The chopper was flying low—lower than it should—an easy target of opportunity.

"We're losing power, and the pilot says we can't make it over the Hai Van Pass. We may go in at Phu Bai. There's an Army MASH unit there, the 22nd Med."

The helicopter crew had assumed the wounded Marines were his men, but the charade could last only so long. The more military personnel he met, the more likely someone was going to call him out. A few minutes later the chopper's engine began roaring. The pilot had increased RPMs. They had dropped even lower, and he looked out the little window as the helicopter settled onto a sandbagged LZ. Two army ambulances stood nearby.

"Where are we?"

"Phu Bai," the crew chief shouted. "Hey, what's this shit these boys are telling us about you rescuing them from the NVA with a bayonet?"

Martin gave him his best sideways grin. "I think the morphine has them talking out of their heads."

The crew chief wrinkled his brow and cast a glance at the two Marines lying on stretchers. Exhaustion, dehydration, and the morphine had left them nearly comatose.

"Oh well. It did seem pretty far-fetched, what they told me, but they almost had me believing it. So, who are you if you're not their commanding officer?"

"I'm an army officer, but my mission is classified."

The crew chief cast a skeptical glance his way, and Martin used the flurry of activity around the chopper pad to wander away across the ramp. He had gone only a short distance when he glanced back to see the Marine helicopter crew talking with a soldier wearing an MP armband. Something wasn't right. He ducked into a cluster of Hueys as another crew ran past, piling into a chopper with medevac markings.

"Where are you guys headed?" he shouted.

The cracking whap-whap of the chopper's main rotor indicated it was about to lift off.

"West about thirty-four klicks up toward the A Shau Valley. The Hundred and First has some wounded up there. We can use some help if you wanna go?"

He didn't. He wanted to go south toward Chu Lai, but he had to leave before the MPs came looking for him. Martin glanced over his shoulder. The Marine chopper pilot was pointing his way.

"Sure," he shouted.

The medevac had already gone light on its skids as he leapt aboard. Within minutes, they were high over the central highlands in a cold mist. The open, windblown cabin of the army helicopter was a stark contrast to the one he had just left, and the crew chief was studying him intently.

"You look like shit, partner," he shouted. "How come you're carrying that AK? You SOG or something?"

Martin nodded. Better to lie than attempt an explanation. The crew chief bent closer and shouted. "I appreciate you helping us out. We've already had four choppers bring in wounded from up there. Two of the birds were shot up pretty bad. Those boys are in a hell of a fix, and it's gonna be a hot extraction. You mind covering that door over there?"

"No problem."

His first thought was how the army might explain his body being found on a crashed medevac chopper in I-Corps. Those worries quickly evaporated as the main rotor began clattering and green tracers zipped past the open cabin. The chopper descended toward a cloud of red smoke and a mountain LZ that was little more than a hole in the jungle. Despite the crossfire of enemy rounds, a paratrooper of the Hundred and First stood in the open, his arms raised, as he guided the helicopter down through the narrow opening in the trees.

With his AK-47 slung across his back, Martin leapt to the ground. The helicopter thundered and swayed in the tiny jungle clearing as he began helping load the dead and wounded. Moments later, the crew chief motioned for him to climb back on board, but Martin grabbed his rucksack instead and waved him off. The MPs would likely be waiting on him if he returned too soon. The crew chief stood staring in disbelief as the chopper lifted away.

Martin walked off the LZ into the jungle that evening as the infinite darkness of a jungle night fell upon the highlands. It was a black night, blanketed with clouds and a thick ground mist that filled the valleys and saturated the undergrowth. The mountain insects were a constant chorus, as he sat listening for the nearby American troops. They weren't making a sound. It was the Hundred and First Airborne. These guys were good. Only the chirps of crickets and the buzz of locusts came from the nighttime jungle as he crawled toward the Americans' perimeter.

With no moon, he was guided only by instinct and his hands as he soon found a tripwire. It was likely attached to a flare. After tracing its path, he eased past it, feeling his way until he touched the first Claymore. Drawing a calming breath, he paused before carefully crawling around it. Moving inches at a time, he thought himself totally silent until he heard their whispers.

"I hear something, dude."

They were close—very close, within three or four meters. It was the voice of some black kid from God only knew where—Detroit, Chicago, maybe, or perhaps Memphis.

"Shut up. I can't hear shit with you talking."

It was another voice—perhaps a white kid from Ohio, or from any of a dozen other midwestern states. Martin crawled past them, continuing until he found a group huddled in a shallow depression. The soft scratch of a radio told him it was the company CP. They were gathered in a circle eating C-rations while whispering to one another. Martin crawled up to their circle.

"Hey, any of you guys got another one of those C-rations? I'm hungry."

Someone tossed him a carton, and he broke it open.

"Hey, I've lost my P-38. You got another one?"

"Who the hell are you?"

The whisper was louder and agitated.

"Just give me a P-38, and I'll be good."

A hand reached out and jabbed him with one of the little can openers. The men resumed their conversation.

"I know we're in a bad way. No need to say that. We've lost the captain, the first sergeant, and nearly a platoon of men wounded or KIA, and battalion says we've gotta get back to the firebase on our own."

"But we can't stand another ambush like that," one said.

"How far is it to the firebase?" asked another.

"Three, maybe four clicks due west, but it just as soon be a hundred miles. These bastards have our number and they're not about to give us a free pass."

"What are we going to do?"

"What do you suggest, Sarge?"

"Divert to the south. Throw them off. They know we're trying to reach the firebase, and they won't expect us to go that way."

It was likely a young lieutenant, probably no more than a year out of West Point or OCS, and his company was in a bad way. Fallen heir to a possible massacre, he had the good sense to ask the older and more experienced NCO for help. Martin eased away and made his way back through the perimeter into the jungle. He would help them, but first, he had to find the NVA.

CHAPTER TWENTY-NINE

A s the jungle came to life with the first light of day, it was again drenched in an early morning mist and birds were screeching in the overhead canopy. Martin lay watching as the point man slowly parted the leaves a few feet away. The young soldier wore the typical jungle sunburn, and his face dripped with sweat. He was clueless as to Martin's presence just in front of him. This was the lead element of the beleaguered company he had visited during the night.

The young paratrooper moved slowly, his blue eyes wide and sharp, darting left and right as he searched the surrounding jungle. Stopping, he used the green towel around his neck to mop his face. Martin had watched only minutes before as the NVA circled up a ridge only a few hundred meters away. They were behind him, preparing an ambush, and the paratroopers had no idea they were about to walk into the kill zone.

The point man's machete pinged against the vines as he hacked a path through the jungle. Martin waited until he was less than six feet away. The paratrooper's face was that of a kid no more than a year out of high school. Yet, it was one hardened by the carnage of war. Sweat ran in rivulets from beneath his helmet. The soldier's camouflaged helmet cover was marked with the usual graffiti—

FTA, Linda, and myriad other notices of love and rebellion penned to an uncaring outside world. His bottle of mosquito repellent and a playing card, the Ace of spades, were secured beneath the band.

"You need to stop here," Martin whispered.

The paratrooper froze as he cut his eyes toward the sound of his voice, not yet having seen him.

"Don't worry. I'm on our side."

The soldier's eyes grew wider and wilder by the moment.

"There's an NVA ambush waiting up there on that ridge just ahead. There's also some more of them down below waiting for the ones of you who run that way."

"Who the hell are you?"

Another paratrooper pushed through the thick undergrowth and stepped out behind him.

"Are you talking to yourself?"

"Shut up," the point man said.

"Send your slack man back. Tell him to bring the RTO and an officer with a map up this way. We'll try to get some air support."

"There're some howitzers up at the firebase. Who the hell are you?"

"Artillery alone won't be enough. You've got a couple hundred NVA regulars about to make minced meat out of your company. We need TAC air in here with nape if we can get it."

"Are you okay?" the slack man asked. "Who the fuck are you talking to?"

"Hell, I don't know. A damned ghost for all I know. Go back and tell the LT we've got a big NVA ambush up here waiting on us. Tell him we need some TAC air with napalm. Go. Go tell him now."

The second soldier backed away, disappearing into the misty undergrowth.

"Who are you, a lurp or what?"

"If your commander does as I say, you boys might make it back to the firebase."

"I swear to God, I don't smoke weed, but this has got to be what it's like. I'm hallucinating. Are you a ghost?"

There came the shuffle of boots as the leaves parted. A lieutenant stepped out and gazed at Martin. Behind him was an RTO who had his antenna taped down and his handset wire inside his fatigue shirt. These boys weren't rookies.

"Are you a lurp?" he asked.

"Someone came to your CP last night and asked for a C-ration. One of you gave him a P-38. That was me."

The lieutenant's jaw dropped.

"Who the fuck are you?"

"There's a hundred or more NVA up there on that ridge ready to ambush you. Give me your map, and I'll show you where they are. You can call in the airstrikes."

"How did you get into my CP last night?"

"The same way I'm here now. Stop wasting time. Give me your map, and let's call in the airstrikes."

The lieutenant motioned the RTO forward while pulling a wrinkled topo map from his cargo pocket. Grabbing the map, Martin unfolded it. After a moment he was able to determine their position.

"We're here. You've got maybe a hundred NVA troops up here and another fifty or so down this way. None of them are more than three or four hundred meters from us right now."

"We can't call in airstrikes that close."

"You don't have a choice, Lieutenant. Back away and they'll know you're on to them. That means they'll attack and probably overrun you. It's your call."

"Okay, show me again exactly where you think they are."

Martin pointed at the map. "Do you see where these gridlines are squeezed up close together?"

"Yeah. It's that ridge up there." The lieutenant pointed toward the rise to their front right.

"That's right. And they're up there waiting on you. The others are down here in this area." Martin drew his finger down the map. "I'd light up the whole AO with nape."

"You know we're right between them, and if the flyboys miss by even a little bit we're going to get a lot of our men killed."

"Lieutenant, we're between a rock and a hard place and out of options. When the jets get close, we'll put out smoke and let the birddog call it. Just make sure they understand how close we are and tell them to keep their ordnance off us."

The red-faced lieutenant removed his helmet and rubbed his head. "Jesus, I hope you're right, mister. I just want to get these boys home without losing any more of them."

He motioned to the RTO. "Get on the command net and tell them we have a large enemy force in a fixed position. Tell them we need TAC air, ASAP."

The minutes seemed like hours as Martin waited. Most of what he was doing was based on instinct and training. If he was wrong, men would die. The Lieutenant's radio broke squelch, and he talked quietly into the handset while referencing the map.

"Roger. Just keep it tight as you can. We're right between them. Out."

He gave the handset to the RTO and turned to an NCO who had walked up.

"Okay, the birddog says we've got fast movers inbound. Pass the word back. Bring 2nd Platoon up on the right and 3rd down on the left. Maintain noise discipline but tell everybody to pop yellow smoke when they get into position. And tell them to break out their ponchos and get under them. The nape is going to be dropped close. Tell them to hurry. Do it now and be quick."

The surrounding jungle remained seductively quiet, as if begging for some small sound to break its spell. A lone bird called—its whistle clear and clean somewhere high up the mountain. Tree frogs croaked in the undergrowth below. It was mesmerizing and deceptively peaceful.

Martin gazed about. A green gecko crawled down a nearby vine, dangling there while its bulging black eyes studied him. The men had popped yellow smoke, and gentle shafts of sunlight filtered through its billowing volume, casting an almost festive array of light beneath the canopied jungle. Martin already recognized it for what it was—the precursor to a circus from hell.

The radio broke squelch again and the lieutenant spoke quietly saying, "Roger, the banana. That's us."

Martin's eyes met those of the lieutenant. The two men stared into one another's eyes, but neither spoke. By now the enemy surely suspected something was up, but the jungle remained quiet. From somewhere far above the mountains, came the distant buzz of the spotter plane. Martin strained to listen, but there was only the silence. The tension was palpable, and the silence was as agonizing as it was mesmerizing.

A shrieking thunderous roar shattered the tranquility as everyone dove for cover. It was the afterburners of an F-4 Phantom only a few feet above the jungle canopy, already climbing skyward. A moment later, canisters of napalm exploded along the ridge only three hundred meters away. A monstrous wave of roiling orange flame billowed down the mountainside. Men hid beneath their ponchos and shielded their faces with their arms as the heat and flames sucked the oxygen from the air.

Just to their front, shreds of dripping napalm poured down through the treetops as screams of agony arose from the surrounding jungle. Enemy soldiers appeared from the smoke and flames, running and tumbling as they tried to escape the hell that had descended upon them. Some were aflame, while others, blackened and naked, ran streaming smoke until they dropped.

The paratroopers opened fire—relieving the poor souls of their agony. Another jet came up from the river valley to the south, streaking across to their front as more flaming clouds of napalm mushroomed from the jungle. Sporadic M-16 fire came from the surrounding undergrowth, as the enemy soldiers fled into the guns of the waiting paratroopers.

After a while a strange silence fell over the hillside and nearly a half-hour passed as the men held their position, watching and waiting for the command to move out. The lieutenant met with his NCOs and ordered the company to sweep the ridge. The smoke-shrouded jungle remained quiet as they moved cautiously forward. Dozens of enemy dead littered the jungle floor but there was no resistance. The survivors had fled, and by midafternoon the column was climbing up the steep trail into the firebase.

The rhythmic thunder of rotors echoed through the mountains near Firebase Berchtesgaden, signaling the approach of inbound helicopters. Martin sat on a wall of sandbags gazing out at the hazy hills. There had been only four American casualties that morning—three with burns from the napalm and one with shrapnel wounds from an enemy grenade that cooked off in the embers. None were life-threatening, and they were being medevaced back to Phu Bai. He intended to go with them.

It wouldn't be long before these men told the brass on the firebase about him, but he planned to be long gone before then. The chopper came in fast and maintained its RPMs as the crew cast wary glances back while Martin helped the casualties climb on board. When they were loaded, he tossed his rucksack inside and joined them. A minute later the warren of sandbags at Berchtesgaden dropped away below as the chopper climbed out over the highlands and swung back toward Phu Bai.

CHAPTER THIRTY

That evening, courtesy of the army helicopter pilots, Martin wore a new set of jungle fatigues and was sitting in the officers' club at Phu Bai sipping whisky and smoking Marlboros. The pilots had assumed he was a lurp working with the Hundred and First, and hadn't a clue otherwise, but the two wounded Marines he rescued from the NVA had apparently been telling their story everywhere around the base. It was the current topic of conversation at the club, but he avoided comment and affected a smiling persona of cluelessness.

The two young Marines had told everyone on the base about the ghost soldier who dropped from a tree and killed their captors with his bayonet, and the more the story traveled about the base, the more it was embellished. Yet here he was enjoying some well-deserved R&R. No one had connected him with any of it, and it wasn't of particular concern until the Marine helicopter crew walked into the officers' club that evening.

"The old Sikorsky is fixed," one shouted over the juke box. "We're southbound for Da Nang in the morning and a base full of beautiful navy nurses."

"Yeah, sure, swabby," one of the army pilots shouted back.

"Maybe in your dreams. Come sit down. We'll buy you a drink before you go."

Martin pulled his cap down low and scooted his chair back into a shadowed corner as the Marine helicopter crew pulled their chairs up to the table. Patsy Cline was singing "Crazy" on the juke box, and he thought he probably was too. This insane mission to find Ray, Joe, and Jake was growing increasingly difficult, yet giving up wasn't an option. The army certainly wouldn't waste time with such a Quixotic mission—at least not without strong evidence of where they might be imprisoned.

"Tell us again that story your boys have been spreading about the army guy rescuing them," one of the army chopper pilots said.

"Oh hell!" the Marine aviator said, slapping the table. "You haven't heard shit, yet. You want to hear something *really* crazy?"

"You mean it gets better?"

"Hell yeah, a *lot* better," he said with an emphatic nod. "We just went by the hospital to tell them we're moving our Marines down to Da Nang tomorrow, and there were four paratroopers there from the Hundred and First they brought in this morning."

"Yeah. That was us," an army pilot said. "We brought them in from Hill 1030, Berchtesgaden."

The Marine pilot's lips turned down at the corners as he threw his head back.

"No shit?"

"No shit," the army pilot said.

"Well, listen to this. Those boys you brought in said some skinny dude showed up just like this other guy did with our Marines. He stopped their point man and told him they were about to be ambushed by a couple hundred NVA. Turns out he was right. He saved their asses."

The army pilot turned to Martin. "Hey, you were up there. Did you hear anything about this guy?"

Martin kept his head down as he fished a cigarette from his pocket.

"No, I didn't."

"Hey, wait a minute!" The marine pilot leaned closer. "You're him. You were with those boys when we medevaced them from up near Dong Ha. You rode back with us, and those guys kept trying to tell us you were him."

"Who?" one of the army pilots asked.

"The ghost. He's the one who took on the NVA with a bayonet and freed those Marines after they were captured. He's the one they're calling the ghost."

An army pilot turned to Martin. "Was that you that warned those boys about the ambush up near Berchtesgaden?"

Martin flipped open the lighter and lit his cigarette while gazing up at the pilots surrounding him. Squinting, he inhaled deeply. It was time to make a deal.

"Yeah, but the story is overblown. I can't say much about it because my mission is classified."

"I don't think the story our boys are telling is overblown," the Marine pilot said. "So, who the hell are you?"

"Like I said, it's classified, but I could use your help if you're willing."

"How's that?"

"I need to get down to Quảng Ngai Province, south of Chu Lai."

"We can take you as far as Da Nang, and once we get there, we can probably hook you up with another chopper crew going down to Chu Lai."

"That'll work."

"So, did you really take on a squad of NVA regulars with a bayonet?"

"Only the two at the rear of the column. I killed the other one with an AK-47."

"Jesus!"

"So, it's really true?"

"Can we keep all this low-key till I'm gone? I'm not carrying any orders or identification, and I don't need to be stopped by the MPs."

"I knew it," one of the army pilots said. "You're with Special Operations, aren't you?"

"Let it go, Hound Dog. Like the man said, *it's classified*."

"We'll depart as soon as the ambulances deliver our guys to the chopper in the morning," the Marine pilot said.

"Thanks," Martin said. "I'll meet you there at first light."

Two days later Martin was on Highway One west of FSB Suzy. It had been little more than two months since he was here last, but it seemed light years had passed since then. The black market was still open, and at least twenty American soldiers were milling about. Their shoulder patches were those of his unit, the Fourth Infantry Division, but he recognized none of them. He found two men standing off to the side and approached them.

"Hey, are you guys from FSB Suzy?"

"Yeah, we're just doing a little looking and hoping to buy some souvenirs. Why?"

"I heard one of your platoons got into some serious shit a couple months back."

"Yeah, that was first platoon. They lost eight men inside of a week to ambushes. Two were platoon leaders and one was the platoon sergeant."

"No shit? All KIA?"

"No. Actually, four of them are listed as missing in action. The scuttlebutt is they were captured by the gooks."

"No shit?"

"No shit. One was a new lieutenant. Don't remember his name. Two were old heads, a guy we called Taco and another one we called Chief. There was another one, too, but I don't remember his name. He was a cherry—hadn't been around long. They were out reconning a village a few clicks over that way." He pointed eastward across a rice paddy.

"Anybody trying to find them?"

"The Marines sent some recon patrols out of Chu Lai and the 75th Rangers sent a couple lurp teams up here to poke around in the highlands, but they say it's like searching for a needle in a haystack. Those guys could be anywhere by now—maybe even Hanoi. Who knows?"

Martin had to replenish his supplies and noticed an old woman with a case of LRP rations. The long-range patrol rations were light compared to C-rations and a hell of a lot better tasting. Problem was he had no money and little else the old Vietnamese woman could possibly want.

"Hey, wait," he said to the two soldiers. "Do you fellows want to buy some souvenirs?"

"What 'cha got?"

Martin dropped his rucksack and opened it. Pulling out an NVA pith helmet and a red star belt buckle, he tossed them on the ground.

"Holy shit! Where'd you get these?"

He gave them a blank stare.

"Never mind. We'll take 'em. How much?"

"Twenty-five for the belt buckle and fifty for the helmet."

"What the fu— We ain't got that kinda money."

"Yeah, we do, Burnie. You got—"

"Shut the fuck up, Parson."

"Okay," Martin said, "fifty bucks for the buckle and seventy-five for the helmet."

"But you just said—"

"I know what I said, but I can go over there to your buddies right now and get that price from any of them."

The two infantrymen stood in red-faced silence.

"Tell you what. Give me eighty-five and you can have them both."

They quickly fished through their pockets.

"Any idea where the rangers are headquartered?"

"Not sure. They're choppering in from somewhere south of here. They were at the base the other day. Those bastards from the 75th Rangers are some badass dudes."

Martin left the black market that day with high-quality binoculars, an extra canteen, heat tabs, and a dozen LRP rations. He also picked up extra socks and a new boonie hat. His westward trek into the hills paralleled the so-called highway. It was a dirt and gravel roadway with little that resembled a modern thoroughfare.

A week later, he realized he was facing casino odds. The misty purple mountains of the Central Highlands rolled away to the horizon in all directions, miles upon miles of double- and triple-canopied jungle. Mostly trackless, the primary avenues were footpaths and animal trails. He could search for years and walk within meters of his friends without finding them. The proverbial needle would be an easier find.

His first week, he had watched an ARVN company in trucks and APCs motoring up the highway into the area, but it returned before sundown that first day. The South Vietnamese knew to stay out of the highlands after dark. He later spotted a column of ROK Marines, but mostly he saw enemy soldiers carrying AK-47s and RPGs. The enemy seemed to have free rein over the highlands, and there were too many for him to follow. The futility of his search slapped him in the face as he contemplated what to do next. He would never find them searching alone. He needed help, and there was but one place he could find it.

CHAPTER THIRTY-ONE

The trek from the highlands back to FSB Suzy took two and a half days. Getting into the firebase and walking into Captain Bowman's HQ office took ten minutes. It was probably the simplest thing Martin had done since escaping the island. He pulled a metal chair up and sat down, while the saucer-eyed captain's face drained of color and his lips parted.

"What the—! Shadows?"

"Sorry to walk in on you this way, sir, but I had no choice."

"But—but where in the hell have you…?"

The captain didn't finish his sentence as he squeezed his eyes shut and reopened them.

"Sir, they say you commanded a company of the 4th Infantry up near Dak To in '67—earned a Silver Star and a Purple Heart, but you got back with most of your unit in one piece. That tells me you probably give a shit about your men. So, I came to ask for your help."

"I'm not helping you with a damned thing till you tell me what the hell is going on."

"I'm an Army Intelligence officer, and I report directly to MAC-V. What I'm going to tell you is top-secret and you can help me by keeping it that way."

"Well, that explains why the MAC-V brass have been all over my ass for the last two months. Where have you been?"

Martin began his story with the day he was first assigned to FSB Suzy. After a couple minutes, the captain reached into an ammo can behind his desk and retrieved a bottle of whisky. He set two glasses on the desk and uncorked the bottle. It was one of the better Tennessee whiskeys, Jack Daniels. Martin talked another five minutes before picking up his drink and emptying the glass with one swallow.

"Like I said, sir, I think our boys are still alive, and I'm not giving up, but I can't do it without your help."

The captain refilled the two glasses.

"We haven't given up on them either. Pamphlets offering a reward have been distributed in every village in the province and probably half of II Corps. We have Marine Recon combing the hills west of Chu Lai and Army Rangers doing the same west of here. At first, we got several bites on the pamphlets, but only one has turned out credible. That came in just two days ago."

"So, they were seen alive?"

"Seems so. At least that's what one village chief claims. One of the ranger LRRP teams went into a village twenty-five clicks west of here. The village chief claimed NVA regulars kept our men in a hootch there for a night a few weeks back. One of them slipped the old chief a dog-tag, but the chief said he gave it to an ARVN officer whose unit came through the following day."

"Any idea who the ARVN officer was?"

"I'm not sure, but it was probably Colonel Nguyen's XO, Major Thanh. He's been running the unit since the colonel disappeared. Problem is he hasn't reported getting that dog tag to anyone. I haven't trusted the sneaky bastard from the git-go. He claims his people patrolled out that road several times in recent weeks and found nothing."

"I think your suspicions are well founded, sir. Thanh was

driving the colonel's jeep that day when we were captured. As soon as we were ambushed, he must have taken off."

"So, what are you proposing?"

"I want to go back to that village as soon as we can with one of the Ranger teams and talk with that village chief. I need to determine if he's legit. I also want you to contact my CO, Captain Palmer, at MAC-V. Tell him everything I've told you. If you can't meet with him personally, make sure you're on a secure commo link. There's too much at stake here. If Major Thanh doesn't know he's a suspect, he might lead us to Nguyen, and Nguyen might lead us to our men."

The captain stared at him with disbelieving eyes.

"This is the craziest shit I've ever—"

"Oh, and before I forget, sir: Privates Robert Greyman and Peebles admitted to me that they killed Lieutenant Branch. I didn't have the chance to report this before I was captured. You probably want to notify CID."

"I need a written statement to that effect before you leave, Lieutenant. If I can't get them hanged, they'll at least spend the rest of their lives at Leavenworth."

Late that afternoon, Martin boarded a slick with six Army Rangers and an ARVN interpreter. Eight more Rangers followed in a second chopper. This *Bull Team* as they called themselves was packing heavy with two M-60 machineguns, two thump guns, and an M-14 sniper rifle equipped with a 3X9 scope and bipod. The Central Highlands were spooky any time of day, but this was Martin's first clandestine helicopter insertion. It took only minutes before he understood why Army Rangers deserved their reputation.

The choppers had flown low through the hills, making several false insertions before the team reached its objective. Once on the ground, they were ghosts—something Martin already knew a lot about. Moving silently through the shadowy jungle, they crossed over the mountain toward the village in the next valley. They were deceptively fast, quiet, and efficient.

At last light, operating mostly with hand signals, they moved into a night defensive position where they maintained strict light and sound discipline. Martin felt he was in his element and with men he understood. After a night's rest, the team moved silently down the mountain to a high ridge where the team leader, Sergeant Tex Stoneman, studied the village below with binoculars. The sun had risen, but there was little activity in the village or on the adjacent east-west highway.

"I don't like it," Stoneman whispered while squinting into his binoculars.

"I see a few cook fires," Martin whispered. He was scanning with his binoculars as well.

"Yeah, but there were more people here the other day—a *lot* more. We need to call C&C with a sit-rep. Let's hook up the long-range antenna and settle in. We'll watch 'em a while. If we don't spot the enemy, we'll ease down there in the morning and have a talk with the village chief about that dog tag."

The men took shifts watching the road and the village. After several hours the activity remained minimal. They had spotted only a few villagers—a woman cutting wood, another hauling water buckets across her shoulders, and an old man feeding a pig in a cage. Two half-naked children sat in the open doorway of a hootch, but there was little other activity. By late afternoon, despite the absence of suspicious activity, Stoneman remained cautious, wagging his head again after studying the village several minutes with his binoculars.

"I still don't like it," he said. "It's almost as if the enemy is somewhere close watching them, and those people down there know it. They don't want to leave their hootches, but we can't sit up here on this ridge forever. If nothing changes before sunup in the morning, we'll ease down and talk with our guy. Do you agree, Lieutenant?"

"Yeah, but I don't want to walk into a trap. Can we have your men set up security outside the village to cover us while just you, me, and the interpreter question the village chief? Will that work?"

"That's pretty much SOP, sir."

"Oh. Sorry. I'm new to this stuff."

"Sounds to me like you know your shit. The CO at FSB Suzy told me some crazy stuff about you escaping an NVA prison and freeing a bunch of Marine POWs with just a bayonet. Is that true?"

"Pretty much. I was captured the same time as these men we're looking for."

"Maybe this village chief can help us find them," Stoneman said, "but don't be disappointed if he's developed lockjaw. There's a whole lot of people missing from that village since the last time we were here. Besides, those boys are prob...."

Stoneman looked away and didn't finish his sentence. It was clear he was filled with skepticism. This mission seemed impossible and destined for failure, but Martin was determined to at least try, no matter how hopeless the odds.

"Thanks for being upfront, Sarge. I appreciate what you're saying, but this is something I have to do."

———————

At dawn the men ate a cold LRP ration, checked their weapons, and drew up a plan. Wasting no time, the team deployed on a rise just outside the village as the first beams of morning sunlight scattered heavenward across the misty eastern sky. One M-60 covered the main village entrance, while the two grenadiers positioned themselves to cover the east and west highway approaches.

"You ready?" Stoneman said.

Martin nodded and the sergeant led the way, as they walked with the Vietnamese interpreter down a trail and into the center of the village. A rooster crowed and pigs squealed, but only a few villagers gazed at them from shadowy doorways. The three men stopped in front of the chief's hootch where an old woman peeked out at them from inside the door. The sergeant motioned silently with his chin to the interpreter and over at the old woman.

"Lai day," the interpreter shouted.

"No need to yell at her," Stoneman said. "That's the chief's wife."

The woman stepped outside her hootch. Her arms were folded across her chest, and her eyes were sunken and bloodshot.

"Ask her where her husband is," Martin said.

The interpreter said something, and the old woman stared at the ground. He repeated himself. Still, she did not respond. His voice became more insistent, and she mumbled something.

"What did she say?"

"She said he died."

"How?"

The interpreter pressed the old woman with more questions, before she began quietly mumbling and weeping.

"She said he tortured by NVA soldiers because he gave metal badge to South Vietnamese officer who was here last week. She said the officer gave it to the enemy soldiers who killed her husband."

"Metal badge?" Martin said. "The dog tag?"

"Reckon so," Stoneman said, "but I doubt they were NVA. VC regulars maybe, but not NVA, not around here."

"Ask her if she saw the Vietnamese officer who took the dog tag. Ask her if she can tell you what he looked like."

After the interpreter again exchanged words with her, Martin noticed the woman rubbing her wrists and pointing at them.

"What did she say?"

"She said his arms have scars from napalm bombs."

"Does your boy have burn scars on his arms?" the sergeant asked.

"That's him," Martin said, "Major Thanh."

"Find that sonofabitch and you've found yourself a turncoat," Stoneman said.

"Yeah, and this pretty much verifies the village chief's story. The sorry bastards killed him for it."

"What now?" Stoneman asked.

Martin turned to the interpreter. "Ask her if she knows where the enemy is now."

Again, the woman refused to look up as she mumbled and motioned slightly with her head.

"She said they have big camp on mountain not far." He pointed westward. "That way she said, maybe four, five kilometers. She said she care no more and only wish to die, too."

Stoneman cast a gaze up the mountain.

"Damned! They're probably watching us right now. Let's back out of here quick before we get into something we can't handle."

After rejoining the team, Stoneman led them back up the mountain, quickly putting distance between them and the village. After an hour of hard climbing, they stopped for a breather. The village and the main road below were still visible. Martin used the opportunity to scan them with his binoculars.

"Hey, Sarge, you better take a look down there."

A column of ant-size figures was moving through the village—enemy soldiers. There were more on the road outside the village. They wore pith helmets. Stoneman studied them through his binoculars.

"What do you think?" Martin asked.

"Those aren't the local boys," Stoneman muttered. "The old woman was right. Those *are* most affirmatively NVA regulars. I can't believe the bastards are this far east."

"What's the plan?"

"We need to keep moving up the mountain and contact C&C. I'm going to suggest we move west and try to locate their basecamp, but we'll have to do whatever our people say."

By sunset the team had relocated four klicks to the west and higher up the mountain where they set up a night defensive position. The light was rapidly dimming beneath the jungle canopy, while Stoneman talked on the radio with Command-and-Control. When he was done, he gave the handset to the RTO, looked over at Martin, and shrugged.

"We have two squadrons of fast movers, some Skyraiders, and Cobra gunships on standby for tomorrow. We'll move down the mountain in the morning. If we can locate that basecamp, they're bringing in enough ordnance to obliterate the whole area. The ROK troops are also being ordered out this way from Highway One. They'll sweep the mountain afterward."

"So, we're calling in an airstrike and that's it?"

He was being betrayed. His brothers were being betrayed. Martin had thought Stoneman was a man of his word.

"Pretty much. We'll set up to ambush any stragglers who try to escape up our way."

"What about our men—the POWs?"

Stoneman's stared down at the ground.

"Sir. This is C&C's call. By now your men are either dead or wishing they were. Hell, if the NVA are doing to them what I think they are, we'll be doing them a favor."

"Can you give me twenty-four hours? That's all I'm asking. I'm going down there now and find that camp. I've got to try and see if those men are there."

"With all due respect, sir, you must be out of your ever-lovin' mind. Even if you find it, you'll never get into an NVA basecamp. Besides, how the hell do you expect to find us after we're separated? I can't let you take one of our radios."

"I have a couple starburst flares and some smoke. Look for a starburst with purple smoke. That'll be me—and hopefully our three guys."

"Lieutenant—I mean, sir—I sure wish you'd reconsider. You're taking a helluva risk for the very unlikely possibility of finding those boys."

"I know it's risky, and maybe I *am* crazy. Hell, if I survive, the army will probably Section-Eight me to a stateside hospital with bars on the windows, but I have to do it."

Dusk faded toward nightfall, while the men lay beside one another. There was a too-long interval of uncomfortable silence before Stoneman sat upright. The only thing visible in the dusky darkness were the whites of his glaring eyes.

"Sir, this is my patrol, and I'm not agreeing to this."

Another lengthy silence ensued.

"There's a chance I could pull it off," Martin said.

"Okay, what the hell is it with you, Lieutenant? Have you lost your—" Stoneman went suddenly silent.

"Look, I don't mean to be disrespectful, sir, but just what the hell are you trying to accomplish? Those boys are dead, and that's why we need to take out that basecamp—so we don't lose more of our men. Don't you see how this whole war is nothing but a political pissing match with no winners?"

Stoneman's blackened face glowed in the shadows. His eyes were those of a wild animal.

"You can't kill them all and you can't save everyone. We're caught in the middle of this shit-show, and as soldiers we have a duty to perform, but look around you. This entire war is based on bogus assumptions. The idiots in Washington use body-count because it's a number they can understand, bend, and inflate when it suits them, but what they don't understand is we're facing an enemy who isn't counting. And now, they say we're leaving. We're turning it over to the ARVN to let them finish it. Hell, they won't last two years before the Communists roll over them. Can't you see? It's all a big farce."

Martin met the sergeant's glare with one of his own. It first occurred to him some weeks back, that he might be going mad—that this war had stolen his sanity—and he now understood what had driven his madness. Stoneman was right. It was the lies. No one spoke the truth, and nothing was quite as it seemed. Everything was based on lies—even the war itself.

The charlatans who found purpose and profit amidst this chaos were on both sides and at all levels. Honest men, like Tim, Paul, Joe Thunders, Ray Lopez, and Jake Randal, thousands of soldiers, and thousands of Vietnamese civilians were nothing to the maestros of this debacle. These people were pawns used to fulfill the greed and power fetishes of depraved reprobates and politicians.

And the more he thought about it, the more Martin understood how those that were morally corrupt were perhaps the smarter ones. They knew all along what he only now had come to understand. There was no honesty in war. It was the ultimate obscenity, and its darkest side was best orchestrated by the most vulgar of men. Even the president had lied to the American people and to Congress. For him and people like him, there was no honor, no transparency—only lies and deceit. They were as ruthlessly corrupt as the enemy, but he couldn't fight both.

The more he thought about it, the more he saw how he had been sucked into a black hole of hatred and retribution—one based on ignorance—one that was destroying him. The war had become a personal thing that he allowed to rule him, but no more. If it was to be personal, he vowed to fight for those things that were important to him—his friends. They were all that mattered. Stoneman was right, but Martin refused to stop until he found them—dead or alive.

"Sir," Stoneman said, "I've lost friends, and I've seen a lot of men die in this war, but you can't personalize it. Do your best. Do your duty, and if you're lucky, you'll go home in one piece. Survival—that's the grand prize."

Stoneman's whispers were becoming raspy and broken. The team leader lay on his back and opened a can of Copenhagen. Taking a healthy pinch of the snuff, he put it inside his lip and cut his eyes at Martin.

"Want some?"

"Hell no!"

Stoneman cast a wary glance his way.

"So, you're still bent on going off on your own?"

"I have to."

"Hell, there might be an entire battalion in that basecamp. What the hell are you gonna do—just walk in like you own it?"

"I am only asking that you give me a little time. Tomorrow, tell C&C you haven't yet located the basecamp. If I'm not back by sunset, then go ahead with the planned airstrike the next morning."

Stoneman replaced the lid on his snuff can and dropped it in his pocket. After spitting to one side, he nodded.

"Do what you have to do, but I'm not making you any promises. I'll do what I can, but the safety of my team comes first."

CHAPTER THIRTY-TWO

It was after nightfall, and Martin had found a trail leading down the mountain, but he could hear someone following quietly behind him. The jungle was as black as the island caverns as he stepped off the trail and held his breath. The person walked past him, followed by another, and another. It was a column of enemy soldiers passing within arm's reach. He couldn't see them, but he heard their breathing and smelled their body odor. His ears told him there were nine—probably NVA regulars carrying AK-47s. When the last man passed, Martin exhaled and stepped out behind him.

Stripped of most of his gear, he carried the bayonet, his AK-47, and a canteen, along with a haversack containing two 30-round magazines, a smoke canister, several LRP rations, and a couple star-burst flares. He hurried to catch up to the column, nearly colliding with the soldier at the rear. The pitch darkness of the nighttime jungle left him dependent upon his senses of touch, hearing, and smell. His only orientation was the downward slope of the trail and the quiet footfalls of the enemy soldier just ahead.

With stealth and silence, he remained behind the column, until he heard the subdued voices of two Vietnamese—behind him! They were close—too close—no more than five meters, he figured. He listened. They weren't moving, and it dawned on him what had happened. He had just walked past them. The two men were on a listening post beside the trail, and they must have thought he was part of the column.

Searching the ground with his fingers, he found their commo wire. It led down the mountain. He was at the basecamp. Looping the wire over his bayonet, he was about to cut it but hesitated. Cutting their commo wire would alert them of his presence. He dropped it and continued down the trail.

Two brushy mounds loomed ahead—likely bunkers. Objects were becoming more visible, and Martin realized a crescent moon had risen. Its soft shafts of light now penetrated the jungle canopy. For eyes attuned to the black of night, it was as good as a sunrise— giving shapes to trees and other objects. The shadows now had definition and the rocks reflected a dull shine. This would enable him to move about and recon the camp, but something caught his eye—a movement. And there came the foul stench of a latrine. He stopped.

A moment later, shuffling footfalls on a rocky path indicated someone approaching. The outline of an NVA soldier wearing a pith helmet appeared. He stopped a few feet away. Martin remained motionless as the new moonlight revealed a cabana of palm leaves and bamboo. The soldier stooped beneath it and dropped his trousers. This latrine had to be near their living quarters. He was now well inside the camp.

Slipping away, he circled quietly as he continued his reconnaissance. All night he moved about, crossing paths with no one. The NVA camp was in a flat basin high on the mountain slope, well hidden beneath the canopied jungle. It was surrounded by a ring of bunkers, and after several hours Martin found what he had been searching for—several camouflaged hootches. This was it—the center of the enemy basecamp.

As the eastern sky began to glow, he climbed to a vantage point high among the limbs of a giant banyan tree where he could overlook the entire camp. Tying himself, his weapon, and his gear securely, he settled in for the wait and closed his eyes in hopes of catching a quick nap.

Martin jerked awake to the keening call of a bird somewhere in the trees above. The sun was already high overhead. He'd slept too long. Peering into the camp below, he realized he was almost *too* close. NVA soldiers were everywhere, milling about and totally unaware of his presence as he studied the camp and its inhabitants.

Four recoilless rifles, a half-dozen mortar tubes, and several .51 caliber machineguns were stored beneath a camouflaged canopy near the hootches. Stacks of wooden crates—likely ammunition, rockets, and additional armaments—were hidden beneath another canopy. There was enough equipment and supplies here for at least a battalion, if not a regiment. It was clear the enemy was preparing for a major offensive, and this was their headquarters. If Ray, Joe, and Jake were still alive, this was where they would be.

After a while, he noticed one hootch with more activity than the others. A sentry was posted outside the door, and the guard stiffened when certain soldiers came and went. He was recognizing officers—another sign of a headquarters unit. He also noticed a second hootch with another sentry at the door. It was directly across from the headquarters, and its entrance was secured with a woven bamboo gate. There was only one reason for the gate. It was a prison cell of sorts.

If his brothers were here, that hootch was likely where they would be, but Martin had no choice except to wait until nightfall to find out. He could only hope and pray that Stoneman wouldn't call in the airstrikes before then.

Shafts of afternoon sunlight penetrated the jungle canopy as he catnapped in their warmth, casting an occasional wary eye on the camp below. It remained quiet, and it seemed now that Stoneman must have delayed the airstrikes. When nightfall came Martin would have to work fast to reach the hootch and hope Ray, Joe, and Jake were there.

Sergeant Stoneman and his team of Rangers probably had the basecamp located by now, and morning would no doubt bring the promised air strikes. A rain of hell would fall here and on a large part of the mountainside. Martin hoped he and his men would be far up the mountain by then. And it came to him how so much of this was contingent upon so many assumptions. The doubts ate at him.

A sliver of the waning moon again rose in the east as Martin stretched his sore muscles. Soft, milky shafts of moonlight filtered through the jungle canopy. Patience was key. Before he made his move, he wanted the enemy to be drugged with sleep. He waited until well into the night when the camp was still. The only soldiers visible were the sentry at the HQ hootch and the other at the hootch where he hoped to find his friends. He formulated a plan in his head. The sentry guarding the prisoners was too close and would hear the slightest sound. He had to be taken out.

Dropping from the tree, Martin walked softly across the open ground to the rear of the hootch where he left everything but his bayonet. Easing forward, he peeked around the corner. The guard was there, five feet away, staring into the darkness. Forty meters across the way, the other sentry stood in the shadow of the HQ hootch. Martin watched patiently and waited. Several minutes passed. He had to do something soon, or he wouldn't have time to escape before the airstrikes began in the morning.

A monkey howled from somewhere high on the mountain, and both sentries cast long stares up that way. Martin sprang. Pulling his bayonet hard across the guard's throat, he quickly dragged him from sight and returned to watch the other sentry. He waited. The other soldier didn't seem to notice his missing comrade. Returning to the rear of the hootch, Martin used his bayonet to carve through the straw wall. Once inside, he found a lattice of bamboo bars bound with rope.

"Who's there?" came a whispering voice.

"I'm Martin Shadows. Who are you?"

"It's me, Ray Lopez. I thought you were dead."

"Who's in there with you?"

"Thunders. It's me and Joe Thunders."

"Where's Lieutenant Randal?"

"They killed him. He was wounded when they attacked us, and—"

"Sshh. It's okay. I've almost got this hole big enough." Martin pushed the bamboo bars apart. "Can you guys walk on your own?"

"Yeah, but we don't have boots and we're both sick as hell. We got dysentery or something, and I think Joe's leg wound is infected."

Martin slipped inside and cut the restraints from their arms and legs.

"Come on. Follow me, but when we get outside, try to walk casually, like you belong here."

Ghosting through the camp, the three men moved with the aid of an adrenaline high as they passed within feet of sleeping soldiers and manned bunkers. It was an exercise in stealth and raw nerves as they crawled, crept, and felt their way through the darkness. Several times they were forced to detour around clusters of sleeping soldiers or drowsy sentries. Martin hadn't told them about the airstrikes, but he could hear the clock ticking.

———————

Dawn was now breaking as the men climbed away from the basecamp. It had taken them several hours to sneak past the bunkers and observation posts on the perimeter. Their progress was slowed further as bare feet and debilitation took their toll on Ray and Joe. Martin could not bring himself to tell them about the impending airstrike. They were doing all they could, but the two men continued falling and occasionally crawling until Martin helped them to their feet.

Their wounds and imprisonment had left both men sickly and ragged. They were emaciated shadows of their former selves. Joe's leg, reddened and swollen with infection, slowed him even more, but he suffered in stoic silence. They had climbed little more than four hundred meters from the enemy basecamp when Martin realized he had to give them a break.

"Okay, let's take five. I want you guys to eat something."

Opening two ration envelopes, he mixed the contents with water from his canteen and gave them to the men.

"Eat."

He didn't have to say it twice. Both men ate ravenously, finishing their meals within a minute.

"Where have you been?" Thunders asked.

"An island prison off the coast of North Vietnam."

"How the hell did you escape?" Ray asked.

"It's a long story. I'll tell you later. First tell me this: Have you seen Colonel Nguyen around that camp?"

Ray's eyes flashed with anger. "Yeah. He's there all right. The sorry bastard is wearing an NVA field uniform. He even told us he was going to visit our buddies at Suzy soon. I think they're planning a full-scale attack on the firebase."

"Has he mentioned anything about other infiltrators or spies in the ARVN ranks?"

"Yeah, he said they're everywhere and a replacement is already running his old battalion. Nguyen's the one that told us they killed Lieutenant Randal, and he's been torturing us bad, trying to find out how we discovered he was a spy."

"What'd you tell him?"

"What *could* we tell him?" Ray said. "I told him it came from higher up, and we had no idea how they knew. He kept asking us questions about you—like you had something to do with it. Did you?"

"We're not out of this mess yet. If I tell you and we're recaptured—well, it's confidential. I'll tell you everything when I can."

Thunders cast a smug glance at Lopez. "See. I told you."

Martin handed the canteen to Thunders.

"Both of you take another drink, and let's get moving."

"My wočhékiye to Ptesáŋwiŋ has been heard," Thunders said.

He put his hand on Ray's shoulder. "I think you should apologize to me now for yelling at me when I chanted my prayers."

"Yeah, but I had to," Ray said. "Nguyen was beating the hell out of us every time you did that. For some reason it scared him."

"That's because he was afraid of the spirits Joe might invoke," Martin said.

Lopez slowly wagged his head. "You and Thunders got some strange juju going on."

Martin stood and pulled both men to their feet.

"You haven't heard the least of it, Sarge. I'll tell you more later. Come on. We've got to keep moving."

CHAPTER THIRTY-THREE

Martin found a game trail in the dim jungle twilight, but progress remained slow as his two partners struggled up the steep mountainside. Visibility was limited, and the jungle was eerily quiet. By now, the North Vietnamese likely had patrols searching for them, but Ray and Joe could move no faster. Martin was again forced to stop while they caught up.

"Where are we going?" Lopez asked.

Although panting and breathless, Ray's face had regained some color, and he was sweating. This was a good sign.

"There's a lurp team up here somewhere—75th Rangers. We've got to find them."

He gave Ray the canteen.

"Both of you drink some more water."

When they were done, he took a swig, recapped the canteen, and paused to listen. Something—a distant sound—had broken the spooky silence. Martin cocked his head as a faint roar came from somewhere back to the east. Possibly that of jets, it quickly faded.

"We've got to move faster, guys. We're still too close to that enemy camp, and I think all hell is about to break loose."

"We're doing all we can," Lopez said.

Martin gazed at his friends. He had to tell them the truth.

"You've got to do more. They gave me twenty-four hours to find you guys. That ended yesterday evening, and there's an air strike coming. Come on. We've got to keep moving."

Sergeant Tex Stoneman nodded to the RTO who held the handset to his ear and clicked the transmit button twice, acknowledging the transmission. The previous day the LRRP team had found a high mountain ridge with a clear view of a basin far below. After studying it for a couple hours, Stoneman concluded they had found a regimental NVA basecamp, and it was going to be easy pickings.

"Blue Rider One-Six is five mikes out," the RTO whispered.

Stoneman nodded as he thought of the young lieutenant from MAC-V. Shadows was a crazy sonofabitch, but if nothing else, he had balls. The idea that he could actually go into an NVA basecamp and rescue POWs was crazy, but he respected him for trying. It was going to be difficult watching the airstrikes this morning. He'd seen them before, and everything in the basin below was about to be destroyed in a mass of flaming napalm.

His team had set out a line of Claymores and taken up defensive positions while the RTO talked to a birddog circling somewhere in the distance. The still morning silence of the mountains was about to be wrecked. Stoneman watched the distant horizon and waited. It was a tactic only recently learned by the air force and other outfits providing tactical air support. They would come in fast, far ahead of their sound at mach-one plus—a tactic that guaranteed they would catch the NVA above ground. Only at the last minute would the birddog fire his marker rockets.

Stoneman had done this many times. Other than birds chirping and insects buzzing in the undergrowth, the jungle was peaceful and quiet, but he knew from previous experience the silence was about to be shattered in a big way. A minute later he caught the glint of a plexiglass canopy as the first jet dropped swiftly and silently into its bombing run back to the east. There came the whooshing sounds of the birddog's white phosphorous rockets marking the target—the NVA basecamp. They were spot on.

———————

Martin gazed skyward through the thick overhead canopy. The jungle was quiet, but his gut said to climb—climb, run, and do whatever he could to get as far away from the enemy basecamp as possible. The jets were coming. Of this he was certain. They were coming with a fury of fire and destruction. But he no longer feared for himself. If there was one reason he had been allowed to live, it was to save his brothers—Ray Lopez and Joe Thunders.

The sudden whoosh of rockets from the spotter plane came first, followed by a single jet that came in on cat's feet, fast, silent, and with no warning. Only when it went vertical and climbed away into the clouds, did its thundering afterburners reveal its presence. They were a precursor to the hell of napalm erupting on the slope below. A cool rivulet of water seeping from the rocks was their only hope as they dove and rolled into a shallow pool. Martin shielded his face as the flames towered above them. The enemy basecamp below was inundated in a massive wall of flames.

"Come on," he shouted. "We've got to keep going."

———————

Tex Stoneman watched through his binoculars while F-4 Phantoms, one after another, roared up the valley and across the mountainside, sending canisters of napalm tumbling from their bellies into the jungle below. Massive mushrooms of orange flame erupted as the heat and hot wind rolled up the mountainside. Propeller-driven A-1 Skyraiders came in next, laden with 200-pounders they dropped along the periphery. Forty-five minutes later, Cobra gunships searched for any remaining targets as their miniguns roared and their rockets whooshed into the ridges below. The destruction was inescapable. Everything in the basin was now smoking ashes and charred debris.

The team remained in place and waited. An hour later, from the highway at the base of the mountain there came the roar of diesel engines and the creaking clank of tracked vehicles. Armored personnel carriers were approaching from the coast. These were the ROK troops coming to sweep the mountain and eradicate any die-hard stragglers. The ROKs were known for their ruthlessness. There would be no survivors.

It was pretty much over and done. Stoneman had seen friends and fellow soldiers die in this war, and young Lieutenant Shadows was just another on the long list of good men who had gone above and beyond only to pay with their lives. Shadows was a man he would not forget. Like so many youthful heroes he had been willing to wager his own life to save his brothers, but he lost. After pulling in their Claymores, the team began moving back up the mountain toward the extraction point.

———————

Thunders and Lopez rolled in fetal balls with their arms over their heads as the blistering heat blew up the mountainside. The smoky oil and soap odor of the napalm filled the air, but Martin would not give up. Stopping now meant certain death. He jerked them to their feet.

"Come on. Get up! There's more coming. We've got to climb higher."

The heat singed their hair and wilted the vegetation around

them. The napalm had yet to hit them directly, but the smoky, oxygen-starved air was only a precursor to what was likely more to come.

"Hang with me. We'll make it if we don't quit."

He again found strength as he recalled another of Two Shadows's visions, when he said, *I saw you with your warriors riding the fiery breath of a great thundering bird into the mountains.* Martin was a true believer. What he once believed were the silly ramblings of an old Indian had now become the revelations of a Lakota wiseman. His only hope was that *the mountains* indicated a place of earthly salvation, where he and his *warriors* might escape with their lives. Leading Joe and Ray on an uphill run, he refused to stop.

Two hours later the three men were sprawled on the ground, their fatigues steaming, their skin reddened, but their souls once again believing salvation was possible. The silence of the mountain highlands had returned, but it was no longer the eerie quiet of the jungle but a God-given silence like that of a church at midnight. There were no more jets, no more bombs, and no more napalm— only the blissful silence of the jungle. They had survived.

Martin opened his eyes. He was on his back, staring skyward as he listened to their breathing. Both Lopez and Thunders were still with him and alive, but he realized it was another sound that had awakened him—the rhythmic thump of Hueys somewhere in the distance. It was probably a dream stemming from wishful thinking, but it seemed so real. He sat up. It wasn't a dream. Helicopters were hovering somewhere nearby. He jumped to his feet.

"Wake up!" he shouted.

His two partners scarcely stirred as he pulled a starburst flare from his pocket and thumbed the trigger. A red, snaking stream of flame shot skyward where it burst high overhead. It was as beautiful as any Fourth of July fireworks he had ever seen, but this time he hoped it was celebration of a different type of independence—freedom from the hell he and his friends were suffering.

"Come on," he shouted. "We've got to find a clearing."

Dodging vines and trees, he scrambled toward what appeared to be an opening up ahead—a place where sunlight shone through the jungle canopy. And suddenly he was there staring at a hole to heaven. It was where the mountain had sloughed off into a deep ravine, leaving a clearing large enough for a chopper to drop through the canopy. He fired the last flare, sending another snaking red streak heavenward where it blossomed into another glorious umbrella of red sparks.

A sudden clacking reverberated against the mountainside. It was the main rotor of one of the choppers indicating it was making a radical turn. They'd spotted the flare, and it occurred to him he had yet to pull the pin on the smoke grenade. Grabbing the canister from his pack, Martin snatched the ring, and tossed it toward the center of the little clearing. Purple smoke spewed into a billowing thick cloud. A moment later the whining roar of a turbine engine preceded a powerful downdraft as a chopper hovered into sight. Tex Stoneman was kneeling in the doorway.

The pilot jockeyed the aircraft carefully downward through the narrow opening until it was hovering a couple feet above the ground. Leaves, limbs, and purple smoke filled the surrounding air as Stoneman and three Army Rangers leapt from the skids. Grabbing Lopez and Thunders, they helped them climb aboard the chopper. Martin followed, falling exhausted between his two friends. With the side of his face against the metal floor, he listened to the high-pitched whine of the Huey's turbine engine as it lifted skyward from the jungle.

Stoneman bent over and pressed his mouth close to his ear and shouted, "Did you go into that NVA camp to get these boys?"

With his cheek still resting against the floor, Martin nodded.

"C&C radioed me and said some colonel at MAC-V called—and these are his words not mine: You've gone off the reservation, and if we find you again, we are to detain you and deliver you to the nearest Military Police detachment."

Martin no longer gave a shit. He'd done what he set out to do. Ray Lopez and Joe Thunders were going home alive.

"And?" he shouted, without moving his face from the floor.

"And screw them!" Stoneman shouted over the thundering rotor and rushing wind. "I'm gonna recommend they pin a damned medal on you."

With the last trace of adrenaline drained from his body, Martin closed his eyes and the world around him faded into blissful sleep.

M artin Shadows stood outside his grandfather's lodge lost in thought as he gazed at the full Montana moon. The winter night sky was perfect—unblemished by a single cloud, and the moonlight pure, with a luminescence unlike any other. They were saying men—astronauts—would soon walk on its surface. Things were changing, racing ahead despite the war and the riots and the uglier machinations of men. He wondered if the moonlight would be the same when it reflected from the footprints of men.

His father and grandfather were inside the tepee building a fire. Martin stepped through the small entrance and pulled the hide back over the opening. His father stood and wrapped a buffalo robe across his shoulders. Their eyes met and George Shadows raised his chin—a sign of deep respect for his son. This was something greater than any of the medals Martin had received. The little fire crackled as it climbed through the pile of kindling, but the yellow flames had yet to warm the interior and the frozen vapor of their breath clouded the air.

Old Two Shadows began packing the bowl of his pipe and the lodge soon warmed as the Montana wind gently buffeted its exterior. After lighting Chanunupa Wakan, the sacred pipe, Two

Shadows passed it to his son, who in turn passed it to his. A few minutes later, Martin was once again certain his grandfather had packed the bowl with something more than tobacco. He wanted to smile but he couldn't. Smiles, laughter, and other shows of mirth were no longer his to display. Gripped by the deep sadness combat veterans share, he hoped for a time when those feelings of happiness—normalcy perhaps—returned.

"Martin, your father tells me you wish to tell us of your time in Vietnam."

Martin drew the smoke from the pipe and exhaled it over the fire. The milky white column spiraled upward into the darkness. He passed the pipe to his grandfather.

"Yes, Grandfather. I want to tell you how your visions came true, and how they helped me survive the war."

Martin began his story slowly, describing the things that occurred in Vietnam and how the mystery of his grandfather's dreams and visions came to pass. He spoke at length, while his father and grandfather nodded but offered little more than grunts of acknowledgement. After a while it occurred to him that he was merely adding detail and verifying something they already knew— that these things had come to pass because they were inevitable. He gazed across the fire at them and gave a solemn nod. They too nodded, knowing it was a shared understanding.

It must have been two hours before Martin finished his story and again expressed his appreciation. A long silence ensued as the prairie winds soughed gently against the lodge's exterior. The fire had died to a bed of glowing coals. Two Shadows relit the pipe and began explaining how his role was merely that of an intercessor, and as with all that is, he was but a small part of the Čaŋgléska Wakȟaŋ—the sacred hoop, and Wakȟáŋ Tȟáŋka—the Great Spirit, which resides in everything.

"And do not forego your mother's beliefs," he said. "The

Jesuits who first came to our land said as much. We are all seeking the Great Spirit, but in different ways. Pity goes only to those who deny him."

With that, Martin found sudden peace in his heart. The tug between cultures was gone.

"As with your father before you, the Great Spirit has recognized your heart is a good one. I already saw this, and I am humbled that Wakȟáŋ Tȟáŋka has allowed me to father two such great warriors. Someday, I hope your father will do as you have done and tell you about his war, because he was given many medals for his bravery."

Martin had known this for a long time. He had found the Bronze and Silver Stars, along with the Purple Heart medal in his father's chest of drawers. His father had seen some terrible combat in Europe, but he had spoken little of it. Only now, after Vietnam, did Martin fully understand the reason for his father's silence. There was nothing that could be said, that truly expressed the experience of combat, war, and the deaths of friends.

"Now, tell me, grandson: What will you do next? You have said your duties with the army remain for another four years. What have they told you?"

"Along with the medals they gave me my choice of duty station. I can go wherever I want. They suggested I become an army recruiter somewhere here in the United States, but I didn't want to do that. They have sent me orders for my next assignment, and I depart again in two weeks."

The dim visages of the old men reflected the curious glow of their dark eyes as they stared across the dying embers at Martin.

"And what have you decided? Where will you go?"

The pipe was passed to him, and Martin again drew the smoke and exhaled before passing it to his father.

"I am returning to Vietnam."

If you enjoyed this story

Please leave your written review of
The Ghost at
www.amazon.com/review/create-review?asin= B0BBDF4YZS
The author and other readers will appreciate your comments. Post
your review and tell others what you like about this book.

Keep reading for a preview of another of the novels from The
Vietnam War Series, *The Birdhouse Man*, a story about a Vietnam
War Veteran and a college coed writing a thesis on his perspective
of the war.

Excerpt from

THE BIRDHOUSE MAN

RICK DESTEFANIS

CHAPTER ONE

Beyond the Ultimate Sacrifice

July 1968
Near a Montagnard Village
Central Highlands, Republic of Vietnam

The North Vietnamese were here, and Sam Walker's long range reconnaissance patrol was doing everything possible to avoid them. The young lieutenant knelt behind his Montagnard guide, who was point-man for the team. The jungle was quiet, and the midday sunlight filtered down into the twilight world of the triple-canopied jungle. All morning they had silently paralleled a trail on the Laotian border, finding enemy signs at almost every turn. The slack man, Robbie Knowlton, dropped to a knee and pointed out from beneath the undergrowth to a hilltop several hundred meters away.

"Out there, sir. See them?" Robbie whispered. "They're long bamboo huts kind of like birdhouses on stilts."

"That's it," Sam whispered. "That's the Montagnard village we're looking for."

The bronze-faced point-man, Khul, turned and nodded. It was his village, one of the few whose people had refused to relocate to the security of the CIDG camps. The indigenous soldiers of the

Civilian Irregular Defense Group were an integral part of combat operations and Sam respected the Montagnards on his recon team. They were dependable and loyal—something that wasn't always the case with some of the South Vietnamese—especially when the chips were down, but these men had proven their grit.

Sam studied the huts with his field glasses. The village was six-hundred meters away beyond a shadowy chasm, and only a couple of the huts were visible back in the tangle of vines and trees. The rest disappeared into the dense forest atop the hill. This village was home to the Montagnards on his team, but after scanning with binoculars for several minutes he found no visible movement. Something seemed amiss, but from somewhere far down the valley came the resonating whoops of Siamang Apes. This was a good thing. The monkeys were relaxed, likely because there were no large concentrations of North Vietnamese troops nearby.

Sam gazed back at his men scattered down the trail behind him. Slowly he motioned them forward. It would take time, an hour, possibly longer, to cross down into the deep ravine and climb out again. Besides his recon mission to locate a well-used trail hidden in this mountain pass, he was to deliver tools and medical supplies to the inhabitants of the little village. It seemed a pretty simple task until taking into account the thousands of NVA troops hidden in base camps throughout the highlands. Sam and his men were in the enemy's backyard.

The plan was for his medic, Lee Miller, to treat any villagers needing medical attention while Sam's Montagnard team members reunited with their families. The next day he hoped to get the hell out of these mountains, but six and a half klicks of jungle undergrowth still separated them from the extraction point. His only communications were with the birddog flyovers every two hours where squelch was broken twice to indicate all was well. In the interim, he and his men were on their own and it was a situation where contact with the enemy could spell disaster.

Sam shot an azimuth to the village, not that it was needed with the Montagnard guide, but it was habit, a habit borne of good military training. They started carefully down into the little valley. A step, two steps, stop, listen, another few steps. The entire team moved with the soundless stealth of the Indochinese tigers that populated these mountains. It was a game of chess where one lax moment could put a man's life in permanent checkmate.

After stopping at the rocky stream near the bottom of the little valley, they refilled their canteens and began the steep climb up through the canopied jungle toward the village. Sam studied Khul, his point man. The young Montagnard had increased his pace, obviously excited about seeing his wife and family, but that was okay. There should be no trouble now. They were well off the trail and getting closer to the village, well-hidden back in the jungle. If there was going to be trouble they most likely would have already found it, but less than thirty meters from the first hut, Khul went to a knee and raised his hand to halt the column. Something wasn't right.

Sam eased up beside him. The little Montagnard's face, only minutes before bright with anticipation, was now rigid and sallow. His jaw flexed and his dark eyes, wide with fear, darted about. Slowly, he raised his M-2 carbine under his arm, but he remained otherwise unmoving.

"What is it?" Sam whispered.

"Something wrong," Khul answered.

The Montagnards built their huts on raised platforms, and the incessant buzzing of flies came from the nearest one. There was not a hint of a breeze, but Sam caught the momentary scent of what he had already begun to fear was there. Just before beginning to degrade toward putrescence, large amounts of blood emit a unique odor that speaks almost viscerally of death. It was faint but he had caught a definite whiff—enough that the hair on his neck was crawling.

Soundlessly, he deployed the men across the slope, and when they were ready he motioned them forward. Not a footfall was heard, not a leaf was rustled nor a branch broken as they moved steadily up the hill into the village. There was only the incessant buzzing of the flies. Sam noticed spent brass scattered about and picked up one of the shells. It was 7.62 Russian—an AK-47 round. The NVA had been here. Khul scrambled up the ladder to the first hut, dropped to his knees and set his weapon to the side. He bowed his head, cradling it between his hands while trembling in silence. Sam climbed the ladder behind him.

The bodies of an elderly woman and two small children were there, soaked in blood and riddled with gunshot wounds. Sam placed a hand on Khul's shoulder. "We need to secure the village first, my friend. Then we will tend to the dead."

Khul nodded and followed Sam down the ladder. The patrol swept slowly forward across the hilltop and through the village searching each hut. The corpses of the elderly, the women and the children were scattered throughout. At the center of the village, bodies of several old men had been bound to trees by their wrists. Eviscerated and mutilated, they had likely suffered a horrible and torturous interrogation before the eyes of the entire village. These were the fathers, grandfathers and uncles of Sam's men who were now using their machetes to cut the ropes by which the bodies were suspended.

A deep anger ached in Sam's gut as he watched his young Montagnards go about the business of gathering the remains of their families. They had brought along entrenching tools to give the villagers, but the men were now using them to dig graves. These innocent mountain people, armed with little more than bows and arrows, were of no consequence and presented no threat to the communist of the North Vietnamese Army. Yet, this was the Communist methodology for capturing the hearts and minds of the people.

Sam had seen it several times before—the killing of innocents for no reason other than what seemed the joy of slaughter. He had also grown to understand that this was a necessity for the communists because they never truly captured anyone's heart or mind. They simply eliminated them, leaving their remains as a form of intimidation. He had grown to hate them during his months here in Vietnam and he was fighting his own inclination to now become like them—a wanton killer.

It was late afternoon when they moved off the hilltop and deeper into the jungle. Sam had to put as much distance as possible between the village and his long-range recon patrol. Should the enemy return to find the fresh graves, they would know the patrol was near and begin combing the area. He also avoided taking a straight-line path toward the extraction point. If they were following, a straight line of travel would tip-off the enemy as to where they were headed. It was dusk when the men crawled into a bamboo thicket and established their night defensive position. Tomorrow they would break radio silence and head for the extraction site.

The jungle had grown quiet, until from somewhere back in the hills came the yelp of a dog. The NVA used tracker-dogs when searching for American patrols, but Sam's tail-gunner, the medic Lee Samuels, had dusted their back trail with powdered CS, probably the reason for the dog's yelp. A nose full of the powdered tear gas would not only prevent the dog from tracking for a time but also burned like fire. That dog was finished tracking for several hours. The question was if the enemy had more dogs.

Sam had to decide whether to make a risky night movement

or wait till morning. The NVA were obviously on their trail, but the jungle was thick, with numerous rocky ledges and steep ravines, and the extraction point was still several klicks away. He waited and listened. There came the yelp of another dog. He had a decision to make.

CHAPTER TWO

Claire's Senior Thesis

September 2018
Boone, North Carolina

The blonde-haired boy held his chin high as if the old man sitting at the table weren't there. The boy's Lacoste shirt was pink, but the old man was certain it had nothing to do with the women's breast cancer movement and everything to do with the boy's sense of stylish in-your-face masculinity. He could wear a yellow tie, a pink shirt or whatever it took to prove his ability to ride a trend at the cutting edge of cool. His hair was perfect and his jaw long ago squared by an orthodontist's artistry. The old man felt sorry for him.

Sam Walker was in his seventies. Many of his students over the years had been much like this boy standing before him. This one fit the profile—not quite one of the childish snowflakes of his generation, but not yet one with the manners and humility required to be a true man. Some men grew old without developing either. Sam smiled, but the young man continued ignoring him while looking over his shoulder—obviously waiting for someone.

Impolite imbeciles were common nowadays and seldom bothered him—no more than this kid did, now. At least that's what Sam told himself, but he was lying. He didn't care for aloof assholes who seemed incapable of at least a polite 'Hello,' or 'How are you?'

Perhaps the boy thought that sitting behind a table selling birdhouses wasn't exactly a pinnacle accomplishment for a man, but it was what Sam had chosen to do since the death of his wife. It brought him a certain sense of peace. Caroline had been his everything since that war over fifty years ago. She was his anchor, and it was her strength that had allowed him to cope with the memories. Now that she was gone, there was only time to mark until he was with her again. The art and crafts festival was an annual event, and the park grounds were crowded with the local university students, many of whom were here only for the extra credit.

The young man again turned and gazed at the birdhouses. Sam shoved one toward him. It was one with his school colors—gold with black trim, and it had a little sign over the entrance that said, "Winners Only." It would appeal to someone like him. The young man picked it up and gave a sideways smirk.

A girl wandered up beside him. She was pretty, with clear blue-gray eyes that said she might be as bright as she was attractive. And she *was* very attractive, but Sam found himself caught in a moment of awareness. There was something more about this young woman, something in her persona that said she was much more of a woman than her boyfriend was a man. Sam attempted another smile but was pretty sure it came off more as a grimace.

The girl gazed across the row of birdhouses at him, and her smile faded. She seemed at first to stare him in the eyes, but he realized it wasn't his eyes. It was his cap—the one with the 82nd Airborne insignia. Her eyes clouded and she picked up a birdhouse, but it seemed more a means of distraction than one of interest. She ran her thumb across its weathered wood surface. After a moment she looked up. Her mouth opened as if to say something but closed again. Sam studied her. Something had upset the girl.

"You want that one?" the young man asked.

"No," she said.

He looked down at Sam and bared his bleached teeth with a grin.

"Sorry, pops. She's a finicky shopper."

Fighting to maintain his best poker face, Sam stared back at him, but the boy took the girl's arm and turned away. She pushed his hand away and refused to budge.

"That patch," she said.

Sam removed his cap and studied it before again looking up at her. "Yeah?"

"What does it mean?"

The young man nudged her with his elbow. "Claire, don't be so crude. What else could it mean?"

The girl turned to him with wrinkled brows. "Huh?"

"That AA on it means he's a member of Alcoholics Anonymous."

The young woman's face paled. "You're an absolute idiot, Brad. I can't believe you just sa—"

"Calm down for Chris' sake. I was joking. I know it's an army hat or something."

Despite a momentary jolt of anger, Sam fought to avoid his *grumpy-old-vet-gonna-kill-you* persona. No sense in creating a scene at a campus arts and crafts festival. The girl looked gut-punched.

"It's okay," Sam said.

Her eyes moistened.

"Really. It's okay."

She tried a failed smile.

"This patch is the unit insignia of the 82nd Airborne Division.

The 'AA' stands for 'All Americans' because when the unit was formed at the beginning of World War I it had at least one man from every state in the union. Later, when the division was re-formed at the beginning of World War II this little crescent patch that says 'AIRBORNE' was added. It means we were paratroopers."

Junior's eyes bugged, "Sorry, sir. I didn't mean—"

"That patch," the girl said, "It's the same one that's on my grandfather's old army uniform. He was wounded in Vietnam. He was my...."

The young woman's bottom lip quivered ever so slightly as she tried to speak. A tear hung on her eyelid.

"Is he...?" Sam paused, not wanting to be himself crude and uncaring.

"He died back in the spring. He was my best friend. We...." Her voice again trailed into silence.

Sam's eyes locked with those of the girl. "I can see that."

"Were you in Vietnam?" she asked.

Staring down at the table, Sam nodded. It was game day at Appalachian State and the rattling beat of the drums from the marching band echoed through the campus buildings. That along with the rippling pop of the flags at the convocation center across the street brought back the memory of graduation day from Basic Training.

The Birdhouse Man is available now in ebook and paperback.
Buy it now: www.amazon.com/gp/product/B086LKMDS1

Glossary

AAR: After Action Report—usually written by an officer involved in combat

AK-47: Russian-made assault rifle used by VC and NVA troops in Vietnam

An Ninh: Viet Cong and North Vietnamese counterintelligence group—spies

ARVN: Army of the Republic of Vietnam (the South Vietnamese)

C&C: Command-and-Control center

Cherry: Newly arrived soldier in Vietnam lacking combat experience

CID: Criminal Investigation Department, U.S. Army

Čaŋgléska Wakȟaŋ: The sacred hoop—represents the concept that everything in the universe is intertwined (Lakota Sioux)

Chanunupa Wakan: The sacred pipe (Lakota Sioux)

Claymore: A remote-fired directional mine that fires over 700 ball-bearing-size pellets

CO: Commanding Officer

Con rắn: Vietnamese for "snake"

Extraction Point: Place designated for helicopter pickup of troops

Frag: Fragmentation grenade/v. to kill someone with a fragmentation grenade

GRU: Grave Registration Unit—where they take soldiers killed in action

Hootch: Slang—either a soldier's living quarters or a Vietnamese hut.

Huey/chopper: UH-1 Helicopter used in Vietnam

Klick: Military slang for a kilometer or one thousand meters

LRP Ration: Precursor to the more modern "Meals Ready to Eat" rations

LRRP: Long Rang Reconnaissance Patrol—sometimes referred to as lurps

MAC-V: Military Assistance Command, Vietnam, controlled all military operations

NDP: Night defensive position

OP: Observation Post

PRC-25: Standard U. S. military radio normally carried on the back by the infantry

RTO: Radio Telephone Operator—the man who carried the radio

ROK: Allied troops from the Republic of Korea

Section-Eight: Military provision for discharging men for mental instability

SOG: Although called the Studies and Observation Group, they were the Special Operations Group in Vietnam made up mostly of Army Special Forces often referred to as Green Berets.

SWAG: Military sniper acronym for Scientific Wild Ass Guess

VC (Charlie): The Viet Cong, also called Charlie, Chuck, and Victor Charlie

Wakȟáŋ Tȟáŋka: The Great Spirit (Lakota Sioux)

XO: Executive Officer—second in command

About the Author

Rick DeStefanis lives in northern Mississippi with his wife, Janet, four cats and a male yellow lab named Blondie. Although many of his novels cross genre lines that include military fiction, southern fiction and historical western fiction, he utilizes his military expertise to produce the Vietnam War Series. *Melody Hill (Book #1)* is the prequel to his award-winning novel The *Gomorrah Principle*, both of which draw from his experiences as a paratrooper with the 82nd Airborne Division from 1970 to 1972.

Learn more about Rick DeStefanis and his books online at www.rickdestefanis.com/, or you can visit him on Facebook at www.facebook.com/RickDeStefanisAuthor/.

Made in the USA
Middletown, DE
14 September 2022

10497624R00168